Willow's Discovery

By

Joanne Jaytanie

Willow's Discovery is a work of fiction. Names, characters, places and incidents are products of the writer's imagination or have been used fictitiously and are not to be construed as real. Any resemblance to persons living or dead, actual events, places, incidents or organizations is coincidental.

ISBN-10:0996700110
ISBN-13:978-0-9967001-1-5

Cover design by For the Muse Design
(www.forthemusedesign.com)
Edited by Ruth Ross and Self-Publishing Services
LLC (self.publishing.services@gmail.com)
Formatted by Self-Publishing Services LLC
(self.publishing.services@gmail.com)

Dedication

For Ruth Ross—

It is a sincere privilege to have you in my life.
Thank you for your continued support and belief in me.
For being the one person I can always count on to bounce around story ideas and still keep me honest.
I am honored to call you my friend and mentor.

The Doberman on the cover is my girl, Maya.
AKC Champion Jaytanie's Made in Basic Black
~ Maya ~

Acknowledgement

Author photography and the Doberman on the cover were taken by Sarah Smith. Thank you for some dearly cherished memories.

Chapter One

Willow palmed her office door scanner at the same time Asia, her petite black Doberman, pushed her snout into the door.

"Wait until…" her words trailed off as Asia bounded into the office. "This is between you and me, girl. Wyatt will have a cow if he finds out I left my door open." She pushed the door open further and stepped inside.

Her jaw dropped; the wreckage of her office stunned her. The entire contents of her desktop littered the floor and were replaced by the contents of her now empty desk drawers. She turned in a slow circle to find nothing spared. The credenza doors and drawers stood open, their contents dumped on the floor. Her bookshelves suffered the same fate. The intruder hadn't even spared her walls, for all her pictures were either knocked askew or added to the mayhem on the floor.

Panic-stricken, she stumbled over the debris, fighting to reach the back of her office. Asia on her heels, stopping momentarily to sniff, whined and followed Willow. Willow held her breath as she placed her right index finger on the minuscule indent on the far wall. A large section of the wall slid back and exposed the hidden, fire-resistant walk-in closet filled with file cabinets. The cabinets housed the files of all the Winters Corporation employees, past and present. They appeared intact. Releasing her breath, she stepped in and randomly selected a cabinet and pulled open a drawer. Nothing looked disturbed. On a quest, she repeated the process over and over until certain the closet wasn't breached. She stepped over to the first cabinet and pulled open the top drawer. Rows and rows of neatly stacked USBs filled the drawer.

"Everything's here. Let's go, Asia." The dog trotted out of the closet. Pressing her finger on the indent, Willow re-engaged the door. It slid back into place, and she sagged against it as relief flooded her system.

Amidst the destruction a sparkle caught her eye; she rushed over to find the picture of her and her family tossed haphazardly among the rubble. Willow gently pulled the treasure free. Tears swamped her eyes as she realized the picture somehow remained in one piece.

"I guess this isn't between you and me anymore," Willow murmured to Asia. Asia leaned against her leg and she reached down to run a hand over her satiny black coat. Willow smiled at her, located her favorite chair, and turned it right side up. She recovered the soft seat cushions and Asia jumped up into the oversized chair, spun in circles a few times, and finally settled down.

* * * *

2

Wyatt placed his cup on his desk and turned on the computer. He had to admit, he enjoyed the convenience of a satellite office situated on the Winters' campus. As long as he could recollect he was an early riser, which served him well in his military career. Ever since he got assigned Captain in Charge of the Special Operations Command or SOCOM teams, it became imperative to be at the office early. The layout of the campus made his morning routine one-stop shopping. He could work out, shower, and jump into his workday in an office supplied with all the latest and greatest of everything. He sipped his coffee and soaked in the silence, a luxury for another thirty minutes tops. By then his brother, Tristan, and the rest of the team would traipse in, destroying his peace and solitude.

Wyatt's cell phone vibrated in his pocket. He glanced at the screen and moaned as the serenity of the morning quickly vanished.

"Good morning, Willow. You're in early. What can I help you with?" He tried and failed to keep the gruffness from his voice.

"I need you here immediately; somebody trashed my office."

* * * *

"Son of a bitch," Wyatt hissed as he stood in the doorway and looked around at the mess. "Are you hurt? Did you see anyone?"

"I'm fine, Wyatt. No, no one. Asia didn't react at all, which tells me the intruders came and went a while ago.

3

"This is exactly why we need to keep this campus on lockdown. Only employees should be allowed on the campus. I'm calling in the team this second." He pulled out his phone and punched in the "SOS" signal to his team.

Willow glared up at him from the floor as she gathered the pieces of her computer.

"Wyatt, this is a place of business. Employees, contractors, and invited public need to be able to enter the campus."

He didn't want to get into a pissing match with her, so he ignored her protest. "Does the computer work?" he asked, as she tried to start her computer.

She typed in her password and the beast roared to life.

"I think so, I'll get in touch with our tech team and have them do a complete diagnostic."

"What do you think they were looking for?"

"I have no idea."

"Did you check your file closet?"

"Yes, no one entered; everything is safe."

"Why would someone search your office? What projects are you working on? Anything controversial? Have you disciplined any employees lately? Maybe they were after a specific personnel file? But whose?"

"I don't know. No projects out of the ordinary. Nothing. No. Your guess is as good as mine." She rattled off the answers to his questions.

"You can't even guess?"

"And how would you suggest I do that? Do you have any idea how many personnel files I have? The entire corporation is stored with me: the London complex, our old complex in town, this new campus. There are easily thousands of files."

"Thousands?"

"We've been in business a long time, Wyatt."

"Do you have electronic records?"

"Yes. The paper files are duplicates of the electronic files."

"Someone could have left your files alone and accessed them on the computer."

"No, they couldn't have. The program for the personnel files is encrypted. I have access to the program here; it is housed off network. When I'm done I save my work and everything is backed up, again off network. That in turn triggers an automatic, off-site backup. If I happen to walk away or stop entering data for over ten minutes, the system shuts down and backs up."

With caution Wyatt ventured in, stepping between piles and climbing over files until he stood behind her chair. He leaned forward to get a better look at the screen.

"I did my last backup before I left last night."

"Last night? What time did you leave last night?"

"Hum...sometime around nine."

"I didn't see your notation in the security logs. How many times do I need to tell you? You need an escort after six, Willow." *This woman is stubborn as all hell*, he thought.

"Asia was with me."

Asia's head popped up from her overstuffed chair. She jumped down, stub wagging, black silky body shaped in a "C," and smiled as she slithered up to Wyatt.

5

"Yeah, a real killer." He shook his head at the dog, squatted down, and rubbed both sides of her silky cheeks.

"Sorry, I'll do better. But we need to keep 'the gates' open." She made air quotes with her fingers.

"We can't do that. You know as well as your sisters the danger the three of you will be in if we continue to decrease security and leave the campus open to the public." He tried to remain professional and patient. But really...*this woman is testing my last nerve*, he thought.

"I didn't say a word about decreasing security. I said people need to be able to get on our campus. It's *your* job to figure out how to make the process painless and secure," Willow scolded him.

Wyatt walked over and flipped a chair right side up and sat down. He crossed his arms over his chest.

"And just how do you suggest I keep the campus secure with this open door policy? We don't know all the players involved with Kaleidoscope Group. We don't know KG's endgame. We don't know when or how they will strike, but we know they will. You are well-versed in the danger the three of you continue to be in on a daily basis. You need to take every precaution every minute of every day."

She waved a hand in his direction as if swatting away an irritating pest. He swore his temperature doubled.

"I know. I *understand*. And contrary to your belief, I do listen. What you don't understand is we need to be able to bring candidates in freely! If I can't find the people to fill our three key positions, you'll have even more to worry about, because we won't be able to keep our doors open."

*Please, give me strength...*Wyatt thought.

"Stop that," Willow snapped.

"Stop what?" He gave her a suspicious look.

"Don't play innocent with me. I know you're thinking negative thoughts. Your critical energy permeated this area from the second you walked in the room. A lighthouse spotlight would be less invasive. I won't even begin to tell you what I'm picking up from your aura."

"Oh for the love of...now you can read my aura? Is nothing private?" Wyatt stared at her. Her special abilities had started to bloom and she didn't even notice. "Victory was right once again when she told us your special abilities would eventually surface. Your ability to read auras—is that something new, or simply increased in strength?"

"I always could. I just never told you before. Actually, I like to see you squirm. And look who's talking about privacy."

"Okay, now you've lost me."

"Stop being coy; I'm aware you read minds. FYI, reading auras is not the same as mind reading. I don't know specific thoughts that run through your head. I'm fairly certain I'm better off not knowing."

"I don't read minds. I share a conduit with my brother, Tristan. No one else. I can't read your mind."

"Potato, potahto. Tell me how many times you've heard Victory's thoughts in your brother's head?"

"What...never. I don't hear Vic—well almost never. We've worked out the glitches. All thoughts are kept only between the two people who are in direct communication. Tristan has created a very intricate set of conduits in his mind; nothing crosses over."

"Then you're saying if not for Tristan's buffer, you would listen in on all my sister's thoughts."

"That's it!" He threw up his arms and leapt from the chair with such force it toppled back. "Dammit. How in the world did we go from your safety is a top priority, to me listening to Victory's thoughts?" He held a hand up as she started to comment. "I've refereed enemies who are easier to work with than you, Willow. I leave for D.C. tomorrow. Tristan is on another project. I'm going to give Noah the parameters we'll compromise on as far as your and your sisters' safety are concerned. I'll leave him the chore of hashing this out with you. May the Force be with him."

"You're not funny."

"I didn't mean to be. Make sure you keep Noah updated, which means tell him immediately should anything come up missing. He'll dust for fingerprints, and Jack will go through the entire security camera footage from the moment you left last night. Have a good day, Willow. My attention is better served elsewhere, dealing with matters I *can* solve today. And whether you agree with me or not, security will be increased today."

Without another word Wyatt turned his back on Willow and left.

* * * *

Willow shook her head and looked down at Asia who was curled up at her feet.

"Why is it I always find the need to goad Wyatt? The past few weeks I've gotten worse. After all, he only wants to keep all of us safe. He just doesn't understand the *private* business industry."

Asia cocked her head as if contemplating the question.

"We squabble like sister and brother, or so Payton says. It's totally different in his world. When he needs a person with a special skill, he just phones General Roberts, and *voilà*, done deal. I wish it were that easy in the private industry. I know," she fumed to Asia. "I've tried to explain it to him, but he just doesn't get it, or he doesn't care."

Asia whined in sympathy.

She looked around the area for the office phone. Deciding it was a moot point, she pulled her cell from her pants pocket. She started to hit the speed-dial button for Victory, but stopped midstream and stuck the phone back in her pocket.

"Let's go for a walk, Asia. I need to talk with Victory in person. If Wyatt gets to her before I do he will blow this mess up into an atomic bomb. You know Victory; she always feels the need to play the mother figure. She'll hound me even more about staying late last night. Besides, I wonder if Wyatt is right about my abilities."

* * * *

Willow and Asia stood motionless in the doorway of Victory's lab. Victory was engulfed in some sort of testing. Willow was positive her sister's current immersion pertained to their mother's formula.

9

Victory was spending her days and part of her nights trying to create and stabilize a DNA buffer for herself, her sisters, Collin, and Morgan. Whatever held her entire attention seemed intense enough that Victory's super-keen hearing hadn't picked up on the two of them yet.

"Morning sis, what's up?" Victory asked.

"Can you read auras?" Willow asked. "Everyone can, right? Wyatt only attempted to provoke me, right?"

Victory chuckled softly.

"I can *sense* people's emotions, but nothing like you. Remember how you said you possessed no special abilities? Well, you do. You always have. Reading auras is so ingrained into who you are that the process doesn't feel *different* to you."

"Huh. So, Wyatt's right, this is my special ability. Well, bully for me. It's not like I can ground others' emotions or magnify them, as Payton and you can. I see color and energy floating in the atmosphere. Yeah, I'm gonna change the world."

Victory raised an eyebrow at her and let out a short laugh.

"Okay, I have noticed my perceptions are much more acute, and they've gotten more so over the past few months. Earlier today I told Wyatt his energy radiated brighter than a lighthouse spotlight. As if that weren't enough, I said I could tell when he communicated with Tristan. Holy crap—I even accused him of listening in on telepathic conversations between you and Tristan! I think I'm losing it."

"Let's sit and discuss this." Victory stretched as she got up from her workstation. She led the way across the hall to her office. Willow and Asia followed and made themselves comfortable on the loveseat. "I'm having tea. Join me?"

Avoiding Victory's gaze, Willow slumped deeper into the loveseat and hugged Asia tight across her lap. "I don't know what's wrong with me. I called Wyatt to let him know my office got broken into. I tried to play nice, but he always brings out the worst in me."

"Wait one minute. Back up to the part where your office was broken into."

Willow explained the events of the morning.

"Don't worry, sis. Everything's fine. Nothing was taken as far as I can tell. Well, I guess I can't really say everything's fine. I acted like a child and as a result of the break-in Wyatt has increased security."

"Even with our high-tech security system someone managed to break into your office? Don't you see? Everything's not fine. It's extremely likely the person who broke in is an employee."

"You're right. I got so caught off-guard with my reactions to Wyatt, I didn't give the situation much thought. But why would an employee do this—did someone bribe them? Are we not safe even from the people we've hired? We should be completely safe with Wyatt's SOCOM team right here on campus. It's possible our current government contracts could be the issue. I never expected Winters Corporation or especially the three of us to be on some greedy madman's radar. Even so, why would *my* files be of interest to anyone? I don't do research!" She sat back and sipped on her tea. "And why on Earth didn't I act this logical when speaking with Wyatt? I must get a firmer grip on my reactions."

Willow noticed Victory was studying her. Blast it all, she wished at times she could read Victory's aura and know what her sister thought of her.

"Explain to me again why I can't get even a glimmer of an idea about what you are thinking?"

"Willow, I haven't discovered anything more than what I've already told you and Payton. It's just my educated guess, but I believe your inability to see our auras is because we're triplets. We were part of one another from the moment we started to grow in mom's womb. Our basic genetic makeup is identical. We seem to be immune, at least partially, to each others' special abilities. I'm still running tests and deciphering mom's notes. With luck, I'll find the answer to this question soon."

"You're brilliant, Victory. If I've learned anything over the years, it's not to challenge your deductive reasoning. Still, it would be wicked to snoop on your emotions and see your aura once in a while—even better than reading your personal journals."

The two sisters broke out in laughter.

"How come you and Payton can get along perfectly well with Wyatt and I can't? I'm not difficult to get along with. I realize I haven't spent nearly as much time with him as the two of you, due to being in England so much."

"You're both natural leaders. You manage all the employees and Wyatt manages his teams. Your missions don't always mesh well and you don't always need the same outcomes."

"You'd think that being natural leaders would bring us together, since we're both the same type of people."

"Not always. More than likely the two of you would butt heads more frequently, which has been the case. And you're right. Payton and I have spent more time with Wyatt. I think we understand him better. Give it time, Willow."

* * * *

"Hey, Willow." Noah's voice floated in from the hall. He stepped into her office. "Wyatt said—holy mother of..."

"Stop right there." She emphasized the comment with the push of her open palm in his direction. "Believe me. I've had my fill of reprimands, and the actual workday has barely started."

"I'm not here to knock ya back. It's just that Wyatt said you had a *little* problem. Hell man, this is more like a typhoon. On the upside, I brought you your favorite latte." Noah handed her a steaming cup.

"Thanks, Noah. Sorry I jumped all over you. But Wyatt acts like I wanted someone to tear my office apart. Yeah, rip my office to pieces, I have nothing better to do than try and put a year's worth of work back together."

"It's not like that. Don't you get it?"

She stopped what she was doing and focused on him.

"Get what?"

"When Wyatt's upset or feels out of control about a situation, he tends to lash out. Sorta his defense reaction."

"Really. Well, then he must be upset constantly, because he's always lashing out at me." She shook her head and went back to what she was doing.

"Tell me what I can do."

"You didn't stop in to survey the damage and bring me a latte."

"No ma'am. Until further notice, I've been assigned to shadow you."

"You're kidding. I thought he just wanted to get under my skin."

Much to her dismay, Noah shook his head.

"Oh, for crying out loud." Willow reached into her pocket and pulled out her phone.

"I wouldn't do that if I were you. The Captain left the campus, and he's on his way back to base to meet with General Roberts. The General made an unscheduled visit, and he wants Captain Wyatt to fill him in on all these events of the past few weeks."

"Great," Willow moaned.

* * * *

A smile creased Willow's lips as the soft snores of Asia and Noah echoed through her office. She looked across the room at the loveseat. Noah lay on his side with his legs bent. Asia curled in a tight ball behind his knees. Noah didn't look very comfortable to her. His imposing frame made the loveseat look like it belonged to a child's play set. Willow rolled her shoulders up and back a few times. She stuffed a few files into her briefcase and stood. Asia lifted her head and Noah stretched and yawned.

"Ready to call it a day? I'm getting hungry." Noah sat up.

"Yeah. I can understand how napping away the day can work up an appetite." She laughed, grabbing her briefcase and another stack of files.

"Hey, I didn't nap *all* day. I dusted and lifted prints off all the surfaces. Jack's gonna run the prints through IAFIS, Integrated Automated Fingerprint Identification System. We should hear from him soon."

"What about the security video?"

"Yeah, about that. Some sneaky bastard knew what they were doing. Jack says it's nothing but two-and-a-half hours of static. Looking more and more like an inside job."

"I was afraid you'd say that."

"So what's for dinner?"

"What are you talking about? It's late. Victory and Payton are both out for the evening. I'm probably going to open a bottle of wine and have some cheese and crackers."

"Cheese and crackers are appetizers, not dinner. I'll make us something simple."

"I would love for you to cook. But I'm sure you have better things to do."

"You're it. Like I said, I'm your shadow until I hear differently."

"You're not staying up at the house with me?"

"I was kinda hoping you'd let me use one of the guestrooms. If not, I'll camp out on your sofa."

"I've got four Dobermans at the house; I'll lock the doors and turn on the security system."

"No can do. My orders are to stick to you 24/7."

"Damn that man. Fine—don't you need clothes and other things?"

"Got everything covered. Logan dropped off my gear at the house earlier today."

"Of course he did. Then you'll be making dinner. It'll keep you out of my hair for an hour."

Chapter Two

"I'm impressed. You sure can grill a great steak, and the rest of the dinner tasted terrific." Willow picked up the wine bottle and filled both wine glasses. She took her shoes off and put her feet up on the empty chair beside her. "You mind if I ask you a question?"

"Shoot…with the understanding that if it's something classified, I won't be able to answer."

"Last year when Victory and Tristan were kidnapped and taken to the Kaleidoscope Group's Hawaiian island, you and Logan staked out the compound. What exactly did you do?"

"We kept tabs on your sister, Tristan, and all the people who came and went from the island. Reported daily back to HQ and attempted to have daily check-ins with Tristan. During those meetings the three of us devised an escape plan, and Logan and I helped execute the escape."

"Where did you stay?"

"We found a nice cave in the forest. We lucked out; I found a warm spring where we could bathe. Usually we bathe in a cold lake or the ocean."

"Sounds homey." Willow grimaced.

"We're used to campouts. I kinda enjoy them myself."

"So, how did you spend your days when you weren't checking up on Tristan and Victory?"

"We mapped out the entire island. We knew every hidey hole and security trap. Even saw Collin sprint through the forest a time or two. Man, when he and Morgan were running full-throttle, they could cover ground like gazelles. You should see them leap up onto something high—really high. I don't know which one can jump higher, but the both of them can easily clear ten feet."

"Are you kidding?" Willow asked as she dropped her feet to the ground and sat straight up.

"No, it's true. Victory and Payton must have told you about the guys."

"They did. But I've never actually seen them display any unusual abilities and I thought my sisters were exaggerating. I've seen them run here on campus, but not jump. I haven't seen them that much, though, since I spent the majority of the last year in England."

"So, how's the transition there going? Your manager, Angie, how's she recovering since her mugging?"

"The doctors removed the cast from Angie's leg, and she started back on half days last week. Her broken ribs are still sore; those can take a long while to heal. She and Carol, the woman who filled in while Angie recovered from the mugging, were working so well together Angie asked me if Carol could stay on as her assistant."

"The London satellite branch isn't very large, is it?" Noah asked.

"No, nothing compared to here, about ninety-five employees. I told Angie to go for it. They're both wonderful assets to the company."

Asia jumped down from the sofa, stretched, and walked over to Willow. When Willow ignored her, Asia poked at her with one of her paws.

"Hah, okay, I get it. You need to go out."

Asia spun in a tight circle.

"That's her 'tell,' the paw?" Noah asked.

"Only if you're not paying attention to her. If you are, she stares you down. Let me take them all out for the night, and then I'll help you clean up the kitchen."

"I'll go with you; 24/7, remember? I'll take care of the kitchen, too. You go do whatever work you need to do."

"Thanks Noah, you're a good guy."

"Aw, shucks, that's what all the pretty ladies say."

* * * *

"Explain this to me. Why am I the only one who needs a shadow?" Willow asked, as she headed out the door of her office building with Asia on lead beside her and Noah on her other side.

"Need you ask?" Noah asked. "Victory has her husband, Tristan. Payton and Collin are nearly always together."

"Yes, but they both work and they both leave the campus a lot."

"When they do, we all keep an eye on them."

"Can't you keep an eye on me…from a distance?"

"Your office was the one broken into this time. Not Payton's, not Victory's."

"Lucky me. You must admit, it's been quiet for the entire two weeks you've played my shadow."

"See, it works."

"Damn, I stepped right into that one."

As the trio reached the lake, Willow bent down and unhooked the leash from Asia's harness. "Not too far now," she said, as Asia took off at the speed of light, a tiny black smear streaking across the countryside.

* * * *

Wyatt sat on out on the back patio of his office building and watched Noah and Willow interact. He wondered why he and Willow reacted like oil and water. He didn't notice any conflict with others who interacted with her. She and Noah were at ease with one another, like they were longtime friends, maybe more? Then again, Noah was easy going. From the start, Noah made a point to get to know all the sisters. Wyatt knew Victory fairly well, since they'd become in-laws. He knew Payton pretty well, too. Willow hadn't been around as much. No, he couldn't blame their entire predicament on her. If he was being truthful, he hadn't made an effort. Prime example, they hadn't even crossed paths in the last two weeks. Because of him or her? Now he found himself between the lady and the General. He knew he would piss her off again, once he told her what General Roberts wanted her to do.

"I might as well get this over with," he mumbled to himself. He picked his phone up and dialed. "Noah, I need to speak with Willow. Ask her to come to the SOCOM offices after your walk."

* * * *

"You needed to see me?" Willow asked as she and Asia stepped into Wyatt's open doorway.

"Yes, thank you. Come in and take a seat. Noah you stay, grab a chair. I need you here too. As you know, I spent some time with General Roberts last week. We went over security and procedures."

"We've done everything he's asked," Willow piped up. "Our security is better than ever. You saw to it."

"Security is fine, Willow. What he now asks is directly related to you."

She frowned and tilted her head slightly.

"I explained to General Roberts about your increasing psychic abilities." She inhaled as if to interrupt. He raised his hand to stop her. "I misspoke, what I meant to say was, your ability to read auras. He would like you to put your unique skills to work by reconfirming every current employee's work history and resumé."

"Why? Every single employee got their government clearance."

"True. But he wants you to go through each one in person. We need your impression; be aware of any negative energy. Think of it this way. This is the perfect opportunity to ferret out the person who broke into your office, assuming it's an employee."

"Do you realize how long re-interviewing every employee will take me? There are over 350 employees on this campus. Don't forget, I do have my own work to attend to. It's not like I am sitting on my hands waiting for you to give me a new project."

Here she goes again, Wyatt thought. *Blaming me. Sometimes it's hell being the boss.*

"Problems, brother?" He heard Tristan's thoughts pop into his head.

Wyatt and his twin brother, Tristan, were telepathically connected since before birth. Their connection remained only between each other, until Victory Winters came into Tristan's life. Now Tristan and his wife, Victory, were also connected telepathically. It appeared highly possible that their link was even stronger than his connection with Tristan. Wyatt never thought that would've happened.

"No problem, just breaking the news to your wife's hothead sister."

"Will the two of you ever learn to play well with one another?" Tristan's baritone laugh vibrated through his skull.

"Very cute. Tell me how one sister can be so reasonable and understanding and the other a spoiled brat who throws unending fits like a five-year-old? For crying out loud, the three of them are triplets. They should be a little more alike, wouldn't you say?"

"Yeah, like we are? Now Wyatt, you know damn well Victory wasn't the easiest to work with when I was on the island with her. You weren't there dealing with her on a daily basis. Be that as it may, I'm glad you find your sister-in-law so easy going."

"Stop what you are doing right now," Willow demanded.

"Shit," Wyatt said.

"*Whoops. Gotta go.*" Tristan laughed and faded away.

"I mean it. If you don't stop it right this instant, I'm leaving."

"I've no idea what you're referring to."

"You're doing it again. I knew the precise instant you and Tristan started to communicate. I know Tristan's energy."

"Then there you have it. Exactly the reason General Roberts wants you to go over every employee's file. No one else can read people the way you can."

"I can see there's no winning this. Fine, I'll start first thing tomorrow."

"Thank you."

Wyatt turned his attention on Noah.

"Now that Tristan and Collin are back on the campus, I have an assignment for you and Logan. You'll still be the person in charge of Willow's safety, when you're on campus, but for the time being we'll all keep an eye on her."

"Yes, sir."

"The two of you report back here at sixteen hundred, and we'll go over your new assignment."

* * * *

Willow had to admit she savored her walk with Asia to the campus alone. She enjoyed Noah's companionship; however, she spent so much of her time around people she cherished the time with only her dog.

"Good morning, Paula," Willow greeted her administrative assistant.

"Morning, boss. I see you finally lost your shadow. Kind of a shame really, I mean, talk about eye-candy."

"Sorry to disappoint you. I do feel freer today."

"I shifted your schedule as you asked," Paula said, as she followed Willow into her office. "I've totally freed you up for the next four days. Except for a couple meetings on Monday you can't reschedule."

"Thanks Paula. Better than I thought. We'll have to work these interviews into my schedule for the next few months. Guess I should get started and use the next four days, wisely. Where did these come from?" Willow noticed the bouquet of daylilies on the far corner of her desk.

"Security gave them to me when I came to work. There's a card with your name on it."

Willow walked over to the lilies and picked up the little white envelope. She pulled out the card and read aloud. "I hope you have a wonderful week—there's no signature." She flipped the card over to look at the back.

"Well, I guess you acquired a secret admirer. How lovely—coffee, boss?"

"Are you making a run to the café?"

"Thought I would, if you don't need me for a few."

"I'd like a large caramel latte, my treat."

Willow turned on her computer and pulled up the employee files. She didn't exactly know where to start. Should she start with the oldest employee, the newest, or a specific department?

"Hey, sis," Payton strolled in and walked over to the overstuffed chair next to Willow's desk that served as Asia's throne to scratch her ears.

"Morning Payton. You left the house early today."

"Tell me about it. Collin took off with Morgan at the crack of dawn. I couldn't sleep after he left, so I decided to start early."

"You've often begun your days early since living with Collin. So, tell me. What's the real reason you stopped by?"

"I can't pull anything over on you," Payton said, with a laugh. "I know you told us we were welcome to stay at the house. We don't want to impose. We can find a new place for the long-term, if you prefer."

"Not on your life. The house is yours, Payton. You stayed behind and held down the fort after Mom and Dad died. Victory and I abandoned you. If anyone is moving it will be me."

"I don't want you to move out. I have an idea. I realize this is out of the blue, since the house was remodeled not too long ago. However, when we remodeled I never imagined our lives would take the sharp turn they did. What do you think about remodeling once again and adding on? Something along the lines of two individual suites, around the central living and kitchen area?"

"I take it Collin is still finding it difficult to spend large blocks of time with others. If he's okay with it, I think it's a wonderful idea.

"For now, we'll stay in his bungalow. You're right; he needs time away from people and we both need to spend time alone, just the two of us."

"I completely understand and agree with you."

Chapter Three

"How's it going?" Wyatt asked, as he popped his head in Willow's doorway. He could swear he saw her snarl at him for a blink of an eye. He extended his arms out; one hand held a cardboard drink tray with two drinks, his other was palm up in a universal sign of surrender. "I come bearing lattes; may I enter?"

"Of course. Don't be an idiot." Willow waved him in.

Wyatt closed the door behind him and she gave him a skeptical look.

"Something tells me this drink has strings."

"No strings. I just wanted to stop by and see how your first day of interviews went."

This time she blatantly glared at him, actually *glared* as she sat in silence and sized him up. Man, he'd been interrogated by some of the best and never flinched, not once. But for some reason, being scrutinized by Willow Winters made his skin prickle.

"What?" *Is that the best you can do, Farraday?* He silently scolded himself.

"How do you know today was the first day of my interviews?" She sat back in her desk chair and crossed her arms over her chest.

"Your email."

His comment got him another look of disdain.

"Okay, I seem to be a real pro at pissing you off, so I'll start over. Hi, just thought I'd stop by and make sure there were no issues with your interviews today."

This time he earned a quirk of one side of her mouth, almost a smile.

"Very funny. However, you seem to be missing my point. How do you know I sent out a company email?"

"Oh that," he said in relief. "I get all the company emails, and I make a point of skimming through them on a daily basis."

His answer resulted in the most-unexpected reaction from her. Her shimmering blonde hair was pulled back on both sides of her head and held by a hair comb which exposed her porcelain earlobes. They started to stain bright pink right in front of him.

"What do *mean* you read company email?"

"Sorry, I forgot how much happened when you were in England. I guess I figured Payton told you. Jack and your brilliant cyber department created a way for him and me to monitor company email. Strictly for security purposes, I assure you."

"You've read every email I've sent to Payton and Victory?"

Now she lost every drop of color from her face. He should relish making her squirm; hell, she did it to him all the time. Only he felt terrible. *What the hell is going on?* he thought.

"*They do have a way of making you chase your tail, don't they bro?*" Tristan popped into his head, his booming chuckle resonating though his mind.

"*Beat it. I've got enough on my plate, trying to keep the peace with Willow. It's like dancing through a field of land mines.*" Wyatt shot back at his brother. Tristan laughed again and faded away.

"No, no. We can't read your personal emails between the three of you. The way the program's set up, the system flags employee names and certain words or phrases. Those emails come to our computers."

"Thank the—" She stopped in mid-sentence.

"You were saying?" Now it was his turn to smirk at her, making her color rise again.

"Never mind—the interviews went fine. However, at this rate, do you realize these interviews will take me about four-and-a-half months to get through all our employees?"

"Yeah, I kinda figured it would be a slow process. Really Willow, if we didn't believe your input wasn't important, we wouldn't ask you to do it. We all know you can read people better than anyone."

"I really wish you would stop saying that."

"Saying what?" Again he felt confused. *This woman is the most difficult person to understand. It's ironic she's the one who can read people,* he thought.

"That right there!" She pointed at him. "I don't read *people*, I read their aura and their energy. Up until Victory explained our special abilities to us, I thought everyone did exactly what I do. I didn't realize I was different—we were different. Believe me, it's not all it's cracked up to be."

"I know and I'm sorry I've upset you. Explain it to me. Tell me what Victory said to you the night she explained to you and Payton about your special abilities."

"Why? You already know." She looked at him quizzically.

"No, I don't. I mean, technically I do know. Tristan updated me that night. He only said that Victory explained to you what she'd found out about your mom's work. He never gave me the details of what she said. The two of us may possess the ability to speak telepathically to one another, but we learned to erect mental barriers and respect each other's privacy before we could even talk."

She studied him. He wanted to say something. To ask her what she saw. But he knew if he did she would shut down. He did the most difficult thing for him to do...he waited. He wanted to hear for himself what exactly she knew and how she would explain it. She studied him a while longer and then took in two deep breaths and started.

"I suppose it started with the loss of our parents. We were an extremely close-knit family, or so I thought. Now that I'm aware of the secrets our mother kept from us, sometimes I wonder."

"She wanted to keep you girls safe. She wanted you to live a normal life."

Willow eyed him with intense skepticism.

"I thought you didn't know the details?"

"I don't, truly. I just understand a parent's need to protect their children, and your mom would have definitely lain down her life for you."

Willow's eyes misted over. She swallowed, took a tissue from the box beside her computer, and dabbed at her eyes. He could see the internal fight. Crap. The last thing he wanted to do was make her cry. He sat very still and scarcely breathed. He felt as though she was a fawn alone in the world for the very first time, and the last thing he wanted to do was scare her back into the forest.

She sat up straighter in her chair and pushed onward.

"Thank you for saying so, Wyatt. You're right; she was very protective."

"After our parents died, the three of us drifted apart. Victory and I lost ourselves in our work and Payton got left behind in the family home. Our way of coping. If I'm honest with myself, running away was really our way of denying the pain of losing Mom and Dad. Anyway, one day Victory called and convinced me we'd lost each other long enough. We needed to save what was left of our family. So we came home to help Payton. She'd left the house exactly the way it was the day our parents died; it was a time capsule. We convinced her to put the past behind us and together we began a remodel. Four long years had passed, and although we still grieved, we needed to move forward."

Asia whimpered, rose from her chair, and went to Willow. She laid her head in Willow's lap. Willow stroked her silken black head.

"Payton finally agreed, and we began our project, with one exception. She'd closed the door to mom's office and insisted the room remain as Mom left it. Victory wanted to transform Mom's office into an office for Payton, a special place where she could go to work and feel Mom's energy. Payton agreed, but couldn't bring herself to help with that room and neither could I, so Victory took on the burden alone. She wanted Payton to have Mom's desk, and for the first project she took on refinishing it. As she stripped down the desk, she noticed a bottom trim piece had come loose. Victory pulled on the trim, and the piece opened like a tiny door. She thought she'd broken it and attempted to glue the trim securely back into place. Her fingers skimmed across a strange bump— something taped to the back of the trim. She pulled on the tape and found the first of Mom's USB drives."

"She didn't tell you, did she?"

"No, not at the time. Victory always feels the need to fully understand an issue before she brings it to us, or to anyone for that matter. To research it, study it, prove its validity.

"She upset the two of you."

"At the time, yes. Now we understand. The USB Victory found turned out to be the first piece of Mom's personal diary. We all knew the stories about how Mom had a tough time conceiving; she told us herself. She was thirty-four when she finally got pregnant with us. However, she failed to mention she'd been pregnant once before with twin girls and lost the babies while she worked in England. In her diary she mentioned working on the fertility drug she used. Victory assumed she fine-tuned the drug to her specific DNA for maximum benefit."

"So the fertility drug resulted in the three of you?"

"Yes, and as you know, it may have given us some unexpected gifts. It was at that moment we learned Mom went to Dr. Ryker for help. He's still a bit of a mystery, wouldn't you say? Since the story is he left for a vacation to England fifteen years ago and disappeared. No one has heard from or seen him since. It came as a total surprise to me. His personnel file says he left the company, nothing more. Not one mention of his disappearance."

"Hum." Wyatt interlaced his fingers together, placed them behind his head, and leaned back in his chair.

"What?"

"The Ryker thing is still left dangling after all this time. I'm thinking we should yank that string and see what we can unravel."

"I've thought the same thing. If only for our piece of mind, we need to settle what his role was in all this and know without a doubt if he had anything to do with our unique abilities."

"Victory also can understand what animals feel, right? And we all know she's got keen hearing, nothing is a secret from her!"

"Yes, and then there's the additional ability Tristan stumbled upon while the two of them were held captive at the Biotec facility on the island. She can amplify others' telepathic abilities."

"Perfect timing. I didn't think Tristan and I would be able to connect telepathically. The psychic force field that enclosed the island was extraordinary. I'm sure glad Victory was on our side. So all this sparked the realization that your mom and Dr. Ryker did something more to the fertility drugs, causing changes in all three of you."

"Pretty much. She tried to convince us that our abilities were special. At first Payton and I didn't believe her. Neither of us displayed any special abilities—or so we thought. Victory explained because we functioned with these abilities since birth and always used them, we never thought anything about them. To us we were normal. I don't know if either Victory or Payton has thought about this, but I find it interesting all of our abilities stem from emotions."

"Really, how so?"

"Victory amplifies others' special abilities. She developed the skill while being held prisoner on the island. Payton grounds others' special abilities. She feels the extreme emotions and can stabilize them."

"And you?"

"I feel emotions, too. However I interpret them in a different manner. Like my sisters, my abilities are also linked to energy, emotional energy. I feel others' energy in the way their auras shift and change, often interpreting this energy via colors. I see a person's aura in waves and shimmers of colors. Other times I become inundated with their overpowering emotional energy. It ripples off them and floods the area. Although on rare occasions I feel nothing at all. So you see, I don't *read* people. I have no way of knowing what they are thinking. I'm not telepathic. I can see or feel a shift in someone's aura and interpret their emotions from that, sensing if they are uncomfortable, hiding something, lying, nervous, or relaxed, for example."

"Well, I can see how your ability would make you the perfect interviewer. If you ever need a change in careers, come see me." Wyatt let out a low laugh. "Tell me, if what you say is true, how is it the three of you never picked up on each other's energy?"

"A good question and like everything else we are dealing with it's a work in progress. Victory's not entirely sure why we don't; however, she thinks it's related to our being triplets. We don't feel one another's energy because our energy's a part of us since before we were born. We are so familiar with each other that my abilities don't affect Payton or Victory; it has a null effect on them."

"Thank you. So, let's circle back to the original discussion. Did anyone or anything spark your interest or throw up flares?"

She leaned back in her chair again, rolled her head from shoulder to shoulder, and glanced up to the ceiling. "Not psychic really, I didn't see anything unusual. I've started a separate file, and I'm taking notes after each interview. I figured if I must go through this process, I might as well make it worth the effort. I write up a recap of what is discussed in each interview. What I felt or 'saw,'" she air-quoted the word. "Any reactions I take note of, *et cetera.*"

"Wonderful. Would you mind giving me access to your files? I know this is your area of expertise, but I might see something you didn't notice. I'll be looking at your notes in a different light."

"I suppose you're right. I must impress upon you my files stay strictly between you and me. Not Jack, Payton, Victory, or even Tristan can know at this point. The two of us are blurring the line of employee rights."

"Understood. I'll ask Jack to set me up a top-secret portal, and only I will be able to see your notes."

She reached out and placed her hands on her desk, stretched her back out, and rocked her head from shoulder to shoulder once again.

"Rough day, huh? If you're done for the day, I'm on my way to the fitness center after we finish.

Thought I would take a swim. Would you like to join me?"

She glanced at him with suspicion.

"No big deal. I feel you and I don't really know much about one another. Looks like we'll be interacting a great deal in the near future and I thought it would be nice to get to know one another better, without a desk involved."

She smiled at him, a genuine smile.

"Why not? Under one condition."

Now it was his turn to give her a suspicious look. He made sure the look proved effective.

"Which is?"

"Noah is still tied up with whatever you assigned him to do. If I take a swim, by the time I'm finished it'll be dark. I take Asia for a walk every night. I know you'll have my head if we go alone—even though she's with me. Would you walk with us?"

"It would be my pleasure." He grabbed the gym bag he had dropped next to his chair and stood up. "Nice flowers."

"Oh, thank you."

"New boyfriend?"

"No boyfriend. No time."

"Hum, secret admirer."

"Maybe."

Chapter Four

"Hey sis, how's your day?" Payton asked, as she strolled into Willow's office.

"Busy, crazy, but all and all, okay," Willow said.

"I'm on my way to the café. I need a shot of some kind of caffeine. Would you like to join me?"

"Sounds great. I was thinking I need to walk a bit. I've been tied to this desk all week. Let me leave Paula a note. I sent her out on a couple errands and I want her to know I'll be back."

They walked out of the building and headed toward the campus café.

"I stop up on the hill on my way to campus each morning. When I look at what the three of us created, I'm filled with a sense of pride and amazement," Willow said. "I think Mom and Dad would surely been proud of what we built."

"I think our decision not to erect a run-of-the-mill office complex, especially since the campus sits adjacent to our home, served the best possible solution. I love the idea of all the buildings constructed out of brick or stone. Each and every one of them is unique and looks warm and inviting. Every time I enter the campus, I get the sensation of stepping back in time into a cozy village. We really hit our mark, sis," Payton said, and reached out to give Willow's hand a squeeze. "It truly is one-of-kind. A community within a company. Our employees are family. You should be proud of that, Willow."

"Not only me, all of us. We all brought this dream into reality. I just filled out the paperwork and checked credentials."

"You know very well that's not the case. You were our true north. You kept us focused and made the difficult decisions with regard to our hires."

"Obviously given our current circumstances, I miscalculated with one individual."

"Don't be so hard on yourself. After all, you're only human. We all make mistakes. We won't allow one person to destroy what we've built. We're still a family."

"With one dysfunctional family member."

"Every family has one." The two women laughed.

"I still get the biggest kick when I walk a new employee around the campus for the first time. I can feel their confusion about why we don't own the equipment or accommodations they expected. Only to be gobsmacked by the cozy exteriors of every building being polar opposites of the interiors filled with the most cutting-edge, high-tech equipment money can buy. Sometimes, it's all I can do to keep from breaking out in a belly laugh," Willow said.

They approached the campus café, one of their favorite buildings. They modeled the café after a picture Willow brought back from England of an English country cottage, built of massive stones, with oversized windows trimmed in white flanking three sides of the building. The back of the café contained wall-to-wall French doors that slid open to let in the summer breeze or to hear the ebb and flow of spring showers. As they approached the café, Willow caught the scents of the array of flowers. The flowers blanketed the yard: delphiniums, snapdragons, lavender, and honeysuckle. The entire entry was awash with color and fragrance from the flowers, ornamental shrubs, and trees.

"Sandra certainly does an outstanding job of keeping up with the flowers. I can't wait to see what she adds in the next few months when all the fall colors are in bloom," Willow said.

"I love warm fall afternoons on the patio," Payton said.

The café theme continued out onto the patio. There were enormous pieces of slate, which lined the ground, and tiny stones filled in between the cracks. Raised flower boxes ran the entire length of the outer edges of the patio and overflowed with flowers in every color nature offered. Tall black antique-looking English gas heat lamps dotted the outer edges and snugged up next to the flower boxes.

"What do you think?" Sandra asked, as she walked up behind them. "My crew finished putting them up an hour ago."

"They're fantastic. I can feel the heat from them standing here," Payton said.

"Aren't they? With the added heat, I might be able to keep the patio open until the first week of October or longer, depending on the rain. What can I get you ladies?"

"Did I see blackberry cobbler as we walked through?"

"You did indeed. I spent last weekend picking blackberries and I thought cobbler would make a nice treat. I hoped it would last for the week. But the way the dessert is going out the door, I'll be lucky to make it until tomorrow."

"In that case, we'll each take a cobbler and coffee," Willow said. "I don't intend on missing out on your famous cobbler. Let's grab the table over there next to the new lamp."

"I got a call from the bank earlier today," Payton said, as she scooped up another forkful of decadent cobbler, popped it into her mouth, and purred with pleasure.

"Is there a problem?"

"Not so far. The potential buyer checked out, so our banker sent the papers to their attorney. If this deal goes through, we'll get an influx of much-needed capital. I find it a bit strange for someone to purchase such a large building and never see it."

"What do you mean?"

"I've only met with the attorney. He recorded the tour I gave him and sent the feed on to the buyer. The buyer never actually stepped foot on the property as far as I know."

"Well, couldn't it be another positive sign? The buyer is so rich he does this sort of thing all the time."

"Maybe, but it still needles me."

"Bittersweet though...selling the original Winters Research facility. I know we need to sell the complex, but it doesn't make the process any easier."

"You're right, Willow. But like you and Victory told me the day you came home, it's time to put the past behind us and move onward. I believe if Mom and Dad were still here with us, they'd love our new campus far more than the old complex."

Payton's phone rang, and she dug it out of her pocket. "It's our banker. I hope something didn't go bad, again—hello." She listened. "Tonight? Fine, what time? No, you don't need to ruin your evening too; I'll be fine. Good night."

"What's the problem?"

"Believe it or not, the *buyer* is in town and wants to walk through the complex tonight at seven. His flight leaves later this evening. He wants to finish the deal before he leaves, but only if we meet and take him through the building. Damn it all. Of course he would pull this kind of thing at the last minute. Collin has special plans. Tonight is the six-month anniversary of our first meeting. He wanted to take me out for the evening, and we planned to spend the night at his bungalow. I've finally moved some of my things down there. I think it consisted of more dog stuff than my stuff." Payton giggled. "It might take Kes and Parker a while to get used to the smaller space. I feel a bit guilty leaving Asia by herself up at the house."

"Don't worry about Asia. She's usually at the office with me. When I do leave her home, Victory and I arrange for her and Dax to be together. Besides, it's not like you're far away. Don't cancel your plans tonight, Payton. I don't have any plans. In fact, I only planned on doing some catch-up on the work I managed to ignore this week, due to these blasted interviews. I'll get all my stuff together in the next couple hours and work at the house later tonight. Leave Parker and Kes at the house since I'll be home most of the time. Now tell me what I need to know."

"Oh, thank you, Willow." Payton threw her arms around her sister and hugged her fiercely. There's really nothing to know. I'll bring you by the keys. You meet the buyer and his attorney at the complex and answer any questions; that's about it."

"Did you get the opportunity to comb through the labs and offices to make sure none of Mom's files or USBs were left behind? I know you said you were going to, but you've been super busy. I can get there early and take a look."

"Don't bother. Collin and I spent an entire weekend a few weeks back and went through the whole place with a magnifying glass. We struck out. Nothing's left. I do have a few more boxes of hers from when we cleaned the place out that I haven't gone through yet. Are you interested?" Payton asked.

"I think I am. I'll pick them up in a couple days."

* * * *

"If you don't need anything else, I think I'll head home," Paula said, as she walked into Willow's office.

"I'm good, Paula—wait, what time is it?"

"It's about six."

"Oh, crap." Willow sprang up from her desk as she shoved files into her briefcase.

"You have somewhere to be, boss?"

"Yes. I need to get down to the old office complex. Our potential buyer wants to take one last look around before he signs the papers."

"Then we can walk out together. Who's going with you?"

"No one. It's still daylight. I should be back in two hours tops. The guys are all out on some training mission, all but Collin. I'm not going to bother any of them with this."

"At least take one of the guards as your escort. Wyatt will have my head if he finds out you went out alone and I didn't stop you."

"Don't you mean babysitter? Fine, I'll stop at the guard shack and get an escort."

"Thank you. Now I won't worry about you all night."

* * * *

"Wait here," Willow said to the guard as he parked the car in the empty company lot. "I shouldn't be long. I'll call you if I need anything."

Dusk had fallen and the street lights flicked on. Willow walked around to the front of the complex and unlocked the door. It felt strange being back here. She hadn't stepped foot in this place since the night of their parents' death. Again, Payton picked up the slack, organized the move of the company, emptied out the building, and put the complex on the market. She felt terrible she and Victory had burdened Payton yet again with one more awful task. Tonight was a small way of thanking her sister.

She flipped the switch on the wall, and the lobby lit up, a skeleton of the one she fondly remembered. When they were young, the sisters played hide-and-seek in the lobby with its great hiding places. Now it stood empty, the gargantuan built-in front desk the only piece of furniture left.

Willow glanced at her phone. She still had twenty minutes before the buyer would arrive. She walked to the bank of elevators and pushed the button. Nothing happened. She pushed the button again.

"Wonderful. Someone turned the elevators off." She headed to the stairway. The basement was two floors down. She could get to the basement, turn on the elevators, and be back up in fifteen minutes. She headed down, switching on lights along the way. She opened the door to the basement, flipped the light switch, and stood in the doorway. Maybe she should've called the guard to come with her. She stood for a moment more looking into the dimly lit basement.

"Don't be a baby," she chided herself. "Flip the switch and go." There was one slight problem, in order to reach the main circuit breaker panel, she'd be forced to walk halfway into the basement. She took in a long, deep breath, squared her shoulders, and stepped inside.

The main panel was exactly where she recalled it. She flipped the switches and turned to leave. She'd no intention of coming back down to turn them off when she left. No way would she make a return trip. Out of the stillness she heard a pop and the basement was thrown into darkness. Willow stopped in midstride and bit her tongue to stop the yelp that threatened to escape.

"Wil—loow. Come out, come out wherever you are." A male voice echoed through the basement.

Willow felt light-headed but fought down the feeling of blacking out. Who was down here with her? For that matter, who knew she came down here?

"Come on out, Willow. I just want to chat." The voice sounded familiar, but she couldn't place it. What she did know for certain was she wasn't going to let whoever he was find her. She slowly and carefully stepped back until she felt the wall. She pictured the last thing she saw before her world plunged into blackness. She couldn't go back the way she'd come; her stalker's voice came from there. She knew of another way out, but it would be difficult to locate the exit in the dark. She wanted desperately to contact the security guard, but if she turned on her phone it would light up her position like a runway landing light.

She heard a rustle. The noise came from somewhere near the stairway. "Come on, Willow. It's just you and me down here. All I want is a little chat."

She knew he meant to flush her out and remained silent. She closed her eyes and pictured the layout of the basement. She thought she was only a short distance from a door leading to the ladder that ascended to the first-floor security monitoring room. She inched her way in the direction of the door, breathing through her mouth and stretching out her arms in the darkness. It felt like hours ticked by; she ran into cobweb after cobweb, tears leaked from her eyes, all her limbs shook, her heartbeat raced and pounded in her ears until she could hear nothing else.

"Willow! You're starting to really piss me off. Come out this minute, or I'll hunt you down, and you don't want me to hunt you down."

Abruptly a small flashlight beam cut through the blackness.

"I know you're near, Willow. Show yourself, let's have a little chat," he whispered.

She pasted herself against the wall and gradually slid down. She moved as slowly as her shaking legs would allow her to keep from drawing attention to herself. The beam of light continued to move around the basement and approached her position. Willow dropped down as far as humanly possible and lay on the floor. She scooted on her stomach, searching for something to hide herself from the wandering beam. Reaching out, her fingers grazed concrete. She had found one of the large support posts. She managed to drag her body to the far side of the post only seconds before the light played over the spot where she stood only a minute before. It looked as if the beam was intensifying. A rustling came from too close behind her. She glued her body against the post and shimmied away from the sound and the light.

"Wil-loow," the intruder whispered. "Must we play this cat-and-mouse game all night? I will find you."

She held her breath as the light and the rustling drew closer still. The beam made large sweeps over the wall and the area around her. For a split second she saw the door she searched for. It was only a few steps from the place she had stood. A few more passes of the flashlight beam played over the walls.

"Where in the hell is that bitch?" he mumbled.

A mental battle of fight or flight raged within her as she fought to slow her breathing as she pressed her palms into the floor to force the shaking to stop. The seconds ticked by. Finally the beam and the intruder turned away from her.

"I've had enough. Show yourself while I still have enough restraint in me not to shoot you on sight."

Now the voice sounded unhinged, as if another person spoke. She could feel the dark emptiness of his aura ooze through the basement. She needed to make her move now. Still on her stomach, she slid across the floor. Her fingers slipped under the door. Soundlessly she ran her hand up the door until she found the doorknob. The intruder was clear down at the other end of the basement muttering obscenities. It was now or never. She prayed the door was unlocked and gingerly placed her hand around it. She tried to turn the knob, but it didn't move. Panic set in and her hand became coated with sweat. She let go, wiped her hand down her pants, and tried it once again, this time placing both hands firmly around the knob and turning it in the opposite direction. Stuck. Eventually with a low grinding noise it gave way. As she pushed the door open, it squealed on its hinges and she slipped through.

"Willow! What are you doing? Where are you?" The man's voice boomed through the basement.

She heard him run, thrash into things, and curse. She grabbed hold of the ladder and climbed as fast as her body would carry her. She reached the first floor, grabbed hold of the door, and pushed it open. She stepped into another pitch-black room, slowly her eyes started to adjust to the darkness and she located the light switch. All but one of the lights was out. The door below crashed open. The howl that rose sounded like a maddened animal. She slammed the door shut and made a frantic search for something to place in front of the door. Large, outdated computer screens sat broken and abandoned. She found a bench and slid it in front of the door. She ran out of the security room, and straight out the front door, into the night, without a single backward glance. Willow headed for the car and jumped in the passenger's seat.

"Start the car; we need to get out of here, now!"

The guard's head lulled back in sleep. She tugged on his sleeve, a little too roughly but there wasn't time for niceties. He slumped in her direction, his three eyes wide open. Wait, now she really was seeing things, but as she stared her brain finally caught up with her eyes, and she realized the third eye dripped with a thick black-red blood. Willow threw open her door and sprang from the car. She looked around the street, but it was deserted. Running around to the driver's side, she pulled the door open and attempted to drag the guard's body from the vehicle. He was a large man and pull as she might, he didn't budge. A flicker caught her eye and she noticed the keys still in the ignition. She shoved and shoved the body until there was enough space to cram herself in. Grabbing at the keys, she turned the ignition. Nothing. No sound, nothing, not even a click. She glanced over at the guard lying across the seat beside her and noticed for the first time the glove compartment open and its contents scattered on the dashboard. Her gaze backtracked to the open compartment; fuses hung out, ripped from the fuse box.

Willow sprang from the vehicle and reached into her pocket to call someone, anyone. Her phone wasn't there. Desperately she searched her other pockets. Her phone was gone. It must've fallen out when she climbed the ladder. Panic started to set in as movement caught her eye. She looked up to see a figure clad in black standing just outside the building. Slowly he raised an arm and the glint of a gun filled her vision. A pop tore through the silence of the night. Willow whipped her head to the right; there was a hole in the top corner of the driver's side windshield, and spiderweb cracks ringed the hole. This madman meant to shoot her. Out of options, she ran into the night.

* * * *

A few minutes shy of midnight, Wyatt reached the Winters' home. He and Noah had stopped at the campus security office, checked the guards on duty, and read the logs. Willow left the campus with a guard at six-twenty. Noah offered to check to make sure Willow got tucked in for the night; however, Wyatt dismissed him and said he would check on her himself. He had an itch all night, the one that always alerted him something didn't feel right. He didn't know why, but he felt the need to check on her personally.

He parked his car and walked up to the front door. As he approached, he heard Parker's deep growl.

"It's okay, Parker," Wyatt whispered on the wind. "It's me. Don't frighten Willow, I just want to check on everyone." Parker stopped growling and began to whine. Kes and Asia joined in. "Shhh." Wyatt calmed them. He looked at the security pad; the system stood armed. He pushed in the code, scrolled through the recent history, and noticed the last time the system engaged was five-thirty in the evening, by Payton. Wyatt's blood chilled. "Aw hell," he said, as he punched in his code and disarmed the system.

All three dogs stood on the opposite side of the door. An extremely scary situation, if they didn't know you. They immediately rushed him; cold noses pushed at his hands.

"Okay, let's put you out back. I'm sure you all need to potty." The trio headed for the kitchen door; Wyatt brought up the rear. He flipped on the back deck light and let them out. He glanced around the kitchen. None of Willow's things were there. No briefcase, no purse, jacket, nothing. He unholstered his Ruger .38 from the small of his back and started up the stairs. Ruger at the ready, he opened each door as he came to it and cleared each room. At the end of the hall he opened the last door, and instantly recognized the essence of Willow. He scanned the room, and then switched on the overhead light. The bed was made and sat empty. A door to what he assumed would be her bathroom was pulled closed. He opened it and found more of the same. No sign of recent use and no Willow. The earlier itch turned into a full-blown icy chill and slid down his neck.

"Where the hell are you, Willow?" He chastised himself for not getting here sooner. He'd felt something was wrong. "*Tristan.*" He sent his thoughts out into the ether.

"*You still up, bro. What's got you bothered?*" Tristan's voice rang clear though his mind.

"*It's Willow. She's not at home. Has Victory heard from her?*"

"*No. She says she hasn't talked to her all night. Did you check with Payton?*"

"*Not yet. All three of the dogs are here at the house. They would be with Victory or Payton if Willow planned to be gone for the night. She left with a guard and company vehicle at six- twenty. Guards on duty say they haven't heard from him since they left."*

"Aw shit! Not again."

Over the past year both Victory and Payton were kidnapped by Braxton and his crew. Wyatt and his team put an end to them, but that hadn't fixed the main problem, the Kaleidoscope Group.

Chapter Five

"Collin, is Payton with you?" Wyatt asked, nearly hyperventilating at the thought she, too, was missing.

"Yes, sir. Is there a problem?"

"A large one, yes. Let me speak with her."

"Wyatt, what's wrong?"

"Payton, when was the last time you saw or spoke to Willow?"

"We went to the café together around three yesterday afternoon. I dropped by the key to the old complex around 4:30. She did me a favor and went to the old office complex in my place to meet with our potential buyer at seven. I texted her at six forty-five to tell her he canceled due to a schedule glitch, but he signed the papers anyway. I'm starting to worry. What's going on, Wyatt?"

"Your time line gives us a starting point. Payton, I'm at the house. Willow isn't here, and her bed hasn't been slept in."

"What?!"

"Breathe, Payton. We'll find her. She left with a security guard, so she has backup in her favor."

"One guard can be overcome! It's after midnight. Something has gone terribly wrong."

He had to give these ladies credit; they were quick-witted and his false comfort had fallen on deaf ears. Sometimes their ability to rapidly assess a situation could be a real pain in the rear.

"Payton, put Collin back on the phone."

"Yes sir," Collin said.

"Get your gear and bring Payton back to the house. I'm calling in the other team to keep watch on her and Victory. We are going to find Willow."

Less than twenty minutes later Wyatt's SOCOM team, which included Tristan, Noah, Logan, Collin, Morgan, and Jack, were assembled at the Winters sisters' main house.

"Jack will stay here. Boot up the computers and be our eyes and ears. SOCOM team Beta is policing the grounds and they'll remain with you until we return," he said, to Victory and Payton.

"This is all my fault. You have to find her," Payton said, to Collin and the team.

"It's not your fault, Payton," Collin said. "We'll find her, I promise."

"You better," Victory said. "With Braxton and his team dead, you're starting from square one. You have no idea who might have taken her or where in the world she could be."

"Don't jump the gun," Wyatt said. "We aren't positive she's kidnapped."

"Just where do you think she is at one o'clock in the morning, then?" Victory asked.

"Are you sure she doesn't have someone she's seeing? Maybe she's keeping him a secret," Wyatt said.

"Not possible," Payton piped up. "Even if she didn't tell us, we would know. We *always* know."

"Okay then. We're heading to the old office complex. We'll keep you updated."

* * * *

"There's the company car," Tristan said, as he pointed to the only car in the parking lot.

They pulled the black SUV up directly behind the car. The headlights illuminated the vehicle.

"It looks empty," Logan said.

The six men jumped out of their vehicle and surrounded the car.

"Son of a bitch," Logan said, as he pointed to the bullet hole in the windshield.

"Looks like we found the missing security guard," Noah said. He opened the driver's door. The guard lay across the front seats. Noah reached in and felt for a pulse. "He's cold."

Logan opened the passenger door as the others inspected the exterior of the vehicle and the area around it. "Check this out." He shone his flashlight beam on the glove compartment. "The asswipe took the time to disable the vehicle."

"Look at this," Noah said, shining his light on the inside car door. "There's a partial bloody handprint. Little, looks like a woman's not a man's. I don't see any signs of a struggle."

Wyatt straightened up and looked around. "Maybe she got away. We need to find her; every second counts." He reached into his pants pocket and retrieved the SUV's keys. "Noah, take the SUV back to the house and bring Asia here." He tossed the keys over the top of the car.

"I'm going to check out the office building while we wait," Tristan said.

"Logan, Morgan, Collin, go with Tristan. Make it quick and get back here." The four men took off at a full run. Wyatt watched until they turned the corner, and then he returned to the car. He planned to go through it piece by piece and with Jack's help see what they could find.

Twenty minutes later the four men returned.

"The power to the elevators was off. Willow went down to the basement to flip the power back on. The circuit panel was covered with dust and webs, except for the elevator breaker. We found these on the floor inside a second exit that leads up to the security room." Tristan held out Willow's purse and broken phone. "Chances are she lost them in her hurry to climb the ladder up to the room."

"Someone must've been stalking her. I can't believe she would leave her phone and purse behind unless she panicked and took off running for her life," Collin said.

"Anything else?" Wyatt asked.

"There was definitely someone else down there with her. There are shelves, boxes, and furniture tossed everywhere. Looks like somebody threw a tantrum," Morgan said. "She knew the other way out. She got to the other side of the basement and found the door with a service ladder that led straight up to the security monitoring room on the first floor."

"Somebody beat on the other side of the door with a lead pipe. She's a smart woman. She had enough wits about her to shove something in front of it," Logan said. "Pursuer must have backtracked and left the basement the same way they entered."

"Backtracking would've slowed the pursuer down by seven, maybe eight minutes tops. But he or she obviously knew where the car was, since they killed the driver," Morgan said.

"By the looks of it, there were two shots fired. The first one killed the guard, and the second went through the windshield. There are no pieces of glass in the head wound. Jack thinks the man turned to his left as the killer approached," Wyatt said.

"The million dollar question is, did Willow get away, or did he grab her at the car?" Tristan asked.

The black SUV pulled up. Noah jumped out of the driver's side, Asia right behind him. He'd put her leash and harness on her to keep her from taking off once they reached the scene. Collin walked up to Asia, held out Willow's purse and allowed her to get a good sniff. The next second Asia whipped around, pulled at the end of her lead, and whined.

"I think she has something," Noah said. "Should I let her run free?"

"No, hand her lead to Collin; he can keep up with her. The last thing we need is for Asia to run in the street and get hit by a stray car. Willow would skin us alive if anything happened to her. Morgan, stay with the vehicles and stay alert."

"Guess those damn dog genes do come in handy," Noah said, as he handed off Asia.

The five of them let Asia take the lead and followed close behind. They fanned out in a reverse vee formation and moved silently through the streets.

Asia led them up one of the side streets for a bit. She took a sharp right and headed into the town park. She stopped every now and again, sniffed the ground around her, and then lifted her nose and air-scented. Each time she would whine and take off again in a dead run. Collin ran with her, the others close behind.

"Think Asia's taking us on a wild goose chase?" Tristan's question broke Wyatt's focus.

"No. She's on Willow's trail. She may not be a trained search-and-rescue dog, but the need to find Willow is like breathing to her. If she's here, Asia's our best bet."

They reached the other side of the park, which butted up to a large expanse of woods. Asia ran up and down the edge of the woods. She leapt and barked and acted almost frantic.

"Okay Collin, time to earn your pay," Wyatt said.

Collin whispered something to Asia, and she took off as if shot from a gun. The two disappeared into the thick group of trees. The men maintained formation and followed yards behind them, each second falling farther behind. They moved deeper and deeper into the forest. Asia abruptly came to a halt and dropped to her belly. She crawled forward and disappeared under a group of rhododendron bushes. Collin waited for the others. All they could see was Asia's back end and her long back legs stretched out straight behind her. Her stub of a tail wagged furiously.

Wyatt dropped down next to Asia and peered into the bushes. Willow lay as deep inside the bushes as she could get, wrapped into a tiny ball, head tucked under her arms. Asia licked her hand, whined, and nuzzled her hair. Her beautiful blonde hair was a mess; it looked as if a bird had used her hair to line its nest. Twigs and leaves stuck out in all directions, mud smeared throughout.

"Willow? Willow, it's Wyatt. Are you hurt?"

Willow didn't move. Wyatt's heart stopped. *"What if we're too late? What if..."*

"She's not," Tristan's voice flooded in Wyatt's mind, startling him.

Willow's head tilted up. Her glassy eyes focused on Asia. One small, shaky hand emerged and she reached for her dog.

Wyatt backed out from under the bushes.

"Noah, radio Morgan. Give him our location. Make sure he has secured the scene and get our vehicle here now."

He slipped back under the bushes. Willow's eyes were closed, her arms rested over Asia's back, and Asia's head lay next to Willow's. There was a large gash in one of her upper arms.

"Willow, it's time to go home. Are you hurt?"

She fluttered her eyes open and met his gaze.

"Wyatt? I knew you would find me." Her eyes closed and her head fell back into the leaves.

"Willow? Willow? Hurry up, Morgan, she's not responding."

Morgan arrived on foot, his arms full of blankets and water. Wyatt wrapped the unconscious Willow in blankets and carried her back to the vehicle. Asia stuck to him like glue.

"The police are at the scene," Morgan said. "I contacted Dr. Russell. She'll be at the house by the time we arrive."

* * * *

"How's she doing?" Wyatt asked Dr. Russell the instant he saw her on the stairs. He'd continually paced the landing at the bottom of the stairs since he left Willow in her room with her sisters and the doctor.

"She's in shock. I cleaned out the gash on her arm and stitched it up. There were pieces of bark in it; best guess is she ran into a broken tree limb. Victory and Payton helped her take a warm shower. We got her into bed and a hot cup of tea in her. She finally stopped shivering."

"Can I speak with her?"

"Not right now. She's been out in the cold most of the night, and it was frosty out there. I gave her something to sleep. She'll be out for at least six hours. You can speak to her then."

He turned around and saw his team all standing in the living room. The six men filled the room.

"Okay, then. There's nothing to be done here for now. We still have a lot to do. Morgan, did you tell the police about what happened in the building?"

"Yes, sir. I told them there was a break-in. That someone chased Willow through the complex and took a shot at her near the vehicle. They want to interview her tomorrow. The Sheriff agreed to give us access to the building. He told me we could come back after they collect their evidence in a couple hours, and go over it ourselves."

"Good work."

"It's 0700 now. You all have one hour to grab something to eat and then get to work. I want the basement dusted and searched stem to stern the minute they let us back in. Tristan, you take the team and get it done, minus Noah. Noah, I want you to go to the security office and question everyone. Check their logs for the last week and make note of all visitors. Jack you go to the office here on the campus. You do the same. Check our logs. I want you two to compare what you find. We need to make sure there's not a leak in the security team to start. The last thing we need is for someone to be leaking the whereabouts of the sisters. We already plugged that hole a few months back. Let's be sure it's holding. I'm going to Willow's office and see what I can dig up."

* * * *

"Good morning, Paula," Wyatt said.

"Good morning, Captain Farraday. I'm afraid Willow is not in yet this morning. Can I leave her a message?"

"I know she's not in, and please call me Wyatt."

She looked at him, worry showing on her face.

"Has something happened to Willow?"

"Is there someplace private we can speak?"

"Let's go into her office." Paula rose from her desk and walked over to Willow's office door, where she pushed in the code for the electronic lock and the door clicked open.

Once the door was securely closed behind them, Wyatt began.

"Someone tried to attack Willow last night when she went to the old office complex."

"What? Oh my God, is she all right? I told her to take someone with her. I left her at the security office.

She promised me she would take a guard. Oh, this is all my fault. I shouldn't have left her."

"Paula, it's not your fault. She did take a guard with her. He was killed."

Paula's open palm flew up to her mouth, and fat tears rolled down both cheeks.

"And Willow? Did she get hurt?"

"She has some stitches, scrapes, and bruises, and she was in shock. I don't believe the perp actually got hold of her, but we won't know anything for sure until she wakes up. Dr. Russell gave her something to sleep. Payton said Willow offered to go to meet their potential buyer. She said they spoke about the meeting at the café."

"I'm not exactly sure what time they spoke with regard to the meeting. I wasn't here when she left the office. She returned at about four-thirty, I think. She didn't say anything to me about the meeting."

"When did she tell you?"

"I always check in with her before I leave at night. I started to get ready to leave at six. I know for sure, because she asked me what time it was. She told me about her meeting then, and so I suggested we walk out together. I made her promise me she would take a guard, that poor, poor man."

"She didn't note the meeting on her schedule?"

"No. I have her schedule on my computer. She made no additions to her schedule before she left."

"Then no one here in the office knew. That leaves the café. Anyone there could have overheard their conversation."

"You may be right. But I can't believe anyone on the campus would want to hurt her."

"Do you know who else has the code to Willow's door?" Wyatt asked.

"Payton and Victory."

"Do either of their assistants have the code?"

"Not that I'm aware of."

"Have you ever given the code out or written it down anywhere?"

"No. My memory is excellent, especially when numbers are involved."

"Thank you, Paula. Please don't let anyone know about this situation. Tell anyone who asks Willow is gone on business for the day. I'll keep you updated."

Chapter Six

"Willow is awake. And against Dr. Russell's better judgment, she's asked to speak to you," Victory said.

"Thank you, Victory. Did she tell you anything?" Wyatt asked.

"Nothing about what happened. She said she needs to talk to you first, while it's still fresh in her head. She wanted to come down to your office, but Dr. Russell and I put our feet down. She needs to stay in bed. Dr. Russell is still monitoring her for signs of shock."

"I'll be there as soon as possible."

"Great. I need to call Payton and update her. Bad part about managing the company, she had to go in to work. See you when you get here." Victory disconnected the call.

"Jack, tell me you found something?" Wyatt walked into Jack's office. It held every piece of current computer equipment known to exist and some that didn't exist. There wasn't one spare spot to put another thing. Jack sat in the middle of the room, hunched over one computer, his desk smothered in files and loose papers. A small office chair crammed next to the desk was draped in more paper.

"What the hell, man? How can you possibly find anything in this place?" Wyatt asked.

"Are you asking as a friend or my Captain?" Jack eyed him suspiciously.

Wyatt clenched and unclenched his teeth, arms folded across his chest.

"Don't be an ass. Give me the truth, really—I'd love to know how you can concentrate in all this chaos?"

"One man's chaos is another man's nirvana." Jack leaned back in his chair, stretched his shoulders back and extended his arms out. "Wanna seat?" He grabbed everything off the chair in one smooth swipe, turned, and stacked the pile on a printer behind him.

Wyatt didn't say a word, only shook his head.

"Give me an update. Willow is awake and asking to see me. I don't want to go there empty-handed."

"Well, the bad news is he left no fingerprints."

"You're saying he wore gloves."

"Nope. I'm saying he left no fingerprints. There are imprints of fingers, but no prints were made. He either had some kind of ultra-fine clear coat on them, or..."

"He has no prints. As in they were somehow destroyed, burned off with acid, or some other fun thing."

"You got it, Captain. I tried every process and program I could think of—nothing, sorry. The cameras and lights were off. I'm tapping into all the cameras within a two-block radius right now. If I can pick him up on a camera, I would have something to go on."

"Shit," Wyatt said. "What about the dead security guard. Is there a possibility our perp left any trace evidence?"

"It's possible. But the county coroner has the body. No telling what stage the coroner is at by now."

Wyatt stood up. "I gotta get up to the house. I want to talk to Willow before anyone else tries to get to her. I want you to call General Roberts. I've already updated him about the situation. Tell him what you told me and see if he can work his magic and get you direct access to the body."

"Got it." Jack picked up the phone and punched in the speed-dial number.

"Jack, keep me updated every step of the way."

* * * *

Wyatt walked up to the house at a fast clip. He could've run in a third of the time, only he didn't want to be seen by anyone. Most employees on the campus knew what type of research went on here. What they didn't know was he and his team also possessed "special abilities," and he wasn't going to advertise and put a bigger target on his back. They had a difficult enough time trying to keep Morgan and Collin under wraps. Collin's wild mood swings made it an almost impossible task at times, although Victory was making headway with her new buffer serum and Payton's grounding abilities helped calm him most of the time.

Before Wyatt could knock on the door, Victory opened it.

"Thanks for coming, Wyatt. She's a bit agitated and spooked, if you ask me. Certainly not herself. I don't blame her; we both know I speak from experience. I'm just thankful she wasn't kidnapped."

Victory seemed out of sorts herself. She rambled, which was not at all like her.

"Calm down, Victory. She's safe; everything will be fine."

"Don't tell me we're safe. None of us are safe. I don't know if we will ever be, and it's all my fault." She walked out the door and sat on one of the lounge chairs.

"Why would you say such a thing? You know it's simply not true." He followed her out onto the patio.

"If it weren't for my blasted research none of us would be in danger."

"I can't believe I'm hearing this from the level-headed woman I've come to know." He sat down beside her. "Braxton still would have done the terrible things he did, only he would be alive to destroy more people. The Kaleidoscope Group would still be out there. The only difference is Collin would more than likely be dead now, maybe even Morgan. No one would've known what happened to Jeffery or Lisa, for that matter. Detective Ken Howard would still be alive and working for Braxton, a dirty cop who killed innocent people—except no one would know of his involvement. You and your sisters would never have built this unbelievable campus, a place I'm sure your parents would be proud of. Most of all, you would've never met Tristan."

She gave him a pensive expression and wrinkled her nose. Now here was the Victory he knew. She weighed all her options before she spoke.

"You're right; I realize as much, and I'm being silly. This is so *damn* difficult. Seeing either of my sisters in pain tears at me in ways I don't even understand. It's one thing for me to be in harm's way. It's a completely different situation if one of my sisters is in any danger because of me."

"Believe me, I understand. We will all take this step-by-step and do everything we can to keep you and your sisters safe. Now, let's go and see Willow. She may have some information that could help us."

Wyatt opened the door to Willow's room. She was sleeping peacefully. He wanted to hear her story, yet he couldn't bring himself to wake her after her ordeal, so he started to step back out of the doorway. Willow's eyelids fluttered open.

"There you are. I've been waiting for you."

She pulled herself up into a sitting position. She looked pale and frail, two words he would never have associated with Willow. She pushed her yellow-gold hair away from her face. He caught sight of the purplish bruise that started in the corner of one eye and spread out to her temple. A slow burn started in his belly.

"I know I must be a sight." She rubbed her hands up and down her blanket-covered legs.

"Not true. You look fine." He dropped his gaze from hers, his mouth dried up like grass in the middle of a hot August day.

"*Wyatt, what's up?*"

Shit, he had lost concentration and dropped his barriers, inadvertently sharing his pain and confusion. *Rookie mistake, Farraday,* he thought.

"Everything's fine. I'm at Willow's. She's ready to talk. By the way, don't work too late tonight. Your wife needs some attention."

"Why? What happened? Is Victory okay?" Tristan's panic shot through Wyatt's brain.

"She's fine—geeze take it easy, Tristan. She's feeling like this situation with Willow and everything else is her fault.

"Damn it all to hell."

"Get a grip, Tristan, especially before you see Victory. I gotta go."

Willow looked at him strangely.

"Is something wrong?" he asked.

"That's my line; did Tristan find something?"

"Hey, you really should rein your aura thing in."

"Can't, it comes naturally."

"At least you haven't lost your sense of humor. Mind if I sit?"

"Please. So should I start at the beginning?"

"You got it; I want to hear everything from the moment you and the guard left the campus."

She told him everything, step-by-step from the minute she and the guard drove out of the campus parking lot.

"You didn't see anyone following you or anyone strange?" he asked.

"Define strange."

"You know what I mean, anyone out of place."

"No. I unlocked the complex door and turned on the lights in the lobby. I was about twenty minutes early, so I decided to go up to some of the other floors and turn on lights. I went over to the elevators, pushed the button, and nothing happened. Since there was plenty of time left before the buyer showed up, I decided to go to the basement and turn on the elevators and check the breakers."

"Willow—"

She lifted her hand in his direction to stop him from completing the sentence.

"Don't even say it. In order to show the building to its best potential, it needed lights and elevators. It'd begun to get dark as I walked into the building. What was I supposed to do, show the building in the dark? You have to understand, Wyatt. I grew up in that complex. I know every inch and every crack and crevice. There was no earthly reason for me to be afraid of going down to the basement alone. I'd done it a million times in the past."

"In the past. This is a whole different ball game, Willow. You need to be on guard every minute of every day you are alone. You brought the guard. He should've escorted you into the building. He should've gone down to the basement with you. Don't ever put yourself—in that type of situation again. Promise me."

"I promise and I'm sorry. I didn't mean to make everyone worry."

"What came next?"

"I turned on the elevators and turned to go back up the stairs when the lights snapped off. Some man called my name. He sounded like we were playing hide-and-seek. He kept calling and calling; he told me I'd pissed him off. All he wanted to do was chat, he said. He tried to flush me out, but I stood motionless for a long while. Then I remembered the door to the ladder, which led to the security monitoring room. I crept over there, opened the door, and climbed the stairs as fast as I could. I didn't look back, not once. But as I stepped inside the doorway of the room, he found the exit door. I slammed the door shut and barricaded it and ran for the car."

"You said he found you. Did you ever get a look at him?"

"No. There wasn't enough light. After I barricaded the door, though, the oddest thing happened; he howled like a wounded animal, a howl so loud and so intense it reverberated off the walls, even all the way up in the security room."

"That's it. You can't tell me anything else about him?"

"There was one other thing…"

"Tell me, what is it?"

"Probably nothing. Only something pulled at my senses. I recognized something in the sound of his voice. It felt familiar to me, but I couldn't place it."

Her words put Wyatt even more on edge. Not only had a lunatic been following her, she could possibly know the crazy bastard.

"Okay, you got out of the building. What happened next?"

"I ran to the car and jumped in. I thought the guard fell asleep. His head was rocked back, resting on the headrest. At first he looked peaceful to me, as if he were napping. I spoke to him and he didn't respond. I grabbed his arm to shake him awake, and he slid in my direction. I saw the third eye then. At least that's what I thought I saw. Right in the middle of his forehead between his eyes was a large hole."

Wyatt could feel Willow being sucked back into the nightmare. He couldn't have her fall apart now. He needed to keep her on task. "You screamed and jumped out of the car," he said.

"What—oh yes—at least I think so. I think I tried to move the guard. I remember trying to start the car..."

"And then? What happened next?"

"I was standing next to the car. Then I saw him! A dark figure, with something—shiny. He held up something shiny. Everything gets blurry from there. I recall reaching into my pocket to get out my phone and it wasn't there. I don't know where I dropped it. I can't remember. What happened next? I don't remember...Do you think that maniac picked up my phone?" She looked down at her hands and twisted the blankets.

"We found your phone on the floor at the bottom of the ladder."

"The ladder? I don't recall pulling it out of my pocket. Anyway, I'm glad you found it. At least the maniac doesn't have it. Do you have it?"

"I don't, no. It was broken into pieces. Jack couldn't salvage your phone. He purchased a new one for you and downloaded everything into it." Wyatt pulled the phone from his pocket. He got up from his chair and walked over to Willow and placed the phone in her hands."

"Thank you, Wyatt. And please tell Jack thank you." A single tear welled up, she brushed it away with a finger.

"We're almost done, Willow. You're doing great. Just a little longer. What comes to mind after you jumped from the car?"

He waited and watched. He could see concentration, confusion, and finally fear play over her face.

"Nothing. I can't remember anything. The next thing I recall was Asia's cold nose and soft whimpering. When I looked up, you were there. Is that normal, the blank parts of my memory? Will I remember as time goes by?"

"Yes, it is normal. It's your mind's way of shielding you from the pain."

"Wyatt, I'm really tired now. Could we continue our talk later? Would you bring Asia up? I want her with me."

"Sure. You did good, Willow. I told Jack to put my personal mobile number in your phone on speed-dial number one. Now you have my business number and personal number. You can reach me anytime. If you recall anything else, or need me for anything, call."

She nodded and slid down into her bed, closed her eyes, and pulled the covers up to her neck. She shut out the world, which made him feel useless. He could do nothing to spare her from what she would suffer through in the next few weeks. He would gladly shoulder the burden himself if he could shield her from carrying what happened last night for the rest of her life. *It could've been worse, so very much worse,* but at this moment that held no comfort for him.

He leaned toward her, gently placed his hand on her head, stroked her hair, and whispered. "Sleep now. Everything will look better tomorrow."

Wyatt turned and left. A few minutes later, he cracked open her door again, and Asia trotted in. He glanced in at her and could have sworn he saw her eyes snap shut.

Chapter Seven

Willow forced herself to return to her office two days later. There was a guard stationed at her house, and as she left the property she felt the shadow hovering a few yards behind her and Asia as they strolled to the campus together. She'd postponed her arrival as long as she could. Enormously behind on her work, she couldn't justify spending another day hiding in her bedroom under the bedcovers. If it were possible, she would give anything to continue hiding away from the world.

Buck up, Willow. Both Payton and Victory were kidnapped, and they got though their ordeal. They continued to move ahead, to live, and to thrive, she thought. After all, she wasn't attacked or kidnapped. She was shot at, and though it frightened ten years off her life, when compared to her sisters, what she'd experienced seemed insignificant.

"Get a grip," she scolded herself.

To relive the whole scenario with Wyatt had proven unbelievably difficult, and, to top it off, he hadn't stopped by or called her since. In a way, she was relieved. She still didn't know how to feel about his attempts to comfort her, to stroke her hair! He'd never shown a trace of a nurturing emotion since the day she met him. She didn't understand why he confused her so. When he came by to question her about the incident, she noticed the strangest thing. She couldn't read him. His aura seemed out of her grasp by a whisker, but she could tell when he telepathically connected to his brother. A misty halo would encompass his entire head. She'd never detected anything quite like it.

She walked up the stairs to her building and stood at the door. Why did she hesitate? Nothing happened here. She closed her eyes, focused on her breathing, and cleared her mind. A ripple of tranquility slid over her and made her feel more centered. She placed her palm on the security pad and entered the building.

Willow walked into her office to find Paula organizing her desk. She didn't know what she would do without her.

"Morning, Paula."

"Willow!" Paula ran across the office and gave Willow a bear hug. "I'm so glad you're back. You've been dearly missed."

"Does anyone else know what happened?"

"No, no one. Everyone who inquired got told you were on an employment scouting mission."

"Thank you." She squeezed Paula's hand.

"I can't take the credit. Wyatt gave me strict instructions, and I followed them to the letter."

"I guess I'll have to thank him. Let's get to work. I'm sure it's going to take me at least the rest of this week to dig out from under my backlog. Where did this English ivy come from?" Willow stared at the large plant sitting in the middle of the credenza directly behind her desk.

"The plant got left on my desk this morning with a note for you. I assume one of the other admins left it, or the cleaning crew brought the plant in, as they often do for us." Paula walked over to the ivy, dug the card out, and handed it to Willow.

"Welcome back." Willow flipped the card from front to back. "Nothing more?"

"I figured it came from one of the departments or an employee. Should I investigate it?"

"Would you mind asking around and see if you can find out for me? You're probably right. I'm just a bit jumpy. I don't want to overreact and hurt anyone's feelings. It's a nice gesture."

Willow booted up her computer and reviewed her schedule.

"Great, this is going to be a long day."

"What's wrong?" Paula asked, as she returned with a cup of tea for Willow.

"It's these blasted interviews. The next department on my schedule is Pharmacology and then Research."

"You could always postpone them until last and interview a smaller department today."

"No, I can't postpone. I sent out an email with the schedule of appointment times. I need to stick to the schedule and not cause my employees any more inconvenience. Besides, for my own piece of mind, if I avoid them, I'm admitting there's one more aspect of my life I can't work through. I'm moving forward, with everything. No more avoidance. Please contact Aimee and ask her to come to my office."

"Yes, ma'am. I'll follow your posted list for the day unless I hear otherwise."

Thirty minutes later, there came a soft knock on Willow's door. Aimee Harrison cracked the door open.

"Good morning, Willow. Paula called and said our nine o'clock appointment was still on."

Asia jumped out of her chair and walked over to greet Aimee. *A good start,* Willow thought, as Asia showed no signs of agitation or nervousness. Aimee gave the dog a scratch under the chin and Asia returned to her chair.

"Yes, please come in Aimee. Can I get you something to drink?"

She lifted her other hand and showed Willow her cup.

"Paula knows I'm a tea drinker." She took the seat across from Willow. "What's this about?" Aimee set her cup on the small table beside her.

"I'm sure you've heard. I'm conducting interviews with every employee. It's a new procedure. Keeps me up-to-date with what's happening with our employees, a chance to find out if there are any issues or problems."

"Yes, I did hear you were doing interviews. I figured since I only just started here a few months back, I would be excluded."

Aimee reached for her tea, when she picked up the cup and saucer her hands shook mildly, enough to rattle the two together. Willow gazed up at her over the rim of her own cup. Aimee's aura glowed a bright yellow, much brighter than the first time Willow interviewed her. A positive sign in Aimee's case and Willow attributed this color to her mental power and clear thinking. After all, she was a researcher at heart, and a yellow aura represents a sign of analysis and organization. Her outward signs conflicted with her aura, proof of Aimee's nerves and uncertainty of herself. *All natural reactions for her current situation,* Willow thought.

Willow put her cup down and smiled at her. "I have to interview everyone, no exceptions. Besides, you and I haven't a chance to touch base since the week you started here. How are things going?"

"Wonderful, absolutely wonderful! My department is outstanding, and the equipment we have is beyond my expectations. Thank you again for offering me a position with your company. I won't let you down." Her initial nervousness had dissipated, replaced with confidence and pride.

Willow smiled once again and nodded her head.

"I noticed from your monthly status reports you've done some major reassignments."

"I did, yes. The department appeared bogged down. They were over a month behind on their deadlines. I observed their daily routines and concluded while they are all excellent employees, a shift in the process would serve for more-efficient production. I reassigned everyone, and I am pleased to say we've been on task for the past month and a half." She smiled back at Willow.

"A brilliant deduction, Aimee. Everyone is productive and I assume happy? Is there anything your department needs, any problems or issues?"

"No problems or issues with my department. However, I did put in a change of address last week. I've moved and decided to use a post office box as my new mailing address. I'm more than happy to give you my physical address, as long as it says confidential."

"I will see to it. Mind if I ask you why the change from physical to post office?"

"The place I was in had no security. Lately I've had the feeling I'm being watched. Not all the time, but enough I decided to move into a gated community complete with a top-of-the-line security system and guards at the gates."

"I'm sorry hear that, but I think you've made a wise decision. When did you start feeling as if someone was watching you?"

"The week after I started working here. It could be coincidence, or maybe I'm just imaging being followed. Either way, I like my new place a lot."

"And if you had to guess who might be following you?"

"Someone related to Biotec, and that irritates me. I fulfilled their contract. I didn't begin working here until three years and two months after ending my employment with them. I should be of no interest to them; however I can't think of anyone else."

"I will see to it your address remains confidential. I'll have to congratulate Payton next time I see her."

"Pardon?" Aimee asked, with bewilderment on her face.

"She convinced both Victory and me that you were the perfect person for the position. Initially, I was against hiring you. My concern was based only on the fact you worked for Biotec. I'm glad Payton swayed me. You are a real asset to our company, Aimee. Welcome to the family. I would like us to get together for lunch soon. I'd like to get to know you better."

Aimee blushed, nodded her head, and smiled. "Yes, I would like that."

"Well, I think I have all I need. I don't want to keep you from your day any longer."

With the most difficult interview over, Willow felt her shoulders relax slightly. Today would be a long day, but it should be smooth sailing for the rest of the day.

* * * *

"Hey Sis," Victory greeted Willow as she and Payton sauntered into her office. "How's your first day back?" The sisters dropped down into chairs.

"Long and productive," Willow said. "I interviewed Aimee today, and I have to say Payton, you were right. I really believe she is an asset to our company."

"I told you, you only needed to give her a chance. She's a brilliant woman. I'm glad you agree with me," Payton said. "The guys are all back on base. General Roberts is in town, again. I'm sure they'll be in meetings until late tonight. We're dragging you out of here and going up to the house to make dinner."

"Sounds good, but I don't think I have the energy to cook."

"No problem. Victory offered to cook."

"I think I've just found the energy," Willow said.

"Hey you two, you're not funny. I've gotten better at cooking."

"You have, yes," Payton said. "You made me grilled cheese the other night and didn't burn the bread."

"Baby steps," Victory said.

They all broke out in laughter.

* * * *

It was well after midnight by the time General Roberts called it a day and let the men leave the base. Tomorrow would prove to be another long day, and Wyatt should have stayed on base and slept at the officers' barracks. Only he knew he would not get one wink of sleep until he checked on Willow.

"You're heading back to the campus, Captain?" Morgan asked, as he gathered his stuff to leave.

"I thought I should make a check on the sisters."

"Tristan left a few minutes ago. I'm sure he'll check to see everyone is okay."

"Yeah, I know."

"Well, there's no sense in going back to your apartment tonight. I've got a spare room at my bungalow. I insist you bunk with me."

"Thanks, Morgan. I'll be there after I'm done."

Seemed his men knew him well, too.

* * * *

Wyatt pulled his navy-blue peacoat tighter. Damn, it was cold. Only the middle of October and already the nights turned icy. He blew into his cupped hands and wished he'd thought to bring some gloves as his breath came out in a frosty white mist. He stopped by campus security to do a spot-check. Everyone appeared alert and on edge. Pity it took the death of one of their own to become vigilant with regard to procedure. He thought they would have taken the policies and procedures seriously after the deaths of their five colleagues a few months back. *People today had short-term memory,* he thought.

He left the security office and walked a few yards. He took in the entire area. As he did so, he could tell the instant his eyes changed to night vision. Like his brother Tristan, he too possessed heightened senses. While Tristan had a supernatural sense of smell, as strong as dogs', Wyatt's ability was vision-based. On a clear, starry night like tonight, he could see the area around him as if it were lit up. The slightest movement was obvious to him, a real benefit when tracking someone or being tracked by an enemy. Before he placed his hand on the security pad that opened the wrought-iron gate, which separated the Winters campus from the sisters' home, he sent out a wave of calm aimed at the Dobermans as he approached. While he couldn't exactly communicate with them as Victory could, he did have the ability to transmit feelings.

All the lights were out at both the main house and the guest house, which now housed Tristan and Victory. He walked the outer perimeter of the yard and surveyed the area for anything out of place. He moved stealthily, not even his footfalls made a sound. Everything looked locked down and secure for the night. He walked up to both the front and back doors of the main house and verified the security system was on and engaged. He started to back away from the house, but a part of him wasn't appeased. Again he sent out a soothing feeling to the dogs, letting them know of his presence and that all would be fine.

He walked over to the evergreen tree closest to Willow's bedroom window and shimmied up the trunk. She left her curtains partially open. A pair of eyes glowed back at him as Asia stood, front feet on the windowsill. He could tell her stub wagged by the gentle sway of her body. She watched him a while longer, got down, and jumped up on Willow's bed. He could see Willow there in the darkness, sleeping soundly. She didn't seem to notice when Asia jumped up and snuggled into the back of her legs. Finally satisfied she was safe, he slid partway down the trunk and jumped.

"Wyatt, go to bed. I have it. Everyone is fine, and Willow is tucked in for the night," Tristan's voice floated in the wind and filled his mind.

"I don't doubt your abilities, little brother. I just had to see for myself. Last thing we need is another sister kidnapped."

"Believe me. Victory had me securing the area forever tonight. It's late. You're keeping me awake. Good night, Wyatt."

"Fine. I'm gone. Sorry I woke you."

Chapter Eight

Before the sun rose over the horizon, Wyatt and his team were gathered in the Situation Room back at the SOCOM building on the base. General Roberts would arrive at any moment, and Wyatt wanted his team assembled and alert.

The men heard the door to the building open and were on their feet before the General appeared.

"Morning men, as you were," General Roberts greeted them. He grabbed a cup of coffee and sat at the head of the table. "We have a great deal to cover as quickly as possible. I have been called back to D.C. and only have today to cover two days worth of material. Let's get to it. Updates."

"We've tracked every lead we know of. Researched every known associate of Braxton's and we have yet to come up with a new connection to Kaleidoscope Group," Wyatt said. "As far as leads go, we definitely would've been better off if Braxton were still alive."

"What about his dead accomplices, Dave Anderson and the corrupt Detective Howard?"

"I've backtracked every thread connected to both of them. There's not one iota of information to run with. They both led mundane lives and made modest incomes before Braxton found them. The perfect patsies for Braxton to mold into his henchmen," Jack said.

"Have you located the woman who escaped in the helicopter when Braxton was taken down? Tessa, wasn't it?" Roberts asked.

"I've programmed an ongoing search. There have been lots of hits for Tessa, no surprise there since I only have a first name. If I were to venture a guess, I'd say she slithered back to KG," Jack said.

"And Second Wave?"

"They certainly existed. I found a couple insignificant referrals to the schools, which are no longer in existence. All of the campuses are deserted and are on the open market."

"They cleaned house," Tristan said. "Doesn't necessarily mean they're not still active, it means we have to start at square one to track them."

"You believe the schools are viable leads?" General Roberts asked.

"Yes. It's our belief these schools still exist. Where they are, we have no clue," Wyatt said.

"I tend to agree with you. Too elaborate an operation not to continue on and too many students groomed for whatever KG has planned. I'm sure they had a backup plan. Unfortunately, I have nothing more to add."

"So now what?" Tristan asked. "Do we play the waiting game? Sit on our hands and wait for Kaleidoscope Group to make their next move?"

"No, Commander. I expect you to keep looking. Collin, you go visit your sister, Emma. There must be something she can tell us about the school. At least get names of other students. Have you exhausted the initial list of students the team located during their mission to retrieve Emma?"

"Yes, sir," Jack said. "About half of the students have returned home. The other half I can't locate. Based on past example, I would say it's safe to assume they are still enlisted in the Second Wave Program."

"Sir, what about the name Payton gave us: Carl Sterling, the CIA Director?" Collin asked.

"That's tricky. I have a couple people looking into him. However, we've no concrete evidence or reason to associate him with KG. Payton's statement is the only thing we have to go on. I'm sure you understand investigating the CIA Director is exponentially more difficult than almost anyone else. We need to be extremely careful we don't expose Payton or our research in any way."

"I do understand, sir. But Jack said there are only a handful of people with the ability to doctor satellite photographs."

"Would you like me to look into Carl Sterling?" Jack asked.

"Like I said, I have a couple people on him. Don't misunderstand me; I would love for you to do your cyber-stuff, but I don't want to alert him or his people in any way."

"I can do it, General. I know more ways to get in back doors and hide my tracks than the entire department of CIA cyber-snobs."

"Don't get cocky, Jack," Wyatt said.

"I'm not, really. I know I can do it. I'll move with such stealth, they won't even know I exist."

General Roberts looked from Jack to Tristan and then to Wyatt.

"What'd you think, Wyatt? He's your man."

"I would trust Jack with my life, when it comes to computers. He's the best I've ever seen. He can do it."

"Okay. But if you get caught, I'm gonna have to leave you flapping in the breeze until I can figure a safe way to get you out. I can't jeopardize my position with Kaleidoscope Group still on the loose."

"I understand, sir. I wouldn't want it any other way. But it's a moot point. They're not going to catch me. I'll stake my career on it," Jack said.

"Yes, you will. All right, you're a go. Now, back to Collin and Emma."

"General, if you want Collin to go see Emma, someone will need to go with him. If these were normal circumstances, I would send his partner, Morgan. However, with the two of them still dealing with unstable DNA, compliments of Kaleidoscope Group, I don't feel they are ready to work as a team on their own yet. I think Logan should go with him," Wyatt said.

"Sir, I don't need a babysitter," Collin said.

"Son, until this foreign strand of DNA is contained, stabilized, or at least totally understood by Victory, you *will* have a handler," General Roberts said.

"Understood, sir."

"How are Willow's interviews coming? Has she learned anything?"

"Nothing yet, General. She is working her way through the employees," Wyatt said.

"It's been quiet since the break-in of Willow's office, then."

"Not exactly, sir."

Wyatt proceeded to tell the General about the night Willow went to the office complex.

"We don't know for sure this situation has anything to do with KG," he finished by saying.

"I suppose not. But it feels too damned coincidental to me," General Roberts said. "Makes me think they might have an around-the-clock surveillance of this facility, or at least of the front gate."

"We thought of that possibility and stepped up security. They've increased the number of guards on duty. Jack and the campus's tech team have continually scanned the surrounding area for energy readings and are performing constant electronic surveillance. They've tightened up the campus's servers and shut anyone out of the system who doesn't change their password on a weekly basis. There is a log of all calls made to all off-campus numbers."

"Sounds as if your team has a handle on this. I would suggest for now you continue to work from the offices on the campus. You're closer to the action. Every one of you needs to stay on your toes. The moment you let your guard down, the enemy will strike."

The meeting continued into the late afternoon with quick breaks for lunch and stretching. Then Wyatt, Tristan, and General Roberts went into a closed-door meeting, where the men filled the General in on Victory's work with regard to Collin and Morgan.

"Just to give you a heads-up," the General started, "it is highly likely D.C. will 'request,'" he air-quoted the word, "an audience and want you to personally update them, Wyatt."

"General, don't you think it's important I stay here?"

"Yes, I do. However, I'm also a firm believer it's to all our benefits to convince the paper-pushing douchebags we are in complete control of the situation. I'll do what I can and keep you abreast of their opinions."

Wyatt walked General Roberts out to his waiting vehicle after ten at night. He returned to the offices and observed his team still hard at it. He could see they were all mentally drained.

"Okay, guys. Today's been a trying day, and it's time to call it done. I want everyone to go home, no excuses," he said looking directly at Jack. "Collin and Logan, make your arrangements to leave first thing tomorrow morning."

As his team filed out of the building, Wyatt returned to his office and turned on his computer. He looked up to see Tristan leaning against the door jamb.

"Problem?" he asked.

"Yeah. Like you said, it's been a long day. What the hell do you think you're doing? Go home, take it easy, watch a game."

"Sounds great. Unfortunately, I have a ton of reports I have to finish...yesterday."

"Wyatt, even you need some downtime. When's the last time you've stayed the night at your apartment?"

Wyatt rented an apartment on the waterfront, only he rarely resided there for more than a half-a-day at a time.

He glanced up at the ceiling and thought.

"Last week sometime. It's easier bunking down at the officers barracks here on base."

"That's no kinda life. Why the hell do you pay rent on the place?" Tristan looked at him with impatience and shook his head.

Wyatt laughed at him.

"What the devil's so damned funny?"

"You are. Less than one year ago, I was the one telling you to go home. Victory has changed your life, bro."

"Yeah—maybe you should give it a try."

"It's hell being the boss. Go home to your wife. I promise I won't stay past midnight."

"I'm checking in at five minutes after. And you know damn well I'll be able to tell if you are feeding me a line of bullshit. So don't even head in the direction of the house to scout it out. I'm there. No one will get by me, I promise," Tristan said.

* * * *

Willow looked at the mess on her desk and immediately started to stack neat piles in some semblance of order. She filled both of her "in" boxes, grabbed another handful of papers, and shoved them in the credenza. She felt like a young girl again, wanting to make a good impression on the next interviewee. She'd worked her way through the research department. Her next employee interview was with

Mary Downing. Mary and her mom worked together on a number of projects. Willow didn't actually know how close the two women were, but she knew they worked together.

"Am I disturbing you?" Mary Downing asked, from the open doorway. "I was told to come to your office for my interview. If you're busy, I don't mind coming back."

"Nonsense, come in." Willow rose from her chair and went over to greet the older woman. "I've been so madly busy this entire week; I have precious little time to organize. Have a seat; can I get you a drink?"

"I have my water, thank you." She lifted a large, glass water jug with a straw.

The gesture carried Willow back years. She remembered running through the lab past Mary's workspace, bumping the table, and Mary scolding her as she caught her glass water bottle just before it tipped off the table.

"Little ladies walk. They don't race around and act like hooligans," she would say to Willow and her sisters. The thought made Willow smile. *My how things change*, she thought.

"Willow, are you ill?"

"Hum…no, remembering how you use to tell us not to race around."

Now a smile creased Mary's lips. "Life certainly has a way of moving on, doesn't it? Well, I'm ready if you are."

Willow went through her list of questions with Mary, who seemed in conflict. Willow felt she was at ease and confident, while at the same time she saw a thin, muted, muddy-yellow aura appear and disappear.

Muddy yellow generally denoted fear, regret, or confusion. Of course, it might also be associated with bitterness and greed. Knowing Mary as long as she had, Willow didn't believe bitter or greedy described Mary.

Nearly an hour passed by the time she'd finished her questions.

"On a personal note, how do you like the new campus?"

"Oh, the campus is beautiful, simply beautiful. Your parents would be proud."

"Speaking of my parents, I know you and Mom worked together on a few projects. I wondered how close the two of you were."

"Very close. Susan consulted me on many things. A couple of times each week, after everyone else went home, we would open a bottle of wine at the end of the day. We'd debate and discuss our latest project. Some of my fondest memories are from those nights together."

"You knew what she was working on? Her ongoing research?"

The muddy yellow aura grew wider and more prominent.

"I'm not sure which you are referring to." Mary's voice cracked and she averted her gaze.

"Are you all right, Mary?"

She nodded her head but remained silent.

"I know about the fertility drug she and Dr. Ryker were working on."

"How—?" The single word stammered out an octave higher as her eyes grew wide. "No one knew, not even your father at first. Susan kept the secret close. In the end, only the four of us knew."

"You knew Mom journaled everything, both personal and professional."

"Pffft." Mary shook her head back and forth. "That woman always was a quandary. Couldn't get her to input her reports and research in the computer, but she would longhand a journal entry day in and day out. Do you know she always carried a journal with her? I would see her sitting alone in the dining hall or in the break room, head down, total concentration, writing away. If only she put as much effort into her computer data." She shook her head in disgust.

Mary stopped and looked directly at Willow. "Are you telling me all her work on the drug is in her journals? I find that difficult to believe. She was adamant about the project being kept a total secret."

"Her drug information wasn't actually in her journals. We found the information on a number of USB drives she hid. Please keep this to yourself."

"Huh...USB drives, you say. So she did update her computer files in secret. Mum's the word. You don't know the weight lifted off me. I've carried the burden since the day we lost them. Have you thought about continuing her work?"

"Your department is working on Collin's DNA, correct?"

"Yes, we are. In fact, a good deal of my time is spent on him."

"Well, Victory is studying Mom's work. In fact, much of what Mom researched, Victory has discovered and re-created on her own."

"Really?"

The muddy aura faded, and Willow felt waves of love and admiration.

"If she needs another pair of eyes, I would be honored to help."

"An excellent idea, Mary. You were there in the beginning. Why don't you plan on meeting up with Victory tomorrow? I'll talk with her tonight and give her a heads-up."

"Thank you, Willow, I would love to. Your mother was a superior molecular biologist; I always told her she was ahead of her time. It's such a shame to lose her and her talent so very young in life."

Chapter Nine

"How's it going?" Willow asked as she walked into Victory's lab.

"Too blasted slow," Victory snapped. "I've run this test over one-hundred times. The results aren't coming out the way they should. I must admit, I feel the pressure to find an answer, now that Payton and Collin are engaged. As if holding *his* life in my hands wasn't enough."

"I wish I could help."

"Hey. I thought the three of us were getting together in an hour to have dinner together. What are you doing here now? You could have waited until later."

"I wanted to talk with you about your results without Payton around. She puts up a good front, but her worry and fear nearly knocks me over when we talk about Collin. I may not be able to see either of your auras, but extreme emotions from either of you resonate through me. Frankly, I don't know if or how she'll cope, should the worst happen and we lose him."

"We aren't going to lose him. I simply won't allow it." Steely determination radiated in Victory's eyes. "I'll find something. My buffer serum is holding for the time being. I have to say, it would be wonderful to have help. I wish we had someone we could trust."

"I just might be able to help you with your problem. You know Mary Downing. She works over in the other research building."

"Yes, she started working years ago for Mom and Dad."

"I interviewed her today. Remember she and Mom did some projects together?"

"Yes. But that doesn't mean anything, Mom did projects with nearly every researcher they employed."

"In her case, it does. I found out during the interview that they worked more than a few projects together. The way she tells it, Mom and she were close. Mary told me Mom confided in her about her work, *all* her work. Victory, she knew about the drug."

"What? What do you mean? How could she possibly know?"

Willow explained the conversation she and Mary had and how she stressed total confidentiality with regard to the drug.

"You're telling me there is actually a live human being familiar with Mom's research? Willow, this could be our big break."

"I told her to come and see you first thing in the morning. If you feel she'll be beneficial to you, she can be a floater and work part-time in your department. I didn't give her any details about where we found the USB drives, or how many there are. Nor did I tell her specifics about the information in Mom's journals."

"I understand. I'll take this one step at a time. I won't tell her anything until I talk with you and Wyatt. I'll give her only enough information to get us on the path to an answer. Let's see what she actually does know. For now, let's keep Payton out of the loop. I've experienced the same feelings from her. Guess it's the triplet-thing. She's got her hands full running this campus and might not even notice the change. But if she does, I'll tell her the truth: Mary's helping me research."

"My thoughts exactly."

Willow's phone rang. She pulled it from her pocket and saw Noah's number.

"Hey, Noah, what can I help you with?"

"I thought you should know your guard has been relieved. I'm back on shadow duty and was wondering when you are planning on heading home?"

"Why? Nothing has happened all week, why now?"

"Because Wyatt got summoned to D.C. today, and we're under orders to make sure nothing bad happens. Collin and Logan are on an assignment; they're gone for three or four days. Tristan's in charge, Morgan will be shadowing Payton, and Jack is doing his thing. He's here for backup. We gotta keep this tight, Willow. We don't want to have a repeat kidnapping, or for that matter give the man who stalked you at the office complex another opportunity."

A frosty jolt spiraled up her spine.

"I get it. Can't say I'm happy about the whole thing though," she said, and all but groaned. "I'm with Victory. I plan to go back to my office for an hour and then the three of us are having dinner. Or should I say the seven of us? Invite the guys up to the house. We'll see you all in an hour."

"Oh man, that's awesome, thanks. Wait…who's cooking?"

Victory looked up at Willow; she saw that Victory's super-keen hearing hadn't missed a single word of the conversation.

"You tell that funny man I don't want to hear one word about my cooking," Victory said.

"I didn't mean to ruffle her feathers," Noah said, chuckling. "It won't be bad. We're used to MREs."

"Funny man," Victory yelled across the room.

* * * *

"How're your interviews going, Willow?" Tristan asked, in-between mouthfuls of spaghetti and meatballs.

"Slow. Although I have to say, I have gleaned a great deal of new information about our employees. This may be something I do every other year. The department heads handle the yearly reviews, but this is a great way for me to stay in touch with the employees. Don't you dare tell Wyatt."

"You interviewed Aimee, and I hear from Victory that you agree with Payton now, she's a good addition to your staff."

"Yes, I do. I have to say I had some reservations since she worked for Biotec. Not anymore. I think we are lucky to have her."

Morgan gagged on his glass of wine.

"Problem?" Noah asked.

"Yeah, there is. Am I to understand we have a person directly connected to Braxton working for you?

If you ask me, she can't be anything but trouble," Morgan said.

"I understand how you feel, Morgan," Payton said. "You have to trust me. I've known Aimee for years. She's the best at what she does. She questioned Biotec's way of doing business and as a result got demoted and sent to an associate's facility where she could be watched."

"What do you mean she questioned their way of business?"

"Aimee said she and Biotec had a difference of opinion. She believed in the code of ethics for her industry. She told me if a product would make Biotec money, they would find a way to produce it, ethics and government regulations be damned. In fact, she worked on our mother's drug the first year of her employment with Biotec. At the time, the testing and reformulating of her drug remained an ongoing project. They were always searching for new ways to improve on what Mom created. She said even though the drug was a top-secret project, she assumed we knew about it."

"Hum, convenient, don't you think?" Morgan asked.

"I suppose, if I were you and had gone through what you have at Braxton's and Biotec's hands, I would feel the same way. Except I've known Aimee for a long time. She's telling us the truth. She also said Biotec's primary source of revenue is to pirate formulas, like Mom's. They rename the drugs and claim the formulas as their own. She said Biotec is notorious for drug piracy, and somehow, someone always covers their butt. Aimee feels it's someone extremely powerful and incredibly rich."

The men all stopped eating and looked at one another.

"Carl Sterling," Jack said.

All the color drained from Payton's face. "Carl Sterling, the CIA Director? The guy Braxton said was his friend?"

"It fits," Noah said.

"I'll look into Biotec's history again. See if I can find a link between them and Sterling," Jack said. "I'm tempted to believe the link will be directly related to Braxton, so I'll follow that thread too."

"Aimee told me she felt as if someone was following her. It scared her enough to move into a new gated community with security and guards. She's not listing a physical address for public knowledge. She did give me her new address, and I've updated my files and listed it as confidential," Willow said. An idea blossomed in her mind. "Do you think there's a possibility she really is being watched and someone broke into my office to locate her address?"

"It's a thought. We haven't made any headway on your break-in. An address of a past employee who worked in Pharmacology might be someone who makes KG nervous," Tristan said.

"Tristan, could you help me bring out dessert and coffee," Willow said, as she rose from the table.

Tristan gave her a quick glance, nodded, and rose. "Certainly, it would be my pleasure. Anyone up for brandy? I'm pouring."

"So, what did you want to tell me you didn't want anyone else to hear?" he asked, as he set a handful of dirty dishes in the sink.

"I've spoken to Victory about this, and we both feel it's best to keep Payton out of the loop for the time being."

"Let me guess...it has something to do with Collin?" He raised one eyebrow.

"It's all connected, but yes. She puts on a good face, but her fear for Collin's life overwhelms her. Both Victory and I are inundated by her worry. Victory thinks it's a triplet-thing; I tend to agree."

"I could've told you as much," he said, chuckling. "It's natural for you to feel her fear; you're sisters. What do you have?"

"I interviewed an employee who's worked for the company for twenty years."

"So your parents hired her. Looking through the employee files, there are fifty or so employees who have been here for a long time. What makes this one special?"

Willow reiterated her story.

"Mary is the first person who can be directly linked to Mom's research. She knows the history and is interested in helping Victory push this research forward."

Tristan leaned against the counter, his ankles and arms crossed in a relaxed manner as he listened. Willow knew Tristan's energy well. Strangers would think he was laid-back, not her; she saw a large cat, tail flicking, eyes tracking, who would spring at the first sign of danger.

"I think it's a good idea you and Victory keep this under wraps. No sense giving Payton any more to worry about. I'm going to tell you the same thing I'll tell Victory: be careful. Careful with what you tell Mary and what you show her."

"We talked about that very thing and decided to only give her what she needs to do the work. Mary is in Victory's hands now. I'll leave it to her to take the lead."

"I need to inform the rest of the team. It's the perfect time now while Collin's gone. I'll tell them we're keeping this on the down low from Payton and Collin for the time being. But I want to get Jack on it first thing tomorrow. I want him digging all the way back to Mary Downing's birth. Is everything else going okay with you?"

"Awe, you're playing the brother-in-law card. How sweet."

She could swear his energy turned from danger to nurture and concern in a breath.

"You are. We're family now, and I intend to keep you all safe. Don't sidestep the question, Willow."

She let out a soft laugh. "I'm fine, Tristan. Nothing unusual has happened since the break-in of my office and the basement incident. There's one thing that keeps needling me though: the voice of the man at the complex. I'm sure I've heard his voice before, I just can't put my finger on where and when."

"Did you tell this to Wyatt?"

"Yes, and got the exact same concerned look from him. And before you say it, I am being careful. I've got Noah back as a shadow; what could go wrong?"

* * * *

"Hey Willow, you wanted me?" Noah asked, as he stood in Willow's office doorway.

"Yes. It's such a beautiful, crisp fall day; I want to take Asia for a walk down by the lake."

Asia jumped off her chair and started turning circles and yipping when she heard the word *walk*. Willow and Noah laughed at her, which made her bounce up and down, enjoying the attention.

"I guess we're committed now," Noah said.

"I hope I didn't pull you away from anything important. But after my tongue-lashing yesterday when we walked home alone, I thought I should call."

"Ye—ah, a real lashing. I think I recall using the words 'please' and 'my butt's on the line,'" he said, chuckling. "Good to know you took it to heart. I happen to love my job. And no, you didn't interrupt anything that can't wait. I'm all yours."

When they reached the lake, Willow unleashed Asia and let her run free.

"She loves coming here. I used to bring her down every day. Between my numerous trips to the England campus and trying to get this campus up and functioning and now all these interviews, I've neglected her. I'm making it a priority now to walk her every day."

"Good for you. You need to take time away from your office. You look tired. Aren't you sleeping well?"

"No, not really. I'm bringing work home at night. If I can't sleep, at least I can get some work done."

"Is it something at work keeping you up at night?"

"No." She looked away from him.

"What's got you troubled, Willow? We're friends, right? You can tell me. I promise to keep what you tell me to myself."

She looked at him and wondered if he would actually keep something from his boss. Yes, she considered him a friend, a good friend. Even so she knew his loyalty to Wyatt and his team might trump his promises to her.

"I won't tell Wyatt, if it doesn't put you in imminent danger. You decide, but I'd say you could use a sounding board."

"I do consider you a friend, Noah, a good friend. I've known you the longest. After all, you were the one who came to London and told me about Victory being kidnapped. You were so considerate and concerned about me. I don't think I've ever told you, but I sincerely appreciated you. You babysat me out there and brought me back home when Victory came home from the hospital. I feel like you're the brother I never had." She could feel the tears well up in her eyes. She refused to let them fall.

"I feel the same way about all three of you. You and your sisters welcomed us all to your campus and into your lives. In return we brought chaos and danger into your lives, and you still treated us like family."

"It wasn't all *your* danger; Victory too got pulled into this whole mess by Braxton and it followed her home."

"Even so, I appreciate it. I've never had much of a family."

She stopped walking and focused her full attention on him.

"Really? If you don't mind me prying, where did you grow up?"

"I don't mind. I grew up in the streets of San Francisco, and I don't mean the old TV show."

"San Francisco is a beautiful city...wait what do you mean by 'in the streets'?"

"Just what I said. The part of San Francisco I grew up in wasn't beautiful, although as I've matured, I can see past the ugliness," Noah said, as he picked up a stick and threw it for Asia.

"What about your family?" She hoped her surprise didn't show, as she fought to keep her expression neutral.

"I was abandoned at the hospital at birth. My mother got brought into emergency moments before my birth and walked away from her room right after. She never even held me. Somehow she got in and out before the hospital staff even got a chance to get any of her basic information. I was put into the system and bounced from foster home to foster home. By the time I turned twelve, I ran away. When I turned sixteen they put me into a boy's home; no one wanted a troubled teen. By eighteen I found myself in a shitload of trouble—sorry," he gave her a little grin. "The courts gave me a choice: prison or the military."

"Oh my God! I'm so sorry, Noah. You're such an easy-going, funny, fun-loving guy, it's hard to believe you had such a tough upbringing. You had a rough start, but you made a good life for yourself."

"Joining the army turned out to be the best thing I ever did. I hate to think where I would be now if not for the military."

"You would've turned yourself around. You're an extraordinary individual, don't ever forget it."

She saw his ears turn red as he shuffled his feet and looked down.

"Thank you, Willow. That means everything."

She stepped directly in front of him and hugged him fiercely. He stood rigid for a few breaths, then finally relaxed and wrapped his arms around her. A helicopter passed overhead. Noah pulled away from Willow and looked up.

"I'll bet it's Wyatt. He updated us this morning and said he would be heading back in soon."

"He's been gone for two weeks; that's an awfully long meeting."

"You never told me. What's been troubling you?" Noah asked.

"It's nothing really. Just seems like every time I close my eyes, I hear the voice of that lunatic at the complex. I know I've heard his voice before and it's killing me! Who is he?"

"I think you should tell Dr. Russell. You need to get your sleep, Willow."

"This time I agree with you. I've been thinking of stopping by her office."

"We better head back. I'm sure Wyatt will call the team in soon. And Willow, thanks for listening. It's nice to have someone to confide in."

"Thank you for listening, Noah. It is nice to have a trusted confidant."

He smiled at her one last time and then focused his attention on Asia. She'd traveled way off to the edge of the forest, and he whistled for her.

* * * *

Wyatt felt as though he'd been gone for months instead of a few weeks. His team was extremely capable to carry on in his absence, but he hated being away this long. He took in the sprawling campus as the helicopter made the approach to the helipad. As the lake came into view, he saw two figures. The two people moved closer and embraced. He watched them as the chopper passed overhead, and he felt a cold grip in the vicinity of his heart as he realized the two were Willow and Noah.

What the hell, he thought. He'd missed his chance—wait, what in the world was he thinking? He and Willow had only just moved to the stage of being able to function in the same room without spats. It's not like they had any kind of a thing going on, he told himself, but he still felt sick to his stomach.

Chapter Ten

"Morning, Paula," Willow said.

"Good morning, Willow. You have some color in your face today. Did you finally get some sleep last night?"

"I did. I wasn't excited about seeing Dr. Russell yesterday, still the pills she gave me worked wonders. I'm not even groggy today."

"Glad to hear it. You have another busy day. Here's your mail."

Willow stepped closer to Paula's desk and took the stack of mail from her.

"My gosh, you'd think just one day my incoming mail could decrease. Instead, it seems to get bigger and bigger each day. How much time do I have until my first appointment?"

"I blocked out an hour and a half for you. Best I could do."

"Thanks Paula, I'll take what I can get." Willow smiled at her assistant and headed into her office. She dropped the massive stack of mail beside her keyboard and went to hang up her coat. "Come here, Asia." Asia looked her way, and Willow could tell she didn't want to leave Paula's stroking hands. Paula laughed and gave the dog a tap on the rear.

"Go on now. I need to get your mom some coffee."

Asia dropped her head and pouted as she walked into Willow's office.

"You are such a big baby," Willow said, as she pulled Asia's fleece coat off. Asia looked at her overstuffed chair next to Willow's desk, and she turned away and leapt up onto the love seat on the other side of the office. Willow chuckled and sat down in her chair.

"Pouting?" Paula asked, as she saw Asia decided to take up residence as far away from Willow as she could.

"Making a statement. She'll get over it, when I take her for a w-a-l-k later."

Asia's head popped up, and she studied Willow.

"I swear that dog can spell." Paula said, laughing, as she set the steaming mug of coffee on the desk and left the room.

Willow started to flip through the stack of mail and pulled out all of the important pieces. She stopped when she came upon a plain white envelope with her name and address, but no return address. The stamp showed the letter had been processed through the town's main post office. She turned it back and forth in her hands. *Odd*, she thought, *someone would mail her a letter instead of sending her an email, or better yet, stopping by.* She grabbed her letter opener and sliced the envelope open. Inside she found a single slip of small white note paper. She unfolded the paper and read:

Things are not always as they appear.
You have a spy in your midst.

No signature, no date...*how very strange,* she thought. What "midst" were they speaking of? Her friends, her family, her company? She read the note again, then placed it back in the envelope, and locked it in her credenza. She resumed looking through the rest of her mail, only half aware of what she saw, her mind continuing to replay the note over and over again.

She snapped out of her haze as she held another letter, this one expected. It was the official confirmation of her attendance to the National Human Resources Conference. She'd missed this conference for the last three years and was determined to be there this year. They were also accepting her proposal to be an official speaker. She was both thrilled and scared at the chance to speak in front of one-thousand plus of her peers. Willow glanced at the date in the corner of her computer screen and realized the conference was two short weeks away. She would have to inform Wyatt, and the sooner the better.

"Should I tell him of the note?" she asked, mumbling to herself. No. The note wasn't a threat; it didn't make a demand. It's harmless. It told her nothing she and Wyatt didn't already know. She certainly didn't want him to think she ran to him with every little thing. She picked up her phone and dialed Wyatt.

"Good morning, Willow. What can I do for you?" Wyatt asked.

He sounded cordial and at the same time cool.
Something must be wrong.

"Good morning, Wyatt. Did you have a good trip
to D.C.?"

"Long, trying, and I'm sure not the reason you
called."

"No…it's not. I just wanted to inform you I plan
to attend the National Human Resources Conference
two weeks from tomorrow."

"I see. Where is this conference being held?"

"New York City. Before you say anything, it's
only four days long. I'll be at the hotel the entire time,
unless I go to dinner with a group of people."

"I see," he repeated himself.

She wasn't sure she liked this side of him. He
acted too formally.

"Wyatt, is something bothering you?" she blurted
out.

"No…why?"

"You just seem—different. I won't need any of the
guys staying there. Noah can accompany me to the
hotel and come back to meet me for the return trip."

"I see."

Her blood pressure began to rise in concert with
her frustration.

"Is that all you can say?"

"What would you have me say? Sounds as though
you've planned this entire trip out, including who will
escort you to and from the hotel. I'll work out the
details and get back to you. I'll be making an addition
to your plan. Noah will be staying in a room next to
you, and I would like you to remain at the hotel at all

times. Including dinners, too." He hung up without even saying good-bye.

"What on earth?" She stared at the humming phone.

"I'm sorry, did I miss something?" Paula asked as she walked into the office.

"No, no. It's not you. Men—I'll never understand them," she said, shaking her head.

* * * *

Willow patted each of the dogs good-bye as Noah leaned against one of the company's dark metallic gray Lincoln Navigators.

"I hate to rush you; security has increased at SeaTac. If we don't get going now, you run the risk of missing your plane."

"I know; I'm coming." She stepped back inside and pulled an oversized rolling suitcase out and set it next to the overnight bag on the patio.

"Willow, you're only going for four days." He ran up to retrieve the two suitcases.

"Yes, and I feel lucky to get everything into only two bags."

Noah put the suitcases into the Navigator and jumped into the driver's seat.

"I've wanted to take one of these for a spin." He smiled and started the engine.

"Boys and their toys." Willow giggled and shook her head.

* * * *

Wyatt stood to one side of the window in Tristan's house and watched the Navigator pull out of the driveway. He'd thought about sending Logan or even Jack with Willow instead of Noah. Only he knew it would be a petty thing to do, and not an efficient use of his team members. Besides, if Willow and Noah did have something going, it would make a no difference anyway.

"What's caught your interest?" Tristan asked, as he walked into the living room carrying two bottles of beer.

"Nothing," Wyatt said. He stepped away from the window and took the offered beer. Tristan looked out just in time to see the Navigator pull away from the front gates.

"Oh, Willow and Noah are heading out. Don't worry, Wyatt. Noah will get her to New York and back safely."

Wyatt took a slug of his beer to keep from snapping out the thought which had popped into his head, but not before Tristan zeroed in on it.

"Aw, damn. You aren't worried about Noah keeping her safe. You're worried about Noah."

"What are you talking about?"

"You know damn well what I'm talking about. Don't even pull that crap on me. I can read your mind, remember."

"Only when I want you too."

"Yeah, keep telling yourself that. What I want to know is, when did you go from barely being able to stand the woman to infatuation?"

"What the hell are you talking about?" Wyatt's face started to flush. "I'm not infatuated with Willow Winters. It's my job to keep her alive and safe."

"Uh-huh. You're not fooling me for one minute. However, since you aren't willing to discuss this with me, let's change the subject. Is Noah staying out there for the four days or will he come back to the campus? I have a couple things he could do."

"He won't be back until Willow comes back. He's staying with Willow and also helping General Roberts get a few things done."

"Makes sense. When she gets back, maybe you should ask her out to dinner or something."

"Ye—ah. I'll get right on that." Wyatt grunted.

"Your loss." Tristan shook his head. "She's an exceptional woman."

"*I know...*" Wyatt's thought drifted into Tristan's mind.

Tristan glanced at his brother. He wasn't sure Wyatt meant for him to hear that, so he held back his comment.

* * * *

Willow was drained by the time the bellhop opened the door to her room. She'd taken the last flight out of SeaTac so she could finish up work at the office. The extremely long and tiring day coupled with the three-hour time change made for three hours less sleep when she needed it most.

"This is beautiful," she said, as she looked around the large, posh room with its king-size bed, huge bathroom, and separate sitting area with a breakfast nook.

"Is there anything else you need?" the bellhop asked.

"No, thank you." She tipped him and locked the door behind him.

She glanced around the room once more and focused on the vase of blood red roses, fruit basket, and bottle of champagne. "That's lovely." She walked over to the trio, leaned forward and sniffed the roses, and found the small envelope tucked into the bouquet. She gently pulled out the envelope and read the card inside.

You and your sisters have been lied to.
Your parent's death was not an accident.

She dropped the card as if it were ablaze and watched it fall to the floor. She stared at the card while popping the cork on the champagne. She knocked back a glass, refilled it, and walked over to the love seat. She drank the champagne while staring at the tiny white card lying on the floor. She walked back, refilled her glass, and bent to pick up the card.

She'd read and re-read the card so many times, she'd lost count. How could that be? Her parents died in an auto accident. They weren't murdered; they were in an accident. *Wasn't it? The police report said an accident.* Who knew she planned to be here? Who sent the card and why did they tell her their parents' death wasn't an accident? How did they know? Did they kill her parents? Did the same person send both notes?

She sat up for half the night trying to decide on her next move. In the end she tucked the card inside the envelope and placed it in her purse. She decided not to contact anyone, but she would research her parents' accident when she returned home. There she could pull out the file she'd started after she'd received the police report. She took a sleeping pill and closed her eyes.

She woke to the sound of a ringing phone.

"Hello?" came her groggy voice.

"Good morning, Ms. Winters. This is the concierge. One of our servers tried to deliver your requested breakfast. She became concerned when you did not answer. Is everything all right?"

"I'm sorry, yes. I guess I overslept. What time is it?"

"It's a bit after nine ma'am. Would you like us to bring you up a fresh breakfast?"

"No...wait. Could you bring me some coffee and a scone, please?"

"It'll be right there."

Willow sat up and looked around the room. She couldn't believe she had slept through her alarm and someone knocking on her door.

"I guess I shouldn't take a sleeping pill with champagne."

A knock on the door sounded. She got up. Threw on a robe and answered the door.

"Good morning, Ms. Winters. You had a very late arrival. I hope you are feeling rested?" the woman asked.

"Yes, a bit too rested."

The woman walked over to the table in the corner and poured steaming coffee into the cup. She arranged a carafe of ice water, two different scones with butter, and a variety of jams, along with a plate of fresh strawberries on the table.

"That looks great. All I wanted was a cup of coffee and a scone."

"On the house, Ms. Winters. My manager said it would be a long morning, and you needed a good breakfast. Is there anything else I can do for you?"

"Yes, there is one thing. I wonder if you could answer a question for me."

"I would be happy to?"

"Do you know who ordered the roses?"

"No ma'am, I don't, but I can try and find out for you."

"Please." Willow gestured to the phone.

The woman picked up the phone and called the front desk. Willow sat down at the table and doctored her coffee, then she took a long slow sip and savored the flavor.

"The front desk manager said the roses were delivered by one of our regular florists. They left no name as to who they were from."

"How would they know I checked in here?"

"No one called and inquired about you. The roses just showed up, and the maid brought them up. Is there a problem with them; would you like me to take them away?"

"No—no, they're beautiful. I just would like to know whom to thank."

* * * *

It pleased Willow that her speech went well. She had to admit, she was slightly taken aback when she walked into the main ballroom and saw it filled to capacity. The person who showed her up to the head table told her there were 1,064 attendees, and everyone showed up for opening dinner and her speech. After dinner, she got approached by people wanting to say hello to her, and others who wanted to ask additional questions. A local group served as the night's entertainment and allowed her the chance to wander up to one of the open bars and order a drink.

"Nice speech, roomie."

Willow spun around when she heard the familiar voice.

"Cassidy?"

"I've gone by that name since birth," Cassidy giggled, using their secret longtime joke as she rushed up to give her a big hug.

"Cassidy, I didn't know you were going to be here. Where have you been? Why did you stop answering my emails? How are you?" Willow fired her questions so quickly; Cassidy had no chance to answer a single one.

"Life happened. You know how it goes. Your speech was wonderful. So great to see you, Willow. Are you staying in the hotel?"

"Yes, and you?"

"Sure am. This is my one and only vacation this year. I would love for us to get together and catch up."

"I would love it, too. How about tomorrow? I need to catch up on some work tonight."

"Sounds perfect; how about dinner? We could head out to one of the local restaurants and have a quiet dinner."

Willow thought of the promise she made to Wyatt. She knew if she left the hotel, even for an hour, Noah would have to inform him, and he would never trust her again. True, she hadn't actually agreed to his request of staying at the hotel the entire time. All the same, she felt like she was on thin ice with him at the moment and that ticked her off. What in the world had she done?

"Dinner sounds great. All the local restaurants are going to be mobbed when this herd of people head out to eat. How about you come up to my room, and we'll order in?"

"Sounds like fun. It's a date. Oh, gotta run. I left some people waiting."

Cassidy hugged Willow one last time and then melted into the crowd. Willow tried to track her movements but got sidetracked by another colleague and all thoughts of Cassidy were pushed to the back of her mind.

* * * *

Willow locked the door to her room, slipped her shoes off, threw all her stuff in the first chair, and headed for the bar. The bottle of merlot she ordered earlier waited, and she couldn't wait to pour a glass. She grabbed her sweats she'd hung over a chair and pulled out her laptop.

"Geeze...I really need to work on my social life." She shook her head at herself and picked up the wine bottle. Under the bottle she found another envelope. "How does this keep happening?" She put the bottle back down, picked up the envelope, and slid the single sheet of paper out.

Trust only those who are close to you.
Please, watch your back.

She started to feel watched. Someone knew her schedule, knew it well enough to know when to drop these notes in her room. She retrieved the first note from her purse and compared the handwriting. She was no expert, but they looked alike, and, more importantly, they "felt" alike. At this point she had only her gut to go on, and her gut told her these notes were written by the same individual.

Chapter Eleven

Willow rushed back to her hotel room. She met up with Cassidy earlier, gave her the room number, and the two agreed on a time to meet. Cassidy left the dinner-ordering decision up to Willow. She'd left her room in such a hurry in the morning, she needed to make sure everything got put away. She also wanted to order appetizers and drinks ahead of time. A few minutes after she placed her order, there came a knock on her door.

"Good evening Ms. Winters. I have your first bottle of wine," the woman from the night before greeted her and brought in a cart. Wine, a couple of glasses, a carafe of water, and a huge tray of cheese, crackers, and fruit filled the cart.

"My goodness," Willow said. "We may not even need dinner after this."

The woman acted a bit nervous, and Willow could feel uncertainty and concern from her.

"You must work every day. You're the only person who has come to my room since yesterday."

"I knew the hotel would be full this weekend, and I asked for extra shifts." The woman fumbled as she placed the plates on the table.

"Are you okay?"

"Yes, ma'am."

"Did you bring up my bottle of wine last night?"

"Yes, ma'am."

"Please, call me Willow. Did you leave the note under the bottle?"

The woman's gaze darted around the room. She pulled at the sides of her apron and looked at anything and everything except Willow.

"I'm sorry if I did something wrong," she said, her voice wavering. "The gentleman asked me to leave you the notes and left instructions on how I should do it. He told me he's your boyfriend. I've never done anything like this before, but he looked so sad. He made me promise not to tell you and gave me three hundred dollars just to leave the notes. I'm sorry if I did something wrong." She hung her head to hide her crimson cheeks.

"You did nothing wrong, and I'm not upset with you. Do you have any more notes?"

"No, ma—Willow. Only the two."

"Can you describe what the man looked like?"

"I can't really recall. He came by a few days before you checked in. Medium build, white guy, dark hair, I think."

"No one's been in my room?"

"No, ma'am. Neither the hotel nor myself would allow such a thing to happen."

"Good to know." Willow thanked the woman, reassured her the matter was closed, and sent her on her way. A few minutes later, another knock sounded followed by Cassidy's sing-song voice.

"Hey girl, open up."

"Hi Cassidy, come on in and take your shoes off."

"You told me casual. You know I take everything literally, jeans and a sweatshirt. I haven't changed my style since college."

The two laughed.

"Don't tell me you didn't bring jeans?" Cassidy asked, as she looked at Willow's wool pants and silk blouse.

"I didn't think I would have any place to wear them. All I have are my sweats and a sweatshirt."

"Well go put them on, girl. We aren't entertaining and we're not going anywhere."

"Right. Help yourself to a glass of wine and food. I'll be right back."

The two girls laughed and teased as they reminisced about their college years together.

"I forgot how much fun the two of us could have together," Cassidy said.

"What happened? I thought we would be lifelong friends," Willow said. "The last time I heard from you, you were to start a new job. I recall it, because your position took you abroad. You were running low on our vitamins, and I'd none left to send you. I thought you were upset with me about the vitamins and stopped contacting me because of it. I tried to track you down but had no success."

"I know. I'm really sorry how I handled the situation. It had nothing to do with you. I knew you didn't have any more vitamins; how could you? You gave me all your bottles the last time we saw each other."

"Then why?"

"I told you I got offered a new position with a foreign company. They were headquartered in Taiwan, a formulation company. I mean, what were the odds? We meet one another in college, become roommates in college and through graduate school, both major in personnel, and both find positions in the drug world?"

"Winters Corporation is a research company, with a branch dedicated to the creation of drugs."

"Yes, there's a difference. What I'm saying is we were basically in the same industry, and even with me traveling halfway around the world, I thought we would remain friends." Cassidy rose from her chair, picked up her wine glass, and wandered the room. "I couldn't tell you when I phoned you the last time, but I'd been ill for a few months. I finally realized the connection to the vitamins, and I started to ration them. I thought my body needed to get used to not having them, and I tried to wean myself off. About six months after arriving in Taiwan, I got deathly ill and ended up in emergency. The doctors had to really work to stabilize me. After they pushed a massive amount of fluids and other drugs into my system, they released me."

"Did you tell the doctors why you thought you were sick?"

"No. I told you the first day you let me try them I would never tell anyone. However, a few weeks later I collapsed in the employee lounge, and the company doctor came out. They admitted me to the company clinic. They even sent a team in to search my flat for foreign substances. The team came across the last empty bottle I'd tossed in the trash. Apparently there was enough residue inside the bottle to test. That was the very moment I lost all control over my life."

"How do you mean? Why didn't you just come home?"

"I was so weak and at times totally out of it, I didn't put up much of a challenge. The doctor did a barrage of tests on me. He even notified Daniel Prescott, the owner and president of the corporation. Mr. Prescott sent his private plane out, and they loaded me up and brought me back to the States, where he and his elite team of researchers and doctors could study me."

"You make it sound as though you were a lab rat. Are you saying you were kept against your will?" Willow was horrified this had happened to her friend. "If only I'd never given you that first vitamin, none of this would've happened."

"This is not your fault, Willow. You told me over and over to only use them when I felt stressed or couldn't concentrate, and not more than two a day. I got addicted. I took them every day and some days as many as five. Remember the day we were packing and you couldn't find your last box of vitamins?"

"Yes, I remember. There were thirty or so bottles in the box. I thought maybe I'd shipped them home. Come to think of it, I totally forgot about the box by the time I got home."

"I stole it. By that time, I was so convinced I couldn't live without them, I actually stole your vitamins. How low could I get?"

"You said they brought you back to the States. Where did they take you?"

"To Mr. Prescott's personal compound in Texas, under guard 24/7 for four months and used as their guinea pig. I had no phone, no computer, no way of contacting the outside world."

"How did you get away?"

"One day they told me I could leave. Guess I was no longer of any use to them. Daniel Prescott told me never to speak of the time I spent at the facility. He said no one would believe me. He had the power to destroy my life and my family if I ever uttered a word."

"That's weird. Am I the only person you've told?"

"Yes. I figured I owed you an explanation. I also want you to know I never told them where I really got the vitamins. They were in those plain brown bottles with no labels and I told them I'd bought them from a street vendor in Taiwan."

"Thank you, Cassidy. I'm sorry this happened to you. You seem happy now; are you doing well?"

"I am. I love the company I work for. It's a graphics design place with no interactions with the drug industry. They're located in Seattle. I bought my first house on Bainbridge Island, and I commute on the ferry to work. I'm happy and I would love for us to be friends once again, if you can ever forgive me."

"You mean you have been in Seattle all along? How did I not know this?"

"Because I didn't want it to be known, and I changed my last name to my mother's maiden name. Before you agree to walk back into my life I have to warn you: Daniel Prescott is an extremely powerful and dangerous man. I will never be rid of him."

"Seems to be going around these days," Willow said.

* * * *

Wyatt watched as Willow and Noah got out of the cart in front of her office building. Frankly, it surprised him she even went to the office. They'd just returned from New York, and it was late in the day. He figured between the time change, long flight, and lateness of the day she would've stayed home.

"Not Willow. I should've known better," he said.

Noah handed Willow her briefcase. She hugged him and walked into her building. That same nasty itch crept up Wyatt's back. *Knock it off, Farraday,* he thought.

"What's the trouble?" Tristan's voice popped into his head.

"Nothing," Wyatt snapped back, a little too irritated.

"Well, it can't be me. I haven't seen you all day. So it just leaves Willow to incite grumbling. Victory said she was coming home today. Has she managed to piss you off already?"

Wyatt could feel Tristan's chuckle resonate through his brain.

"It has nothing to do with her. Get out of my head and get back to work."

"How's it feel, bro. Used to be you were the only one of us able to intrude into my mind. Now, with Victory's grounding ability, I can come and go as I please."

"Not quite you can't. Only when I'm distracted and, by the way, what happened to our agreement not to intrude?"

"*Yeah, yeah. I stick to our agreement most of the time. Even so, I need to make up for all the past years.*"

"*If you don't leave this instant, I am going to assign you to the most shit job I can find...Tristan?*"

"*Gone. Just don't come crying to me.*"

Wyatt knew his brother would always be there for him. He was only flexing his telepathic abilities and, after all, Wyatt did have a tendency to invade Tristan's thoughts. But that was pre-Victory. He'd let it go—for now. His phone vibrated, and he pulled it from his pocket. *Well, whadya know.*

"Hi, Willow. Did you enjoy your trip?"

"It was a great conference. I made a ton of contacts. I need to speak with you and the guys about something important."

"Okay, how about at our offices tomorrow morning?"

"I really don't want to wait; how about tonight, if possible? I've already contacted Victory and Payton. Could you all come up to the house around seven-thirty? We'll order takeout from that Italian place you guys like."

"You got it. See you then."

* * * *

Everyone gathered around the dining room table and enjoyed the spread the women brought in. Wyatt glanced over at Willow. She caught his gaze and smiled. She tried to play it cool, but he could tell by the way she fidgeted something weighed on her.

"Willow, why don't you tell us why you wanted us all here tonight. You know these guys, they won't stop filling their faces until every last crumb is gone," Wyatt said.

She placed her silverware on her plate, wiped her hands on the napkin in her lap, and cleared her throat. Definitely agitated and *he* didn't even need to be able to read auras.

"Remember when Victory told us about Mom's *vitamins?*"

"Ahh, we weren't there," Logan said.

"When we were very young, around the age of five, our mother started to formulate vitamins for each of us. She insisted we take them and impressed on us never to use each other's vitamins or share them with others," Victory said. "She drew blood from each of us every six months, and, according to her journals, the vitamins she'd created were uniquely formulated to each of our DNA. Constant adjustments were made to each of the formulas based on the results of our blood tests."

"I discovered this information when I found the USB in the clock Mom left to Victory. She'd documented every year of our lives and any changes she noticed," Payton said. "When I found this information, we believed she tampered with our DNA, trying to enhance our abilities."

"I soon discovered that wasn't the case," Victory said. "All those years, she tried to suppress our abilities. She was trying to curb what Ryker had done to us and stabilize our systems. The vitamins she created for us were a DNA suppressant. After she died, we continued to take them until they were gone. The buffers eventually started wearing off. That's why the changes in our abilities. We each changed at different rates, but the longer we went without the buffers, the more our abilities evolved."

"Are you saying you created the same formula your mother formulated all those years ago for Collin and me?" Morgan asked.

"The formulas have differences; nevertheless, they are based on the same principles."

"When Victory told us about the vitamins being more than just vitamins I mentioned I'd given some of mine to my college roommate, Cassidy," Willow said.

"Now I know you didn't fill us in on her," Noah said.

They all sat in silence as Willow told them about running into Cassidy and spending time together over the weekend. No one spoke a word until she finished.

"Wait a minute," Payton said. "Did you just say Cassidy's kidnapper was *Daniel* Prescott?"

"Yes, Daniel. Why, do you know him?"

"I've not personally met the man. Even so, his company and legal team purchased our complex."

"Oh, that can't be good," Noah said.

"Did you check him out?" Willow asked.

"Our legal team took care of all the details. I met the attorney at the complex the first time and gave him the tour. Prescott is who you were supposed to meet that night," Payton said.

"Jack, look him up, would you?" Wyatt asked.

"This Prescott guy has a number of achievements mentioned all over the Internet. There are lots of pictures with him and a variety of powerful people. The particular one that caught my eye was taken last year. Daniel Prescott and Carl Sterling were photographed getting out of a limousine together, and they looked quite chummy." Jack said, as he turned his computer around so the others could see.

"It would seem Daniel Prescott fits the Kaleidoscope Group mold quite nicely," Tristan said.

"My thoughts exactly," Wyatt said.

As they all studied the screen a "breaking news" alert popped up.

"What's the article say, Jack? I can't read the screen from here," Morgan said.

"Mr. Daniel Prescott, new owner of the original Winters Corporation facility, has just been named President of Biotec."

"Are you shitting me?" Collin asked.

"I'm sorry," Payton said. "I should've paid more attention to the interested buyers."

"Don't beat yourself up, Payton," Willow said. "You're busy. Victory and I are just as much to blame."

"None of you is to blame. They would have figured another way to get close, if this one didn't pan out," Wyatt said. "Look at it this way. We have our first big lead."

"And a concrete connection to Sterling," Collin said.

"So this guy that stalked Willow through the basement was a henchman for Prescott?" Tristan asked. "If that's the case, what was the dickhead supposed to accomplish?"

"I'd like to know the same thing, and, what about Cassidy?" Morgan said. "I can't believe she's really safe. Should we bring her in?"

"No," Willow said. "He's left her alone. She's built a new life for herself. She's out of the drug industry; she even changed her last name. We are rebuilding our friendship. Please don't get her involved unless there is no other alternative. There is her family to worry about."

"We'll leave her out, for now. I'll assign one of my guys from Beta Team to check up on her a couple times a week, at a discreet distance." Willow started to protest, but Wyatt raised his hand and gave her the universal sign for *just one minute*. "Willow, this is what we do. Believe me, Prescott may have left Cassidy alone up until now, but when he gets wind of her reconnecting with you, that'll all change."

"We need to know the moment the two of you plan to get together. You do understand the importance of the situation?" Tristan asked. "You can't go off on your own and not tell us. Both your lives could be in danger."

* * * *

"Good morning. Thanks for fitting me into your busy schedule." Wyatt handed Willow her usual drink.

"Thank you," she said, as she took the cup. "I figured if you needed to see me, it must be important."

He sat in the chair across from her desk.

"Nice plant," he said, before blowing on his hot coffee. "I don't recall seeing it last time I visited; same secret admirer?"

"I'm not sure."

His interest was piqued. *Could it be from Noah?* Wyatt made sure his mental barriers were up before the thought crossed his mind.

"A new boyfriend?" He fought to keep the tingle of resentment under control.

"If so, I'm not aware of him," she said with a chuckle.

He stiffened, his jealousy stomped out by impending danger. "What did the card say; it should've given you a clue."

"'Welcome *back.*' No one signed the card. Paula and I decided the ivy was a gift from some of the employees."

"*Son of a bitch!*"

"*Come on, really.*" Tristan's response floated into Wyatt's mind. "*I left you at the café not ten minutes ago. Are you trying to tell me the two of you got into it already?*"

Knock it off. This has nothing to do with us getting along. I need you to organize your team. I want you and Jack here in Willow's office ASAP. I think she has a bug in her plant."

"*What plant?*"

"*The green one.*"

"*Oh, that helps. Can you be a bit more specific?*"

"*I don't know what the hell kind of plant it is. But it's the only one in her office, behind her desk. Check it out; sweep the entire office. See what we have.*"

"*Want us to disable the bug?*"

Wyatt watched as a flash of agitation flushed Willow's face. He brought his index finger up to his mouth. She pressed her lips into a thin white line and squinted her eyes at him. He held out a hand palm up and with the other hand made a writing gesture. Her features softened, and she searched her desk for a pen and paper as he continued with his mental multitasking.

"*No. Keep this all under the radar. I don't want anyone knowing we are looking for bugs or found one. Leave the bug where you find it but inform Paula. When you're done with Willow's office, I want the team to check Payton's and Victory's offices. Make sure you go over Victory's lab with a microscope. Give her a heads up.*"

"*Got it. I'll keep you updated.*"

Willow handed him the scrap of paper. He scrawled a quick note and passed it back.

I'll explain later. For now, please take my lead and act normally.

As she glanced up, he noticed her normal peaches-and-cream complexion had turned ashen. He winked at her, and the unexpected reaction from him brought an instant smile.

"You know, you've been cooped up in a hotel for the past four days. I feel like I haven't seen the outdoors in over a week. What do you say we take a walk and continue the conversation in the fresh air?"

"Sounds like a wonderful idea. I heard it's going to start raining later tonight. We better enjoy the sun while we can."

* * * *

"Are you going to tell me what that was all about back in my office?" Willow asked, as they headed to the lake.

"Your office might be bugged."

"What are you talking about?" She stopped; Wyatt turned toward her. He walked back, gently took her by the arm, and kept walking.

"Keep moving. We don't know who's watching, and we're supposed to be out enjoying the fresh air."

"You tell me my office might be bugged, and I'm supposed to act like nothing happened? When, how? This place is locked down tighter than the White House."

"Your plant. Is that the first plant you've received?"

"Technically."

"What the hell does *technically* mean? Stop playing games with me, Willow, I haven't the time or patience."

He quieted, and she felt the familiar energy of her brother-in-law infiltrate the immediate vicinity.

"They located the bug. I told Tristan to leave it alone. We don't want to give whoever it is a heads up."

"We all know who it is."

Wyatt gave her a sideways glance.

"Okay, so we don't actually know *who* it is, but we know who they work for."

"You're right. We don't know *who*. Hopefully this will lead us to the *who*. You never answered my question. The plant—is it the first one you've gotten?"

"No, do you recall the flowers? I didn't know who sent those either. The note read '*I hope you have a wonderful week,*' with no signature on the card."

"Why didn't you tell me?"

"Tell you what? I received flowers and a plant from some of employees? It hardly seemed worth mentioning."

"When did the plant arrive?"

"The day I returned back to work after the complex incident."

"Shit. Why didn't I see it? The flowers were the dry run. If the flowers found their target, then it's safe to assume they could send in the real thing with no trouble. Son of a bitch. Think back to what you've done since you came back and who you talked with. Thank goodness you spent those four days out of your office. Did you do or say anything that might be dangerous in the wrong hands?"

Willow shook her head. "No. I had a ton of emails and work to catch up on. I did a few interviews, but nothing of any relevance...oh no. I interviewed Aimee first thing when I got in the office. She told me about being followed. She gave me her new address. What if someone from Biotec is still keeping tabs on her? If whoever broke into my office was searching for information on Amiee, I handed it right to them. What have I done? Wyatt, I've put her in danger."

"She'll be fine; don't worry. I'll assign a detail to her. We'll move her into one of the bungalows here on the campus until we can sort all this out."

"The least I can do after the mess I've gotten her into. Could we walk over to her building now?"

"Yes. Let's go over and explain everything to Amiee. I'll get someone assigned to her before we leave there. They can take her back to her place and help her pack whatever she will need.

"After which I'll drop you off back at your home office, I've got a meeting planned with the team."

"If you leave the ivy in my office, how am I supposed to get anything done?"

"I want you to work from home until we figure this thing out. Postpone the interviews for the rest of the week; I know that breaks your heart." Wyatt smiled at her.

When he smiled at her the way he just did, Willow felt like she was the only person in his world. The feeling warmed her to her center and made her feel safe. And the wink he gave her in the office, she still couldn't figure out what that meant. His crystal blue eyes sparkled like the ocean on a warm sunny summer morning. She glanced up at him. He really was eye-catching with his blonde hair and matching five o'clock shadow. She knew for sure he made all the ladies drool.

"What's wrong? Do I have something on my face?" he asked, as he rubbed a hand over his chin.

"No, just rearranging the rest of my work week in my head." *Wow, talk about lame,* she thought.

Wyatt dropped Willow off at her back door with a warning. "Don't go anywhere without someone with you."

"I know the drill. And Wyatt…"

He turned back to face her. She felt him stiffen as if he expected an argument.

"Thanks." She smiled up at him.

He stood there for a second without moving or saying a single word.

"It's my job. Don't forget, you have my numbers if you need me."

* * * *

"*It's your job. Good one, Farraday, best you could do, right? No wonder you don't have a girlfriend,*" Tristan's voice rang through his head.

"*I don't recollect inviting you into my thoughts. Don't you have something better to do, because if you're bored I can find more for you to do, little brother.*"

"*I just got here. I planned to update you. But I didn't want to break the mood. Guess I didn't have to worry. You did it all on your own,*" Tristan's laugh rang between Wyatt's ears.

"Shut the hell up." Wyatt spoke the words out loud. "Save your report and get your ass and your team to the office."

Tristan didn't say another word, and Wyatt felt the instant he left. What distracted him and ruined his control around Willow? He'd made the rookie mistake of dropping his mental barrier once again.

Chapter Twelve

"Willow?" Victory called out from the kitchen as she and Payton came in the back door.

"I'll be right down," she yelled from her office.

"Are you okay?" Victory asked, as she grabbed a bottle of wine and Willow pulled three wine glasses out of the cupboard.

"I'm fine. How are the both of you?"

"A little shaken the guys found a bug in your plant. Tristan searched my office and lab from top to bottom and didn't find a thing," Victory said.

"What do you think they hope to hear?" Payton asked.

"I don't know for sure, but my gut tells me they're trying to locate Amiee. I think its someone connected to Biotec and Kaleidoscope Group, which means we're talking about a bunch of egotistical, rich maniacs," Willow said. She watched as a look of panic filled Payton's features.

"Don't worry, Payton. Wyatt and I went over to explain everything to Amiee. He assigned a full-time guard to her. He took her back to her house to pack everything she needs. We've move her to a bungalow, and, for now, she's not to leave the campus."

"Oh my gosh. How is she handling it?" Payton asked.

"She didn't really seem all too surprised. She has agreed to all Wyatt's restrictions and actually thanked me for helping her. Let's change the subject. I'm glad the three of us get to spend some time together tonight." She followed her two sisters into the living room.

"All the guys are in a meeting. They'll probably be tied up until late, so this is perfect timing," Payton said.

"I vote we order in pizza and salad and spend our time relaxing," Victory said.

"Of course you do," Willow said. "It's your turn to cook. Wait a minute; what am I saying? Yes, pizza sounds great and edible."

Willow and Payton giggled as they looked at their sister.

"Ha-ha. You two are a couple of clowns. You have to admit, my cooking skills have improved over the past year," Victory scolded, frowning at her sisters.

"You're right, sis. Willow, we shouldn't pick on her. At least she's trying. I did notice, however, you want to order the salad too."

"Only because I don't want to spend any time in the kitchen tonight. Thank goodness for takeout. Okay Willow, spill it."

Willow looked at her sisters. She got up from the sofa, grabbed the wine, and refilled all the glasses.

"This is definitely going to be a two-, maybe three-bottle night," Willow said, as she started her story.

"Wait, one minute. You mean to tell me Wyatt wants to leave the bug in your office? How creepy to be spied on. I wouldn't even be able to concentrate if I were you, never mind get any work done," Payton said.

"And that's why I'm going to work from here for the next few days. Give the guys time to formulate their plan. There's something else bothering me even more than the bug."

"It must be a *huge* something," Victory said.

"It is. I thought at first my imagination played tricks on me. Today my fears were proven. Over the past two weeks my ability to see Tristan's and Wyatt's auras has dwindled."

"What are you saying?"

"I'm saying I can feel Tristan's energy when I'm around Wyatt and the two are telepathically communicating. Tristan's energy is so familiar to me, even comforts me, sort of the way your energies do. I used to *see* Tristan's aura as clearly as a flashing stop light. But his aura has faded."

"And you're saying the same is now true for Wyatt, too?" Payton asked.

Willow nodded her head and took another drink of her wine.

"How utterly interesting," Victory said.

"Gee, how did I know you were going to say that?" Willow said. "I'd only begun to understand Wyatt's aura, but now there's almost nothing to glean. Same as Tristan, I still feel Wyatt's energy; it's powerful, but not his aura. Do you think it has something to do with the changes you told us about? Now that we no longer have Mom's vitamins to stabilize our powers, I'm losing my abilities?"

"Absolutely not."

Willow felt her chest tighten. Her eyebrows furrowed.

"Um—it's worse? I'm getting sick, just like Cassidy. How can you be so certain when you haven't even finished your testing?"

"I'm certain because like I told you both before, the lack of Mom's vitamins caused our abilities to magnify, not decrease. What you are experiencing is something different. Your mind has accepted Tristan and Wyatt into your inner circle. You now see them as family."

"You must be wrong. I couldn't possibly— Tristan, okay, but Wyatt? You've got to be wrong. We're only now becoming friendly and only part of the time."

"That's what your mind is telling you, sis; your heart says something different," Payton said, piping up. "The two of you might be like oil and water a good amount of the time, but deep in your soul where it counts, you would trust him with your life."

"But—I—no. It simply can't be."

"Tell me, can you see Noah's aura?" Victory asked.

"Yes…wait, come to think of it I can't. His energy is strong; his aura is the same as the brothers—faded from what it once appeared."

"There you have your answer. You see Noah as a friend, someone you trust, maybe even like a brother."

"Really?" Willow thought about the notes now locked upstairs in her safe. *"Trust only those who are close to you. Is that what's meant by the note?"*

"Willow, are you okay?" Victory asked. "You look as if Jack the Ripper is outside our window."

The doorbell rang, and all three of them jumped. *Saved by the doorbell,* Willow thought as she rose to pay the pizza delivery guy. She hated lying to her sisters and if she didn't answer, then she wasn't lying, right?

By the time Payton and Victory left, the rain had started to fall. The air smelled clean and crisp. Willow's mind drifted off in too many directions to even think about sleeping. She headed to her office to catch up on some paperwork. She dug through her briefcase and realized she'd left the small container of all her active USBs on campus, in her locked desk drawer.

"Darn it." She mumbled as she looked at the time. It was well past eleven. She didn't want to bother Noah or Wyatt. She could jump in the cart, go pick up her USBs, and be back in under fifteen minutes. She would take Asia to keep her company. "Come on, Asia. We have to make a quick trip." The dog jumped down from the loveseat and stretched her front legs way out in front of her with her head between them and butt high in the air. She followed that with an exaggerated yawn.

Willow opened the back door, and Asia sniffed the air. The deluge submersed the patio and made it impossible to see more than a foot or two out. "Let's go." Asia back-pedaled, ears straight out to the sides of her head. Whenever she did that, she reminded Willow of an airplane. "You won't melt, honest." Asia lifted her top lip, scrunched her nose, and gave Willow a huge Doberman smile. "Fine. Some guard dog you are, afraid of a little rain." She pounced from side to side and continued to smile. Willow pulled her raincoat tightly around her, locked the door, and headed for the cart.

The lights on the campus glowed like hazy spheres. Thunder broke the silence, followed by a dazzling flash of lightning which filled the night sky. Willow parked the cart as close to the front stairs of her building as possible and ran up the stairs, placed her soaked palm on the security pad, and entered the building. She flipped on light switches as she continued to her office and went directly to her desk drawer and retrieved the small box she had come for. As she reached her office door, another bolt of lightning screamed through the atmosphere at the same instant a startling, explosive boom of thunder rattled the building. The lights around her popped out and plunged Willow into total blackness.

"Great. I guess this wasn't my best plan." She reached out for the wall and followed it slowly back to the door. The rain fell in sheets and blocked out all possibility of moon- or starlight. She bumped the door with the tip of her boot and felt for the lock and handle. "I should've at least thought to bring a flashlight," she said, scolding herself. She stumbled down the steps, nearly falling on her face a time or two. She must be within inches of the cart. The cart was here; it had to be. This is where she left it. She shuffled in one direction and then turned and traveled back in the opposite direction. She left the cart here, right here.

Murky, dark energy overwhelmed her senses, except the energy didn't feel natural, it felt—synthetic; at this precise moment she realized…she was not alone. *"Oh my god – Wyatt!"*

* * * *

"I'm awake," Wyatt said, and popped up as he came fully alert. He'd fallen asleep on the cot in the break room. He meant to go home right after the meeting; instead, he downed a couple of aspirin for the blasted headache that continued to linger the entire day and decided to rest his eyes for a minute or two. Blackness filled his vision, and he rubbed his eyes to make sure they were indeed open. He closed his eyes, focused, felt the change, and opened them once again, his surroundings as clear as midday. Still, he must've dreamt, because he could swear he heard Willow.

"*Wyatt!*"

"What the hell?" Not possible. He actually heard Willow's voice. He pulled his phone out of his pocket and squinted at the glowing screen, the light much too bright for his night vision. He thought maybe his phone had connected to Willow's and he heard her on speaker. But the screen was blank. Panic slithered down his neck and made him twitch. He punched the speed-dial button.

Willow took off at a full run. In the pitch black it was nearly impossible to stay upright. She managed to widen the gap between herself and the hideous energy. Her phone vibrated in her jeans pocket. She debated answering, but she didn't want the person who pursued her to see the light; the glow would shine like a beam. She stumbled, fell, and rolled down a small hill. Once she regained her bearings, she knew where she was and crawled sideways until she came in contact with the first sword fern. She crawled into the ferns as the phone vibrated again. She reached into her pocket and fought to free it from her drenched jeans.

"Wyatt?" she barely whispered into the receiver.

"Hi Willow. I know it's late and I'm sorry, but—"

"Please help me! Someone is chasing me! I can't see them but I know it's someone menacing and..."

"I'm on my way. Where are you?" he asked as he jumped into his boots and threw on a camo rain slicker.

"I ran out the front door of my building. I thought I headed toward the security shack; somehow I got turned around. I'm in the large grouping of sword ferns—"

"I know where you are. Stay down, stay quiet, and don't move. I'm coming in hot—it means I'll have my gun drawn—so stay put."

He disconnected the call, grabbed his .40 caliber Glock from his desk, double-checked the gun was ready and loaded, and jammed it into his leg holster. He shot out the door in less than two minutes. He stopped for a split second to allow his sight to adjust. Even with the torrential downpour, it was lighter outside than inside the closed building. A sliver of the moon peeked through the clouds. The rain reflected tiny specks of light indiscernible to the human eye, yet for Wyatt's sight, they served as beacons to show him the way. He took off at top speed and headed to Willow's office. He saw the intruder first; the man sported night goggles and appeared entirely absorbed in locating his target. He searched behind every tree and bush. Wyatt detected Willow's movement before the intruder located her. As he feared, her movement caught the attention of her pursuer.

"*Remain still.*" He sent the command with as much mental force as he could in the hope he might connect with Willow. She froze, even her breathing slowed.

His initial thought was to engage the intruder. No, he needed to protect Willow. Get her away from here as fast and far as possible.

"*Tristan. There's an intruder on the campus. He's got Willow pinned down in the large group of ferns a few yards outside her office. Alert Morgan, he's the closest. Tell him I want the intruder alive.*"

"*Done, he's on his way and so am I. I may be farther away, but you know damn well I can be there in seconds. What in the hell is she doing out in this weather and alone?* Tristan hissed.

"*I haven't had the chance to ask her, but believe me, I will. Morgan can distract the intruder—I'm going in for Willow. I'll take her back to her house and watch over her tonight.*"

"*You sure? I can call Noah.*"

"*No, I'll be fine. Morgan's here, gotta go.*"

Morgan shot past Wyatt, a blur in the night. The intruder took off running. An instant later they heard the sound of an engine and a motorcycle appeared out of the darkness. The bright headlight blinded both men for a flash. The intruder jumped on behind the driver of the bike and they peeled off, Morgan scant inches from making contact. Undiscouraged, he kept up his inhuman pace and disappeared into the rain.

"Willow, he's gone. You can come out now," Wyatt called to her.

She stood and turned in the direction of his voice. Her teeth chattered, and she shook from head to toe. In an attempt to warm herself, she wrapped her arms around her body.

"Stay right there. I'll come to you."

She nodded in understanding.

"You're soaked to the bone."

Willow jumped at the sound of his voice right beside her.

"Sorry, I didn't mean to startle you."

"How can you see—oh, Payton *did* guess right, you have special abilities too. Why didn't you tell us?"

"We can discuss all this after we get you out of the rain; let's go." He effortlessly lifted her into his arms.

"What are you doing?"

"No sense in wasting time trying to keep up the charade and lead you back in the dark to the house. Hold tight."

She wrapped her arms around his neck, and he took off. He didn't put her down until they were in her bathroom. He gently lowered her to the floor and turned the shower on hot.

"Get in and warm up. I'll be downstairs waiting."

"What about you? You're soaked too."

"Only my head and pants. I'll grab a towel. Call if you need anything."

* * * *

"We missed them," Tristan said, as he stood in the kitchen with Wyatt. He handed Wyatt a bag with dry clothes.

"How is that possible?"

"They dumped the bike at the fence and went over. With the electricity out, it served as an easy escape. I highly doubt we'll recover any prints with the damn rain. It'll have washed away any information."

"Jesus. This place is supposed to be locked down tight and yet infiltrators appear to come and go as they damn well please. What the hell happened to the backup generator? The fence should always be hot. I don't care if there's a freaking earthquake, I want that fence hot. There should've been emergency lights, too."

"Yeah, about that…Morgan checked the generator when we discovered the fence was cold. Whoever these guys were, they were efficient. They busted into the generator shack and ripped the wiring out. Made a real mess."

"It's a weak spot. Tomorrow we bring in a bigger generator and a backup. I want the backup installed in the existing shack. Then put the main generator in a new shack built next to the main security building. I want the new shack impenetrable."

"Gonna cost some money, bro. We need to run the upgrades by the sisters."

"You just did," Willow said, as she entered the kitchen. "I witnessed this flaw firsthand. We still have funds in the maintenance account. Do whatever you need to do. I don't want to worry about our enemy prancing about the campus."

The brothers looked at one another and smirked.

"What?" she asked, indignantly.

"I highly doubt the intruders were prancing," Wyatt said, and busted out in laughter.

"Very funny, boys." She walked to a cabinet and pulled out three glasses. "Brandy?"

"Sounds great," Wyatt said.

"None for me, Willow. I want to get back to Victory. She's having a bit of trouble with her latest research test, and you know Victory. Her work consumes her thoughts. I want to take her mind off work as much as possible."

"Please, spare us the gory details."

"You're just jealous." Tristan flashed a dazzling smile.

Willow smiled, walked over to her brother-in-law, pushed herself up on her tippy-toes, and kissed Tristan on the cheek.

"What's that for?" Tristan asked, his cheeks noticeably colored.

"For being a wonderful husband to my sister and a pretty great brother-in-law, too." She hugged him.

"Thanks. Believe me, I'm the lucky one. If you need me, call. See you later."

Wyatt followed Willow into the living room. He'd turned on the gas fireplace when he came downstairs, and the room was now warm and cozy. Asia stretched out mere inches from the fire, where she lifted her head in acknowledgment and then went back to sleep.

Willow took the love seat closest to the fire; Wyatt sat in the chair directly across from her. He watched her play with the rim of her glass and gaze into the flames. It didn't matter how many times he saw Willow or what she was dressed in, she took his breath away, so much so that a hitch caught in his chest. Her straight blonde hair fell loose down her back and shimmered with the fire's light. She looked up at him, and he realized her eyes were the color of a perfect aquamarine, a prismatic color of light blue merging out into indigo. They reminded him of the aquamarine necklace his mother use to wear. Willow wore blue sweatpants and a mint-green pullover, and still she glowed. She surprised him when she broke the silence.

"Before you start your reprimand, I want you to know I'm sorry. You told me not to go anywhere on my own, and I did. I had a cart. I only needed to run to my office to pick up a box of USBs I needed. I figured I'd be out fifteen minutes, tops. I'm sorry and I won't do it again."

Wyatt was stunned silent. He never expected this from Willow.

"Glad to hear it. You took the wind out of my sails. No belaboring the issue. I want you to know, however, I'm holding you to your promise. Don't make me regret it."

"I won't. How did they know I would go to my office?"

"They didn't. I'm sure with the bad weather they figured not many people would be around, and they planned to use the opportunity to gather intel. That's not happening again."

"You told me you'd explain your abilities. Why have you kept them a secret? What are your abilities?"

"You witnessed firsthand my ability to run quicker than an average human. I'm not nearly as fast as Collin and Morgan; still, I can hold my own. I can communicate feelings to animals, similar to Victory, yet not as strong. I can't read them anymore than someone who understands animal behavior. I have night vision, and along with my heightened vision, I can detect the minutest movements around me. That's about it…until tonight."

"What do you mean?"

"You contacted me telepathically, don't you remember?"

Her gaze darted from side to side. "I *felt* your presence close to me. I didn't think I actually contacted you."

"You did, and I'm pretty sure you heard me when I told you to stay still."

"No, I have no telepathic abilities. I felt your energy. It filled the area."

Wyatt decided to leave this discussion for another time. He didn't want to push her. She'd experienced a dramatic event on top of all that'd happened to her over the past couple months.

"A while ago, Payton told me she believed your entire team possesses special abilities; is it true?"

"We do, yes."

"Were your supernatural abilities the reason General Roberts brought you together?"

"No. He based his choices on our performances. He had no way to know each of us possessed abilities."

"Does he now?"

"Yes, and now so do you and your sisters. No one else knows of us."

"Your secret is safe with me."

"I do have one question for you."

She stared into his eyes and waited.

"Have you told me everything? You explained about Cassidy, and you told me about the plants, or should I say I pulled it out of you. I need to know the truth, Willow. Are you hiding anything? Has anything else out of the ordinary happened? Even if you believe it's not relevant to the current situation, you need to tell me. Otherwise, we will continue to play the part of defense."

She hadn't moved a muscle. He locked on to her piercing blue gaze and held it. He could swear he watched her thought process from somber to questioning by her expression. She put her snifter on the table and ran both her hands through her hair. She folded her arms and placed her hands in her lap, where they fidgeted, twisting the fabric of her sweats between her fingers. She cleared her throat.

"Something—unusual has happened."

Chapter Thirteen

Willow rose and walked over to the dining table where her briefcase lay open. She reached in and pulled out a letter-size manila envelope and handed it to him.

"I didn't share these with you, because I wasn't positive they related in any way to what is currently happening. These feel more *personal* to me, based on the content. It started me thinking, who could I really trust?"

Wyatt opened the envelope and pulled out the three notes. The top corner of each note was numbered.

"I numbered them in the order I received them. You'll notice they aren't dated; the first one did come in the envelope and there's a postal date."

Wyatt read them in order. He looked over at her and read the notes out loud.

"'*Things are not always as they appear. You have a spy in your midst*'...I suppose you could take this as personal. '*You and your sisters have been lied to. Your parent's death was not an accident.*'" He studied her. "Tell me, Willow. Why wouldn't you trust me with these? Do you believe I have lied to you? Do you think I know the details of your parents' death and choose to keep them from you? Can you *honestly* think that little of me?"

She winced in reaction to his harsh words.

"*'Trust only those who are close to you. Please, watch your back...'*" This note stabbed him like a pin in a balloon. His puffed-up attitude deflated. His straight, stiff shoulders slumped, and he fell back in his chair. "I suppose you have no reason to trust me. I haven't exactly gone out of my way to be approachable. Every situation we find ourselves in seems adversarial."

"Except for tonight. I needed help tonight, and I reached out for you. Strange, don't you agree? You were the one I thought of and you responded...no questions, no judgment. Thank you. I believe our relationship has evolved."

He was stunned. The more time he spent with this woman, the more surprised he became. He realized deep down he truly liked her. He didn't know what to say, where to start, or how to feel. He resorted to his safety zone.

"These notes are important. They may be personal in nature, but at the same time they are relevant to your situation. It's been a long night. Let's call it done. Tomorrow we can approach them with a clearer head. I'll be here on the sofa if you need me."

* * * *

Willow woke to the aromatic smell of coffee and bacon. A smile formed on her lips. Payton must be home. She reached out to rub Asia and found an empty space. She got out of bed, threw on some clothes, and went down to the kitchen.

"Morning Pay—Wyatt? Did you cook breakfast?" Wyatt leaned against the counter and sipped out of an oversized mug.

"I did, yes. Hope you're hungry. I fed Asia too."

"How did you know—?"

"I helped Tristan out many times over the last year with the dogs when you were out of the country. I might not have spent much time with them, but I did learn how to feed them. How are you feeling?"

"Surprisingly great. I'm relieved I showed you the notes. You're right; I should have trusted you, if for no other reason than you are Tristan's brother and I trust him with my sister's life. I also agree with you. The notes are directly related to the current events. I became too emotional over the mention of my parents and the thought of being lied to. The notes made me doubt myself and those around me."

"I'm glad to hear you've found some trust in me. Eggs?"

"What—sure, eggs are fine. Is that all you have to say? You're glad to hear it?" *Take a breath, Willow,* she thought. *What was he supposed to say–hallelujah, praise the lord, she's come to her senses? Come to think of it, it was probably exactly what he thought.*

"No. What I mean to say is, at least we're now on the same page. We can work together and move forward. I have a few pressing things I need to get done today. Noah will be here to keep an eye on everything while I'm gone. I'll bring my computer with me when I return and work from here as much as possible."

"No need, I'll be fine."

155

"Yes, you will."

"Um, do I smell bacon?" Noah asked as he strolled in. "Is there any left?" He smiled as he sat down at the table and rubbed his hands together. "Oh, eggs. I would love some eggs." He winked at Willow.

"Boy, you're lucky I'm in a good mood today," Wyatt said, as he cracked a couple eggs into the frying pan.

"And toast."

"Don't push it."

* * * *

Willow spent the entire day up in her office. By late afternoon her lack of sleep started to wear on her. She got up from her desk, circled the room a few times, and finally decided to round up Noah and take a trip to the campus.

"I'm not sure about this," Noah said, as the two started for the campus.

"Wyatt requested I stay clear of my office for the next few days. He didn't say anything about not setting foot on the campus. Besides, I have you. What could happen?"

"Yeah, right. No disrespect, but lately you're a beacon for trouble. At the very least, can I interest you in taking a cart? We'll get down and back much quicker."

"I want to walk. Part of the reason I'm heading down there now is to get a little exercise. I promise I only want to chat with Victory. After I'm done, we can walk directly back here and you can tuck me inside the house safe and sound."

* * * *

"Hey sis, I'm surprised to find you in your office," Willow said.

"I know; I spend most of my day in the lab, but I'm at a wait-and-see stage in my latest test and figured it's as good a time as any to tackle some of my in-box. I'm surprised to see you here. Tristan told me you are confined to home office duty. How are you doing after last night? The guys have spent the day beefing up security. I swear it's going to be tougher getting on our campus than into Fort Knox," Victory said.

"Wyatt didn't specify I couldn't come to the campus; he asked me to not go to my office."

"Good luck with that one." Victory smiled and shook her head. "Really, how are you feeling? It must have been frightening."

"I'm doing fine. Wyatt made sure I stayed safe and spent the night at the house. And yes, between last night and the event at the old complex, I think I've lost five years off my life. Last night is the reason I wanted to talk with you. The strangest thing happened to me. I told you before that each day it feels like Wyatt's aura gets less clear to me, remember?"

"Yes, I do. Did something change last night? Is his aura vivid to you now?"

"No, in fact it's dimmer. Something strange took place last night; at least, I *think* it did. I'm still not sure what happened. Wyatt questioned me about it, and I avoided answering him. So I guess it must have happened; either that, or we're both crazy."

"What?"

"When I fell down the hill in the dark, I could feel the ominous aura of the intruder engulf my mind. Victory, his aura is one of the two darkest, murkiest auras I have ever experienced. I was petrified he would find me. I thought of Wyatt and shouted his name over and over in my head, as if he could hear me call out to him. Only then the most bizarre thing took place...he answered me. An instant later, he called my mobile to locate me. I keep thinking I made it all up in my head, except Wyatt says he heard me."

"You aren't imagining a thing, Willow. You did call to him and being your soul mate, he answered you."

Willow felt her mouth drop open; her heartbeat raced as she jumped up from her seat.

"What in the world are you talking about? Wyatt and me—no. Where did you ever come up with such a crazy notion?"

"Sit down, Willow. Let me explain. Do you have any recollection of when Payton or I telepathically connected with Collin or Tristan?"

"As I recall, that happened when you were on the island with Tristan. Payton told me she was on the island when she first connected with Collin. What does that have to do with what happened to me last night? I've never set foot on the island."

"It has everything to do with last night and nothing to do with the island. Both of us connected with the men during a time of extreme emotion, pain, and fear. We mentally reached out for the one person we felt a deep connection to. I believe it's in our genetic makeup to telepathically connect with our true soul mate."

"For the first time in my life I believe your thinking is flawed. There is no way Wyatt is my soul mate. Stop saying this; we have only stepped up to friendship."

"Willow, you do realize relationships can begin with friendship and work into love?"

"Well of course I do. This, however, is not one of those times."

"Believe what you will. I predict this is the beginning of a lifelong mental connection."

Willow rose from her chair again. She had come down here to understand what happened and to have Victory tell her everything would be fine. Not this. *This time you're wrong, Victory. Wyatt Farraday is nothing more than a friend,* she thought.

"Give yourself time. You'll work it out. You can always come to me with any questions."

Willow's phone rang and she pulled it out.

"Hey Paula, what's up?"

"Where are you?" Paula asked.

"With Victory, is there a problem?"

"I hope not. An interoffice package arrived from the London office. It's from Angie and marked 'Personal and Urgent.' I didn't want to leave the package in your in-box. I'll be right over."

"I'm just leaving. Can we meet at the café? I need to go over a few items with you."

"Anything wrong?" Victory asked, after she ended the call.

"I don't believe so. Paula has some mail for me and I thought it would be a good time to coordinate our schedules. Thanks for the information, sis. I'll give what you said some thought."

Willow kissed her sister on the cheek and headed out to see Noah. She wasn't ready to tell her sisters about the notes. Besides, she didn't know enough yet. They both had enough to worry about, adding the notes would be piling on.

"Ready to go?" Noah appeared from nowhere.

"About that…"

"How did I guess this wasn't going to be easy?"

"Sorry, only one more stop, I promise. Paula has some important mail for me. I told her we would meet her at the café. Look at it this way. Sandra is bound to have some luscious treat."

"Yum, I guess it'll have to do. You have to pinky promise me we'll head right back to the house after you meet with Paula."

"I promise, straight back."

Paula sat at a table in the far corner of the café, a hard-cover case on the table next to her.

"Hi Paula, thanks for calling me."

"I'm glad you were on campus. You saved me a trip up to the house. I started a pile of some other things I thought you would want. Everything is in here, locked, same combination as last time."

"Paula, have I told you you're one in a million?"

* * * *

Willow placed the case on her desk and dialed in the combination. She pulled out all the papers and looked for the mail from the London office. On the bottom of the case lay a box marked "Personal and Urgent." She picked up the box and noticed it was taped around the entire outside. She pulled a letter opener from her drawer and carefully sliced the sides, opened the box, and stared at the envelope which filled the entire inside. On the envelope, written in her mother's handwriting, was one word: *Willow.* Delicately she pulled the envelope free from the box and noticed it too was taped around all four sides. Willow placed the envelope on her desk and stared at the handwriting. She lost all track of the passage of time as she simply stared at the plain tan envelope.

"Willow. Are you all right?" Wyatt asked, from the doorway. "I'm sorry to barge in, but I was concerned when you didn't answer." He remained where he stood, not wanting to intrude.

"Wyatt? I didn't hear you. Please come in and sit." She felt as if she'd been ripped from the past and forced back into the present. "Did you stand there long?"

"I've knocked for over five minutes. I could hear Asia whine from the other side of the door, and for a split second I worried something had happened. Are you sure you're okay?"

"Yes, I'm fine. A tad bit off balance but nothing to be concerned about."

He walked over and sat in the chair next to her desk. She saw him glance at the envelope.

"It's from my mother," she told him before he could ask. She watched as bewilderment played across his features. He waited for her to continue. "It came in the interoffice mail today from London. Angie sent it. I'm not sure why she had it. I haven't had a chance to ask her."

"Would you rather I leave?"

"No. I'm grateful you're here. Please stay."

Casually he leaned back. He rested his elbows on the arms of the chair, folded one hand over the other, and placed an ankle on his other knee. Then he calmly waited for her to proceed. She studied him for a time and realized his patience was one of the characteristics that made him such a good leader, along with his ability to know when to allow someone else to set the pace. Willow picked up the letter opener and ever so slowly sliced one end open. She looked in, saw papers, and poured the contents onto her desk. Newspaper clippings, handwritten notes, and a USB slid from envelope. She peered inside to make sure it was empty. She spread the pile out and spied a legal-sized envelope. She opened it and read:

My Dearest Willow,
If you've discovered this envelope, it means two things. First, I didn't have the chance to transfer my notes onto a USB; and second, I've been murdered.

Her stomach clenched and her breaths came fast and shallow. She felt chilled and the outer edges of her sight started to dim.

Chapter Fourteen

Wyatt watched Willow's entire body stiffen. Her eyes widened and the color in her face went from peach to a white that reminded him of a first snowfall. She turned to him and attempted to speak, immense pain creased her face as she forced each word from her lips. "My—parents—were—murdered." Her breath caught, and she grabbed at her throat.

Wyatt sprang out of his seat and yanked her chair away from the desk. He placed one hand on her upper back, forcing her to bend forward and place her head between her knees.

"Breathe, Willow, just breathe. Take slow deep breaths."

It wasn't working; she wasn't listening to him.

"Damnit Willow, listen to my voice, slow your breathing or you will..."

He felt her body go entirely slack. Ever so gently, he pulled her upright in her chair. She slumped like a marionette cast aside by its puppeteer. She was out cold.

"Son of a bitch!"

Wyatt scooped her from the chair and carried her over to the sofa. With great care, he laid her down. He went into the bathroom and wet a hand towel with cool water. He filled a glass, and went back into the office, and placed the cool cloth across her forehead.

"Willow, wake up, please."

She didn't so much as stir.

"Willow—honey—please. You're making me nervous. Do I need to call Dr. Russell?"

"You do and you're a dead man," she said, moaning softly.

"That's my girl. I'm gonna help you sit up a bit and I want you to take a couple sips of water."

To his total surprise, she didn't argue and did exactly as he requested. Her eyelids fluttered open; her pupils were dilated.

"Come on. I'm gonna help you to bed. You're through for the night. You can deal with this mess in the morning. It's not going anywhere tonight."

"No. I have to read the letter. I'll only lay awake all night if I don't."

She started to get up, and he placed his hand on her shoulder.

"You stay right here." She attempted to rise off the sofa again, and he lightly pushed her back down. "If you have to read the blasted thing tonight, I'll get it."

He went back over to her desk and picked up the letter. As he approached her, he held the letter out to her. She didn't reach for it. He stood less than an arm's length away but she stared at the letter as if it were a serpent.

"Would you mind reading it to me?"

She felt fragile to him. He thought if he did something wrong, she might crumble. He grabbed the side chair, slid it closer to her, and sat down. Wyatt took in a deep breath and began.

My Dearest Willow,
If you've discovered this envelope, it means two things. First, I didn't have the chance to transfer my notes onto a USB; and second, I've been murdered.

He swallowed hard and looked at Willow. She lay propped up on the throw pillows, eyes closed. He thought for a moment she'd fainted again. She reached out and placed her too-cool hand on his leg. The feel of her touch both thrilled and terrified him, so he pushed it from his mind and continued.

I'm so sorry to leave you with this mess. I understand you will need to tell your sisters, and I want you to; you shouldn't carry the burden of my death alone. I also know you will be the one to spend time here in the London office after I'm gone. Be careful my love. I fear there are traitors about, not only here but back home in Washington.
Enough, I must tell you what I have discovered. You must guard this information with your life and take care not to tell anyone but your sisters until you have gathered all the necessary information to put Edward Ryker away once and for all.

Wyatt stopped, gaped at what he just read, and mentally reviewed the words. He felt the warmth of Willow's gaze on him and looked up to meet her turbulent blue eyes. She willed him on with her look.

I wish your father and I would have told you girls everything, writing this in a letter seems so cold. I gave birth to twins before you came into the world and I was told they died at birth. I say "was told" because I never got to see them, never told them I loved them, never held them or kissed them. I slipped into a coma during their birth and my babies were buried before I woke. Dr. Ryker double-crossed me. I went to him, thinking him a friend, and asked him to help me to conceive. I created a formula based on a fertility drug and changed the initial formula to fit my unique DNA. The drug was to serve the purpose for me and only me to conceive. I brought in Edward to help me with the final fine tuning. I became pregnant with you girls, the three of you were born, and my world filled with love. Edward convinced me to continue my work in order to help the thousands upon thousands of women who, like me, could not have a child. I thought it a noble cause and soldiered on. This was not a quick or easy process. A new drug takes years of testing and then years of clinical trials. I continued on with my testing, even though Edward had left to carry on with his own projects. I got careless and didn't keep tabs on him. Like I said, I thought him my friend and the idea of him stealing my formula never crossed my mind.

Approximately a year later I came across information that shook me to my core. I discovered Edward had stolen my formula and taken it to a man named Lawrence Braxton. Braxton owns a company called Biotec, and together they produced and distributed my formula without my consent or knowledge. Willow, I found information that proved he and Braxton somehow conducted a mass-market distribution throughout four states. I have no idea if or how they got the funding or approval to conduct such a test. I believe the women given this drug were not aware of the consequences. At the time, I wasn't even aware.

I want you girls to know the reason I keep coming back to London is not because you aren't all important to me—it's because you are everything to me. I'm trying to secretly research Ryker's work. I know now he tampered with the drug. He made an adjustment which somehow caused a change in your DNA. I've kept notebooks on the three of you since the first time I noticed the changes. It's become my life's work to buffer these changes happening to you until I can create a drug to permanently stabilize you.

I have been attempting to locate the women who were given the drug. Their offspring will also need my help. I've recently made great progress and feel I am on the threshold of discovering an answer.

I must go now, my darling. I will keep updating you as I gain more information. I have been keeping notebooks of all my work, which are in my home office. I have also saved the most important information on two USBs and have them hidden at the Washington complex. I will continue to update all as time passes.

My love to you all, always, Mom.

Wyatt looked up at Willow. Tears trickled freely down her cheeks; the front of her blouse was soaked. She looked devastated and disillusioned. A hundred questions swirled through his mind, but they could keep. He went to her, slid her legs off the sofa, and sat beside her. He reached out and pulled her close; she fell into his arms and wept. The immensity of her pain spilled from her soul and his heart ached with the hurt of it. He rocked her gently and whispered to her.

He continued to rock her long after her crying subsided and she held on to him.

"You've had enough for tonight, Willow. You need your rest. I want to lock the letter and the contents of the envelope in your safe. What's your combination?"

She didn't answer him right away. No doubt deciding whether or not to trust him, he knew. At first he was angry, but quickly he reminded himself he would have done the same. She finally answered him, and he rose, collected everything, and locked it away.

"You can change the combination tomorrow," he told her as he scooped her into his arms and carried her to her bedroom. He sat her on her bed and stepped away. "I'll make sure everything is locked up tight before I leave." He didn't plan to go far; he would spend the night camped outside the back door. He smiled down at her and headed for the door.

"Wyatt."

Had she spoken his name? The word was so soft, he turned in uncertainty.

"Payton's not been staying here at the house lately; she's spending her nights down at Collin's bungalow. I have Asia but...I guess what I'm asking is, will you stay with me? I don't want to be alone, at least not tonight."

His insides melted yet he managed to maintain his professional façade. "Of course. You get yourself ready for bed and I'll lock down the house."

He returned to her door a few minutes later, Asia at his heels. He cracked the door open to allow the dog to enter and peered in to see if she'd fallen asleep. She sat up in bed with the covers drawn up.

"Can't sleep?"

"I hate to ask this, you're being so good about this entire thing. Would you mind sitting with me until I fall asleep?"

He went to the bed and she shuffled over. He yanked his boots off, put his Glock on the nightstand, and sat down beside her. She curled into him.

"Thank you, Wyatt."

His mind a jumble of questions, he felt Willow fidget and knew she picked up on his energy. He willed his mind to calm. A few minutes later her breathing slowed and became more even. He decided he would stay for a while longer. Being next to her sparked feelings he hadn't felt in—ever. He relaxed, scooted farther down into the bed, and closed his eyes to soak in the experience.

Something cold and wet rubbed against Wyatt's cheek. Still half asleep, he reached up to brush the cold away and came in contact with a wet tongue.

"What the—" Confused, he opened his eyes and found himself face to face with Asia. She had wedged herself between him and Willow. Willow stared at him.

"If someone told me a week ago you and I would wake up in the same bed, I would've told them they were insane," she said, and broke into a smile.

He smiled back; he couldn't help it. A tiny sense of relief trickled though him to see she was taking this with a sense of humor.

"I would've been right there with you. But this isn't a big deal."

"Maybe not to you, to me it's a really big deal, and if I didn't say so before, thank you."

"You did. Believe me, there's no way I would have left you alone last night. I planned on spending the night out on your back porch. Your bed is much more comfortable. I hate to be the bearer of bad news, but we need to work on a plan."

"I know. I'm truly grateful I don't have to do this alone. I'm gonna grab a quick shower. You can use the bath in the hall. Let's meet in the kitchen for a quick bite to eat."

By the time Willow got down to the kitchen she was greeted by Wyatt, Tristan, Victory, Payton, Collin, and the rest of the SOCOM team. Her eyes widened when she saw the whole gang chatting.

"Sorry to spring this on you, Willow. I figured this was the safest place to update everyone and make our plan," Wyatt said.

"We brought breakfast," Payton said.

Willow felt overwhelmed and stood glued to her spot.

"If you want to take your sisters into the living room alone to give them your news, we'll wait here," Wyatt said.

Payton stopped emptying the boxes of breakfast and looked from Willow back to Wyatt. Victory's gaze followed suit. All commotion in the kitchen abruptly stopped and the room fell silent.

"I received a package from Angie yesterday. The package contained a letter to me, written by Mom."

Payton let out a tiny gasp, Collin by her side in a flash. Victory took hold of Tristan's hand, and he covered hers with his other.

"The guys are going to need to hear this, too. However, we can read it by ourselves first, if you prefer?"

Victory glanced over to Payton, who gave her a nod. Collin leaned back against the counter and pulled Payton to snuggle against him.

"If we all have to hear what she wrote, let's hear it together," Victory said.

Wyatt pulled the letter from the file he held in his hands. "Would you like me to read it?"

"Thank you for offering. I need to read it this time." She took the letter, sat down in the chair he pulled out for her, and read her mother's words aloud.

The men remained silent as the sisters processed the information they were given. Payton cried silently and Victory shook her head.

"But Mom and Dad weren't murdered. They were in an auto accident," Payton said, sniffling.

"We'll need to investigate the accident. There is every possibility their death was staged to look like an accident," Wyatt said. "Jack."

"I'm on it," Jack said. He opened his laptop and began his search.

"This confirms my suspicion that Mom really tried to aid us and not use us as test subjects. Somehow she discovered Ryker double-crossed her. Do you think Ryker killed them?" Victory asked.

"No one's seen him in over fifteen years. He could very well be long dead," Payton said.

"He could be a recluse," Tristan said. "Maybe he has taken a new name, created an entire new persona." "I've had the time to digest this information. We must find out which four states were involved in the testing and when," Willow said.

"We might find what we're looking for in here," Wyatt said, as he raised the folder.

"Then let's get started." Payton wiped at her eyes with the back of her hands and stood up on her own two legs.

"Not to be insensitive or anything," Logan said. "But do you mind if we do this over breakfast?"

"Thank you," Noah said. "Finally, I'm not the one asking the question."

The pressure valve in the room released and the tension lessened as they all laughed at the two men.

After everyone got their plates and found a chair, Wyatt opened the folder and spread its contents on the table. Everyone reached in and took a slip of paper.

"I can't speak for you all, but most of this is above my comprehension," Noah said.

"There are a lot of formulas, at least partial ones, and the status reports are pretty dense," Victory said. "Looks like Mom kept all her 'doodling' if you will."

"Huh, and I thought doodling was stick figures and tic-tac-toe." Noah shook his head.

"Put all of this stuff in a separate pile. I'll look through it later."

"Hey, look what I found." Logan held a slip of newspaper up. "It's part of an article." He scanned through it while everyone stared at him. "This is interesting. They're talking about an increase in multiple births and births in general immediately during and after the use of a new prenatal vitamin. Says here the company states the vitamin is one-hundred percent safe and being donated to doctors to give out to their patients."

"One-hundred percent safe my ass," Tristan said. "Does it say where the vitamins got distributed or what company distributed them?"

"Uh...yep, right here. Vitamins were distributed in the states of Washington, California, Texas, and New York. Oh yeah—jackpot. The company was Biot...the rest of the name is ripped away. I think we can safely assume it's Biotec."

"What's the date on the newspaper?" Payton asked.

Logan scanned through the article again, flipped it over, and looked on the back side.

"There's no date showing."

"California, Texas, and New York are the three highest-populated states," Willow said.

"We were born and raised in Seattle," Tristan said.

"I was born in Texas," Logan said.

"Seattle," Jack said.

"San Francisco, California. At least that's what my birth certificate says," Noah said.

"I bet it's no coincidence," Collin said. "Morgan, weren't you born in California?"

"Yes, I was. I also had a twin sister."

The entire group gaped at him.

"She died when she was only six months old."

"I'm so sorry," Victory said. "I'm surprised I haven't come across the information before now."

"I'm sure it's in my personnel file."

"It's not," Wyatt said. "And I find it very odd. Makes me wonder when your file was changed and who changed it."

"Collin was born in Washington State, too," Payton said.

"That's of no importance, since I never displayed any special abilities prior to the wolf DNA."

"None that you were aware of," Victory said. She crossed her arm over her chest, rested her other elbow on it, and tapped a finger on her chin, eyes staring up, focused on nothing. "I took your word for it—the fact you didn't have any special abilities. Why didn't I think of that before? Payton and Willow also thought they had no special abilities, but they do."

"If what you say is so, then why am I having such a difficult time adapting? Morgan doesn't have trouble."

"He does have issues, Collin. They're different problems, and the rate of change is slower, nothing more. I need to go back to the beginning with you. This might be the answer. Chances are you also possessed some types of abilities and what we are truly dealing with are heightened or enhanced capabilities."

"You think you could actually find an answer, Victory?" Payton asked.

"I'll do everything I can."

"Miracle prenatal vitamin will not hit the open market," Morgan read. "Company claims market research resulted in a lack of revenue and has, therefore, made the decision to discontinue the vitamin. I don't see a date on this either. Jack, you can take these and locate the dates, right?"

"I can find anything," Jack said.

"While we don't know the dates of the articles, we do know we were all born within four-and-a-half years of each other. I would venture to guess it's a high probability we were all conceived during the time the vitamin was being used, and it's a good possibility our mothers took them," Wyatt said.

"Looks like the rest of this stuff is in Victory's wheelhouse," Tristan said, as he flipped through the papers. "What did you find on the USB, Jack?"

"More scientific mumbo jumbo. I'll make a couple copies before I give them to Victory, so she won't have to bother."

"And the accident?" Willow asked. "Did you find anything more?"

"I did. Look here." Jack turned his computer so everyone could see the screen.

"What the hell?" Collin asked.

"That is a redacted police report."

"What do you mean, redacted?" Victory asked.

"See all those black lines throughout the report? It's all information they blacked out, so the public wouldn't see it."

"It can't be," Payton said. "Both Willow and I have a copy of the police report; it's complete and that's not it."

"Jack—" Wyatt started.

"I'm way ahead of you, Captain. I'll get a copy of Payton's report and figure out what changes were made."

"Okay, on the bright side we have a ton more information today than we did yesterday. On the downside, we're still playing defense," Wyatt said.

"Could you guys ask your moms if they took the vitamins?" Willow asked.

"Well, Tristan and I could ask; so could a couple others who know where or who their mothers are. I thought about it, and I don't think it's the best idea. They will wonder why we are asking and probably not even recollect something as trivial as the vitamins they took. This is a top secret assignment. We involve our parents—no longer top secret. We're gonna have to figure this out on our own."

"I assume you do have a plan?" Tristan asked.

"I do. I will meet Willow in her office later this afternoon. She is going to tell me she needs to go to London for a few days to help with..." Wyatt looked at Willow for help.

"Ahh...I need to review personnel reports with Angie and check on how everything is running, make sure Angie is not overdoing it."

"That's it. After a few minutes of *arguing* back and forth, purely for our audience, I will agree to let her go. Under one condition, Noah travels with her. Now our *friends* will be looking for Noah. After a couple days there, he will be called away on an urgent assignment, thereby giving our *friends* the perfect opportunity to snatch Willow."

"No you don't," Victory and Payton said in stereo.

"You are not using our sister as bait," Payton said.

"I won't let them get near her, I promise. I plan to shadow Willow every step of the way. She will fly out on Sunday. I'll be leaving tonight, going back to D.C. But really. I'll head out for London, scope things out, and be in my hotel room two days before she arrives," Wyatt said.

Victory and Payton attempted to talk Willow out of the plan. Finally she raised her hand to quiet her sisters.

"I do need to talk with Angie. I need to find out where she found this envelope, or if our mom gave it to her, and I actually do have company business. I'm in. I have one last question for Victory. If all the moms took this vitamin, doesn't it mean you are searching for a stabilizer not only for Collin, Morgan, and the three of us, but all the guys as well?"

"I never could get anything by you," Victory said, scowling at her sister. "Yes, if the men were exposed to Biotec's vitamins, their DNA is also manipulated. I'll need to get blood samples from each of you as soon as possible."

"Why? We were all born with it. We're all stable," Logan said.

"You are in the same situation as we are. Your changes will be much slower, but you will continue to change. Your DNA must be stabilized. Have any of you noticed *any* changes over the past week, month, or years?"

The men looked at one another.

"I figured, along with my maturity, I was learning how to hone my abilities," Noah said.

"My night vision has become a bit more acute," Wyatt said.

"I rest my case. I need everyone's blood by tomorrow at the latest. Don't you dare leave this campus before I have a filled vial in my hand." Victory looked from Noah to Wyatt.

Chapter Fifteen

Willow always enjoyed her visits to the London complex. The Winters Corporation offices were located along the bank of the River Thames at the outer edge of the city. The views from the complex were stunning. Unfortunately, the circumstances of her current visit weighed heavily on her mind, and the sights she always adored were a faded backdrop.

"Willow, are you alright?" Noah asked, as he held the taxi's door open, waiting for her to exit the vehicle.

"Yes—I'm sorry, I guess I must've been daydreaming." She thanked the driver, grabbed her briefcase and purse, and headed for the complex.

"Each time I come to London, I find the city more spectacular. Of course, my last trip was so quick, your flat turned out to be my only stop. Man, when one of you sisters makes up your mind about something, there's no stopping you." He chuckled, reached the entrance door, and opened it.

She gave him a sideways glance.

"The last time you were here, you came to escort me home. Victory had just been shot; naturally, I was packed and ready to go when you arrived." She gave him a sisterly punch in the arm. He winced, rubbed at his arm, and played up the injury.

The foyer was grandiose with its muted coffee-colored marbled floor with veins of black running throughout. The marble continued halfway up the walls in a slightly lighter tone. The centerpiece of the area was an oversized marble fireplace complete with a crackling fire ablaze, which gave the enormous area a cozy feel.

"Good afternoon Ms. Winters, it's a pleasure to see you again," a man in a pristine suit said, greeting them.

"Good afternoon, Henry. You're looking well, and the family?"

"All good, thank you for asking. Angie asked I meet you. She's running a bit late with a client and I'm to escort you up."

"How's Angie feeling?"

"She's well, as long as I force her to take breaks every now and then."

The elevator doors opened at the top floor and the trio exited.

"She's in the conference room and asked that I take you to her office, unless you would rather wait in your office?"

"No, no. Her office will be fine."

"Can I get you something while you wait?" Henry asked, as he held the door for the two. "Perhaps a nice cup of tea with a shot of brandy? The London wind can chill you to the bone this time of year."

"Sounds lovely, thank you."

He nodded and left the office.

"Nice place." Noah said, as he surveyed the office. They stood in a corner room, and two of the walls sported massive windows that framed the awe-inspiring view of London. "Is the entire building yours?"

"Yes, my parents purchased the building a couple years after they started business. It's only seven floors but serves the purpose well. The labs are all on the first four floors; the top three floors are mainly office and conference space. The dining room, a few small rooms for overnight stays, a workout area, recreation and relaxation lounges are all located on the far side of this floor. If we grow any larger, we will be forced to find a new place, but I believe with our new campus in Washington it shouldn't be an issue. We can accommodate any overflow projects there."

"And what's Henry's official position, head butler?"

"No—well kind of. He's Angie's assistant."

"Hum. I thought Carol was her assistant."

"Carol is the assistant manager, second-in-command. Henry is Angie's administrative assistant and bodyguard. There are only a handful of us who are aware of his second duty."

"I see. Well, given past activities, I would say he is a wise choice."

Henry returned with three steaming cups of tea, a full pot, and a small decanter of brandy. As he placed the tray on the table, the door flew open and a petite Asian woman entered.

"Angie, it's so good to see you."

Angie crossed the office and threw her arms around Willow.

"It feels far too long since we enjoyed a movie and popcorn Saturday at your loft," Angie said, as she hugged Willow tighter. She pulled away and flashed Noah a brilliant smile. "A pleasure to see you again, Mr. McNab."

"Please call me Noah. I'm surprised you remember me. We only spent about two minutes together before Willow rushed out of her flat. Thank you again for staying with her until I got there."

"No need to thank me, Noah. Willow is like my sister. She's done so much for me; I would do anything for her. Let's sit and enjoy our tea. You can fill me in on the plan."

"First I need to know where you found the envelope you sent." Willow accepted the cup Angie handed her.

"I stumbled on the envelope purely by accident. I needed another file cabinet and Henry sent a couple of janitors to locate one. Unbeknownst to Henry, they took one from the wrong storage room."

"The one storing all Mom's equipment and furniture."

"Yes. I didn't realize it at the time; I've been so busy. Friday evening I found an hour to sort through some of my files." Angie got up and walked to the far corner of her office. A row of four-drawer file cabinets filled the corner. "It's this one. She pointed to the dark wood one on the end. I haven't had a chance to get it returned to the storage; I'll send it back this week."

"No. The cabinet fits in well there. We need to go through the rest of the storage room. The time has come to move ahead. I may even want a few pieces."

"Are you sure?"

"Yes. We all need to move on. Mom would want us to. You were saying?"

"Right. I filled the bottom drawer and attempted to pull out the next drawer. It put up quite a battle. I couldn't figure out what was wrong. The drawer felt jammed, only I wasn't sure where. I got on my hands and knees, flipped on a flashlight, and tried to see if I could fix the problem without involving Henry. I saw something on the bottom of the drawer way in the back. After numerous attempts to pull the drawer out, I finally emptied the bottom drawer, took it out of the cabinet, and wormed my way under the stuck drawer. I got far enough under to pry the envelope free. I immediately recognized your mother's handwriting— I didn't open the envelope. I sealed it in the confidential package and sent it directly to you."

"Has anyone entered the storage area since?" Noah asked.

"No. After I sealed the package, I called for Henry. He took the package and locked it in his office safe and then reset the security code for the storage area. He also oversaw the installation of security cameras down in the basement the following day. It was the only floor without cameras. Until then, it didn't seem a priority."

"Good to know. Nothing out of the ordinary has happened since?"

"No, nothing."

Willow tried to stifle a yawn.

"I'm sorry," Willow managed to say as she fought the second yawn. "My day started extremely early, and we haven't stopped once. I think I need to head to the hotel, call for room service, and soak in a warm bath."

"You're not going to your flat?" Angie asked.

"No, I wanted to stay closer to the office and with Noah here, it's just easier. I would like to meet for breakfast, if it works for you?"

"Henry cleared my schedule when I found out you were coming. I'll be in the complex every day."

"Great. I'll see you in the morning."

As they waited in the lobby for their car service, Noah asked, "Do you trust her?"

"Yes. Angie's a loyal and honest employee. I consider her my friend."

"Is it possible your friendship might cloud your judgment?"

"Why do you ask? Did you pick up on something?"

"No, just covering all my bases. That's my job."

* * * *

Willow listened intently to Angie as she ate her breakfast. She couldn't quite put her finger on it, but something simply felt off to her. Was Angie sick, thinking about resigning, or worried? Willow saw her aura now, and the colors weren't her regular bright pink and blue, which represent kindness, compassion, and composure. Willow had known Angie for a long time and grown accustomed to the range of her aura. Now Angie's aura was shifting back and forth among yellow, gold, and blue, all muddy in appearance and all connected to fear. There were, of course, other possible meanings to these colors: indecisiveness, regret, a need to hide. However, fear was the common connection.

Angie stopped talking, picked up her fork, and played with the food on her plate.

"Angie, are you okay?"

"Yes." She responded a little too abruptly as she bit at her lower lip and blinked rapidly.

Willow contemplated her response and watched as Angie's aura shifted again, still within the same primary colors.

"Why do you ask?"

"You just feel a bit off. Did something happen?"

Angie looked around the restaurant and raked a hand through her straight blue-black hair, once, twice. They were seated in the far corner of the room and the nearest table to them sat empty. Noah had a seat at the bar where he casually sipped tea as he read the morning paper. As if somewhat calmed by what she took in, Angie forced her eyes to focus on Willow's.

"Willow, do you trust him?" She gave a brief nod in Noah's direction.

"Who—Noah?"

Angie nodded again.

"Like a brother. Why—" She stopped short as the pieces started to come together in her mind. "Angie, did you send me those notes?"

Angie lifted her gaze from the tablecloth she'd been studying and locked onto Willow's. Her Belgian chocolate eyes were fringed in thick, jet-black lashes.

"We can't speak here, too many ears. Let's go back to my office. You say you trust Noah. I would still like to have this conversation privately between you and me."

"What's got you so spooked?" Willow asked. She sat in one of the chairs in Angie's soundproof office and watched Angie patrol the room like one of her Dobermans. "Come on, Angie. Please talk to me."

Angie turned away from the outside view and leaned against one of the file cabinets. She crossed her arms, uncrossed them, and crossed them again.

"You asked me about the notes. Yes, I sent all three of them."

A thousand questions popped into Willow's mind. Instead, she practiced her professional persona and maintained a neutral expression, as her emotional side pushed for Angie to continue.

"I'm afraid for you and your sisters. I stumbled across some information which leads me to believe the three of you are not one-hundred percent safe. Not even on your campus."

"You know I trust your intuition. I also trust Noah with my life. He needs to hear this, too."

"Well, if you really believe it's best, then by all means."

Willow left the room and returned shortly with Noah.

"He's up to speed, Angie. Please tell us what you've found."

"A few months back I spent the night here in the complex. Instead of sleeping in here, like I often do if I stay the night, I slept in one of the overnight rooms. I didn't tell anyone I planned to stay, not even Henry. In fact, I sent him home early that day and promised to take a car service home before I decided to stay here. I left a stack of confidential notes and reports I needed to shred the next morning here on my desk. I woke during the night and was unable to get back to sleep, so I took my pile of papers and headed to the shredding room.

When I entered the room, I noticed a piece of paper hanging out of the machine, like someone left in a hurry before making sure all their papers were shredded. Only about half a sheet was left; the words on the page froze my blood. It said there was a spy on the Washington campus, and you were being watched. There were segments of other information which didn't make a lot of sense to me; test subjects were sent inside, KG remained solid, and a couple words regarding the old complex in Washington."

Willow straightened as she listened to Angie's story. She felt a sudden chill as a cold sweat broke out on her body. After Angie finished she swallowed hard and asked, "Do you still have this note?"

"No. I panicked and accidently knocked the power button on the machine. The machine chopped the rest of the page into confetti before I could stop it."

"Do you know who wrote the page or if it was addressed to someone? The text, handwritten or printed?" Noah asked.

"I have no idea who wrote it or for whom it was intended. The paper was printed off a computer and the top half of the page was gone. There wasn't a heading that showed it to be an email, so it could've been only a printed note."

"And that's when you started sending me the notes. Who delivered them to me?" Willow asked.

"I sent them all to a longtime friend of mine. He's also in personnel. You'd mentioned this year you wanted to go to the conference, and I hoped you'd make it there. My friend has no idea what I wrote. All the envelopes were sealed. I told him your birthday was coming up, and the employees had a big surprise for you. I asked him to stick the last two notes in flowers and send them with wine, to make my story legitimate."

"And you sent me nothing more?"

"Nothing."

"Smart woman," Noah said.

* * * *

Willow told Angie she had a headache, probably from the jet lag, and needed to go lie down. No one outside of the sisters and the SOCOM team knew Wyatt was in town, not even Angie. Willow and Noah left the complex and headed back to the hotel. They needed to update Wyatt and the team. They entered Willow's suite and immediately noticed the door adjoining the two rooms stood open.

"Hope you don't mind, I camped out here all day. That thing they call a desk in my single room isn't big enough for a five year old," Wyatt said. Files and slips of paper littered the top of her dining table.

Four short weeks ago, Willow would've been steaming at his lack of boundaries. Now she smiled at him.

"Feel free to make yourself at home."

"I would've picked up a bit, but I didn't expect you two so early. What's up?"

"Angie's the one who sent me the notes."

Before the statement left her mouth, Wyatt hit the Skype button.

"Hey, Captain." Jack greeted him.

"Is the team all there?"

"Yes sir." Jack waved at the men, and they gathered behind him.

Willow reiterated the meeting with Angie. She also briefed the team about where she found each note and what was written on them.

"Looks like General Roberts was on the right track—again," Tristan said.

"Looks like," Wyatt said.

"Hold on." Willow raised her hand to quiet the group. "Are you saying General Roberts already knew we had a spy and didn't tell us? Now I understand. He wanted me to interview everyone to locate this spy, not verify information."

"He did—does want every employee verified. And no, he didn't *know* there was a spy, he went on a hunch. You more than anyone should understand, Willow," Wyatt said.

"I haven't come across anyone who deceived us in such a manner. I can't believe I will."

"How about Amiee?" Logan asked.

"What is it with you and Amiee? She's loyal and trustworthy, and currently living on the campus, since I potentially put her life in danger. It's not Amiee," Willow said.

"Willow, we need you to continue the interviews when you get back," Wyatt said.

"Where? I still have that darn bugged plant in my office."

"I think it's served our purpose. When you get home, come up with a reason to move the plant. We'll continue on with the plan here in London. We still might flush someone out, especially now, because we know there is someone to flush out."

"Do you think the reference to the 'old Washington complex,' has to do with the attack on Willow?" Collin asked.

"I think it's highly likely," Wyatt said. "I've also given a lot of thought to the guy on campus the night the lights went out. Morgan, you got the longest look at this guy. What's your take? Any chance he had heightened abilities?"

"Now that you mention it, he was good and fast. Yes, I'd have to say even faster than a regular SEAL Team or Green Beret. Are you thinking KG is using the Washington campus as a testing ground for incursion exercises?"

"Why the campus? I can think of a lot less dangerous training grounds," Noah said.

"Two reasons. One, they pit enhanced abilities against enhanced abilities. Two, another way to needle the sisters and show them who's really in charge," Wyatt said.

"You think KG would do all that simply to get under our skin?" Willow asked.

"I wouldn't put anything past Kaleidoscope Group. At this point it would appear our upgraded security is holding them at bay."

"For how long?" Willow asked.

Chapter Sixteen

Noah returned to the States and left Wyatt solely responsible for Willow's safety. Wyatt was staked out directly outside the front door of the complex. Willow only had one more day in London, and she felt it was imperative to get down to the storage room before she left. She decided to play it safe and stopped by Angie's office on her way down.

"Angie's on a conference call. Would you like me to interrupt her?" Henry asked.

"Don't bother. I wanted to tell her I'm on my way to the storage area. I want to go through Mom's stuff."

"Would you like an escort?"

"No, I'm fine. Hard to believe all the time I've spent here at these offices, I've never ventured down into the basement."

"Why would you? Are you sure you don't want me to come with you?"

"I'm sure. If I get lost or turned around, I can ring you on your mobile."

"I'll keep it close." He patted his breast pocket. "This is an old building and there are some dead zones down there as far as camera and cell coverage. Watch your step."

The elevator doors opened to the basement, where the hall was lit, albeit poorly, with a single bar of fluorescent lights. A couple of the bulbs flickered every so often, as if they wanted to go out altogether. Willow stood in the elevator and surveyed the scene.

"Oh joy, another basement. At least this one has lights, if that's what these dinosaurs are called." She made a note on her phone to have the lighting on this floor brought up to the current century.

The doors to the elevator began to close, and she jumped out into the basement. She peered down at her phone again. Henry had texted her the storage room number and lock combination. A few feet down the hall, she reached the first door and realized the room she wanted most likely would be on the next hall over. She picked up her pace and headed to her destination. The hall ended at a "T," and, according to the two rooms she could see, she needed to turn left. Willow passed a number of doors before she reached the room she wanted.

She punched in the code and opened the door. Inside she found a black hole. She felt along one side of the wall and then the other in search of a light switch, keeping her foot wedged in the doorway to prevent the door from closing her inside. She flipped on the light. The room turned out to be much larger than she thought. There were file boxes, tables, a couple desks, file cabinets, chairs, copy machines, computers, and even some lab equipment. Every last thread of her mother's belongings had been gathered up and brought to this room. She stepped forward, and the door closed behind her. A sudden panic welled up inside her as she yanked on the doorknob and pulled the door open. Her heart rattled her chest.

"Take it easy. I'm fine. I will take a quick look around and be out in an hour tops," she mumbled.

She grabbed the nearest chair and propped the door ajar. Willow started with the desks. Pulling all the drawers open, she got down on her hands and knees and used her flashlight to make sure nothing was attached to the bottom of a drawer. All the drawers were empty, as were the file cabinets and lab tables. Next came the search through the boxes. Most held old files of completed projects. Many were recognizable based on Victory's computer files. She found some historical boxes containing information on the creation of the company, news clippings, awards, and photographs. She'd have these boxes shipped back home. She also ran across a few more boxes full of her mother's notebooks and she added those to the boxes she wanted shipped home and put them together on one side of the room.

Exhausted, she dropped down into one of the chairs and looked at all the boxes left to be gone through. Finally, she decided to have all remaining boxes shipped home where she could take the proper time to go through each of them. From where she sat, she noticed a reflection of glass and got up to see what it might be. Tucked behind more boxes she found a stack of framed pictures. One was a picture of her sisters and her as small girls, one the entire family, a couple of her mom receiving awards, and some with people she didn't recognize. These all needed to be returned home; they were a true find. It surprised her that these pictures ended up in storage in the first place.

But the three of them were so devastated after their parents' death, none of them could deal with going through their parents' personal belongings.

A shadow box sat among the pictures. Willow couldn't recall ever seeing it before. She pulled it from the stack, and as she did, something inside the box slid. With reverence she placed the box on the nearest flat surface. She flicked on the flashlight and inspected every inch of the box. Not one thing looked out of place; all the same, something was loose. The black velvet covering the back looked securely attached. Slowly she picked the box up and watched the objects as she continued to lift.

"There it is." Something loose slid behind the velvet. Feeling like a treasure hunter, she turned the box over, released the back from the frame, and pried free one corner of the glued velvet. As she did, she caught a glimpse of the corner of an envelope. "What do you have for us this time, Mother?" She cautiously worked the velvet loose the entire length of one side and pulled the envelope free. She put the box back together and replaced it in the stack.

Way off in the distance she could swear she heard the elevator doors slide open. She looked at the clock on her phone. She'd been down here for a couple hours and Henry had most likely become concerned. She unbuttoned her blouse, tucked the large envelope in the back of her waistband, and buttoned the blouse back up. She switched the light off, moved the chair away from the door, and closed it. Willow had taken only a few steps when someone called out to her.

"Wil-loow, seems we meet again."

193

Willow's legs went weak, and she clenched her jaw. *It couldn't be,* she thought.

"Don't play games again, Willow. Show yourself."

It's him! She screamed in her mind. The voice haunted her nightmares. She yanked her phone out of her pocket and punched the speed dial. Nothing. She looked at her screen and read the two tiny words, "No service."

* * * *

Absolute terror tore through Wyatt's skull like a dull spike. Both hands flew up to press his temples and he forced himself to breathe through the pain.

"*It's him!*"

"Willow." He barely stammered through gritted teeth. The fear ebbed and allowed him to clear his mind and breathe. "*Willow, where are you?*" He pushed the question out into the ether, willing his words to find their mark. As Wyatt's mind continued to reach out for Willow, his legs carried him up the stairs and into the foyer. He punched the button for the elevator at the same time he searched the area for a stairwell. "*Willow, you need to tell me where you are. I'm here.*"

"*The basement.*"

The same instant the elevator beeped to announce its arrival, Wyatt spotted the door to the stairwell in the farthest corner. He went through the door and started down the stairs before the door to the elevator even opened.

"*I'm coming, Willow. Give me an idea of where in the basement?*"

"*I was in storage room number 649. The man who chased me through the basement at the old complex called out to me, and I headed in the opposite direction.*"

He could hear the terror in her voice as he reached the door to the basement. Quietly, he opened the door and assessed where he was. The door to his right read "Janitors Closet, Do Not Enter." He pulled the door open to find exactly what he wanted. The breaker box. He located the switch for the basement at the same time he heard an eerie voice call out.

"Wil-loow. Come out, come out, wherever you are."

Willow. Wyatt got no response. Panic flooded his mind. Wyatt shook his head, cleared the fear, and tried once again. "*Willow, I'm here with you. You're not alone. Do you hear me? Focus on my voice…*"

"Wil-loow."

"*Only my voice. Do you hear me?*"

"*Wyatt?*"

"*Yes, I'm here. Nothing is going to happen to you. I will get you out of this. Find a place and stay put. I'm going to turn the lights out on this lunatic.*"

"*But then I'll be in the dark! I won't be able to see. What if he finds me?*"

"*He won't; trust me. Find a spot to hide now.*"

She found a door open and slid inside the room.

"*I'm inside room number 810.*"

"*Good girl. Stay right there. Don't move. I'm coming to you.*"

Wyatt pulled the switch, and the entire floor went black.

"What the hell! Willow, you are really starting to piss me off," said the intruder.

The man banged around madly in an attempt to find his bearings. Wyatt took that cue and raced down the hall to room 810.

"I'm here Willow. Right outside the door. Don't make a sound; I'm coming in to get you."

Even with his warning, she startled when he touched her.

"Wyatt?"

"Shhh. *Use your telepathic connection. Don't speak.*"

He guided her to the door.

Wait. He opened the door and listened for the intruder. He could hear him, but he didn't see him. By Wyatt's estimation, the man floundered about in the next hall, muttering obscene comments to himself.

"We can move faster and quieter if I carry you."

She nodded her head.

He lifted her into his arms and shot out the door and back down the hall from where he came. He never stopped as he ran up the flights of stairs with Willow in his arms.

"Where are we going?"

"For now, back to the hotel."

She didn't argue, didn't utter a word. He placed her on her feet before he opened the door to the foyer, and she followed him out into the late afternoon sun. Wyatt chose to grab a taxi as opposed to hailing the car service. They didn't stop moving until he had them locked behind her suite door. He turned and studied her. She stood by the bank of windows, gazed out, and rubbed her hands up and down her arms as if trying to chase away the chill.

"I need to call Henry and let him know I left for the day. He will be heading down to look for me at any minute." She pushed the button on her phone. "Henry, it's Willow. I wasn't feeling well and decided to head directly back to the hotel...no, don't worry about me; it's a migraine. No. I wasn't still down there when the lights went out...yes, I'm fine. I'll be back in first thing tomorrow...yes, I'm staying another day." She turned around and looked at Wyatt and silently asked for confirmation. He nodded. "What...I have a project I need to oversee before I leave. I'll fill you in first thing in the morning. Good night, Henry."

Somehow Willow managed to stick to his conditions, in a manner of speaking, and still wind up in trouble. For the love of...he couldn't decide whether to scold her or take her in his arms. Her color had yet to return and the paleness of her skin made his decision for him. He covered the distance between them, gathered her up in his arms, and hugged her fiercely. He loosened his hold and widened the gap between them. She stared up at him; her faceted blue eyes pierced his soul.

"You better not be reading my aura. You might not like what you find."

"Funny you should mention it because I can no longer read your aura. However, I can still feel your energy. You know, its Victory's theory that the three of us develop a telepathic connection with our soul mate. I think she's crazy. I've come to consider you a friend, maybe more, but—"

"You and Noah *are* more. I won't come between the two of you."

Confusion clouded her expression.

"I love him, yes. Noah and I are like brother and sister. Why would you think we are lovers?"

"The two of you always appear so comfortable with one another. You always smile when he's around. I just thought—"

"You thought wrong, Wyatt. I treasure Noah. He's an important part of my life, just like Tristan, Collin, Morgan, Logan, and Jack. I love him; I'm not *in* love with him."

The vise encompassing Wyatt's heart broke free. He leaned down and claimed her lips with a passion and a fire he had never in his life experienced. Willow pulled her pinned arms from between them and wrapped them tightly around him; she grabbed handfuls of his shirt in an attempt to bring them closer.

"You may not think us soul mates; even so we have passed the stage of just friends. I think of you every waking hour, A rúnsearc."

Willow pulled away slightly and studied him. He felt his heart miss a beat as he waited. Her hands cupped his face; she pulled him toward her and kissed him tenderly. He lifted her off her feet and carried her into the bedroom where he laid her down and towered over her, one hand on each side of her body.

"You have to stop doing that to me. Each time you put yourself in danger you make me crazy."

She said nothing, as she continued to stare up at him.

"Should I order us some dinner? Or maybe you'd rather have a drink first? What can I get you, Willow?"

"I have all I need."

To his utter shock she reached up and unzipped his jeans. Her soft, cool hands ran around the waistband of his boxers and brought him to instant attention. Never in his wildest dreams did he think she would make the first move; he thought he'd pushed his luck by kissing her. He must have looked as surprised as he felt, because she smiled up at him and began to unbutton her blouse.

"Just to make sure you understand precisely what it is I want."

That was all the invitation Wyatt needed. He pulled her hands from her shirt and continued the process. She sat up and he pulled her free of the blouse. As he did, the envelope fell free.

"What's this?"

"Oh, I forgot about the envelope. I found it inside a picture down in the storage room. Whatever the envelope holds, I've waited this long. I can wait a while longer."

He tossed the envelope on the floor, never taking his eyes off her as he unzipped the back of her skirt. Gently he laid her back down, and pulled her skirt from her waist.

She lay there dressed in only in an icy blue lace bra and matching panties. The color intensified the heat in her eyes. Her glossy golden hair fanned out around her exquisite face. With extreme effort he pulled himself away from her and stood to remove his shirt and jeans, kicking off his shoes as he did. She sat up and scooted to him. In one smooth motion she dragged his boxers down his legs and he sprang free. She took him into her hands and began a slow sensual movement, her hot palms cupping and rubbing. He could swear all the blood drained from his head. He nearly fainted as she leaned in and blew her warm breath along his length. Her tongue toyed with his tip and it took every ounce of his will to keep from plunging himself into the warmth of her mouth. She relieved him of his struggle and took him in. She nipped and licked until he could no longer remain still or standing.

He laid her back on the bed and ran his hands down the sides of her body. He drew his hands back up to her breasts and cupped both. Then he bent down and took one into his mouth. She arched to meet him and her movement spurred him on. One hand slid slowly back down to her waist, lazily circled her belly button once, then twice before his hand made its way to the vee of her legs. She was hot and damp for him and felt like satin in his hand. She arched again and he plunged a finger deep inside her and was rewarded with a moan. He continued to explore as his fingers played over and inside her most feminine part.

"*Wyatt...*"

Her telepathic plea nearly made him come undone. He pulled away from her and the dark lapis pools of her eyes transfixed his gaze. He nudged her legs wider apart with his knee, and without breaking eye contact drove himself into her. His fingers entangled into hers, and he stretched her arms out wide, slid them up over her head, and pinned them to the bed. He thrust into her until he felt her begin to climb. Willow's eyes glazed over as he drove himself inside her again and remained deep within the grip of her hot velvet embrace. He took her mouth and kissed her thoroughly and set a deliberate, leisurely pace, first totally withdrawing and then plunging inside her, over and over until he drove her up and over, not once but twice, and finally he followed her down the other side. Wyatt rolled over, taking Willow with him, their bodies slick with sweat. She melted over the top of him and he felt the thump of her heart against his. He could now die a happy man, except he wanted to spend a million more nights with her. Every day he learned something more about this extraordinary woman, yet he knew he'd merely scratched the surface. Willow Winters had depths the likes of which he'd never before known.

She lifted her head and rested her chin on his chest.

"Wow!"

He couldn't help himself as he smiled up at her. Her lips were still slightly swollen from being kissed, her face aglow, and she still breathed deeply from the exertion.

"I have to say I'm beyond shocked we ended up here, but ecstatic. Ironic, isn't it? A month ago you and I fought like cats and dogs."

"Sexual tension." Her smile widened like a Cheshire cat.

"Let me guess. My aura or my energy?"

"Maybe a little of both. But you seemed to be on my mind even when you weren't around needling me. I default to my psychology background."

"Yeah, right." He chuckled. "I'll stick to the cats and dogs scenario, although I might have to give your idea credence. I was so sure you and Noah had 'a thing.' Every time I saw the two of you together, it screamed relationship to me."

"You weren't wrong. You just weren't right." She pushed up and kissed him caressingly. Then she rolled to one side of him.

He propped himself upright against the headboard, dragged her up and nestled her beneath his arm, grabbed the nearest blanket and covered them both. For now it was best to leave this subject alone, until he could wrap his mind around his feelings.

"Hungry?"

"Starved."

"How about I order us up some dinner and wine, and you can read what's inside the envelope. Then you can tell me what else you found in the storage room and why you want to extend our stay—although I don't mind extending it at all."

Chapter Seventeen

"I need to make sure everything in the storage room is packed and shipped back to the States before I leave."

They sat out on the terrace, finished their meal, and savored the London sunset as Willow finished explaining the events step-by-step to Wyatt.

"I agree. Let me touch bases with the team and let them know we are extending our stay two more days in case we hit a snag and can't get the shipment out for a day."

"You don't mind staying with me?"

"Willow, I wouldn't have it any other way. Starting tomorrow the jig is up. I'll be escorting you everywhere you go. No more long-distance stakeout. There's someone after you. I'll be damned if he gets any more shots. Besides, your sisters would kill me. Now about the guy that followed you; are you certain it's the same person?"

"Absolutely. His voice has haunted my nightmares since the night it happened. I'm also certain I've heard his voice before. I wish I could place it."

"He's not the same person who broke onto the campus?"

"No. I didn't know him; his aura was unfamiliar to me, almost synthetic." Her eyes widened. "I think the man on campus that night might be genetically altered with regard to his aura and energy. Collin and Morgan's auras appear off-balance at times, but never like this man's. I've noticed it more so with Collin, because of his massive mood swings."

"Which are hugely due to the foreign DNA. According to Morgan, his partner, Collin was a pretty even-tempered guy before the injections."

"You're right. I haven't experienced nearly as many episodes since Collin and Payton have become involved. Why would someone want to alter a person's aura? It makes no sense."

"I have no idea. Although I'm sure KG has a good reason. Now I understand. At the time you were so confused when I asked you about the intruder. You had no time to process what you picked up from his aura. You never experienced it with any of us?"

"No. I've sensed powerful auras from all of you, but never like his, not synthetic or chemical in nature."

"Hum. Is it safe to say whatever he's been injected with is different?"

"Probably. But Victory would be the one to answer your question."

"True. Although you too have a natural instinct, Willow. Don't ever doubt yourself."

Willow shivered and rubbed her hands up and down her arms.

"Do you mind if we go inside? It's gotten chilly. I think I'd like a shower to warm me up."

"Are you going to read what's in the envelope?"

"I don't think I can tonight. I've about had my fill. You'd think I would want to know what my mother has in store for me, but I just can't deal with anymore tonight. The shower is sounding better by the minute."

"I'll be in my room, catching up on a couple of things if you need me."

"Can't it wait until the morning?"

"Well, I guess, but..."

She wagged an index finger at him and watched as her question clicked in his brain.

"Oh...yes, it can wait. Let me deadbolt the doors and I'll be right there."

She smiled to herself and walked into the bathroom. For such an intelligent man, he could be a bit slow at times.

* * * *

"Good morning, Henry," Willow greeted him as she entered his office. "Is Angie in yet? This is Wyatt; he heads up security for the government contracts in Washington."

"Nice to meet you, Wyatt, and yes she is; go right in."

She knocked, waited a beat, and then cracked open the door. "Angie? Are you busy?"

Angie waved them in as she finished up a phone call. "Good morning. Oh, who is your companion? I don't believe we've met."

"This is Wyatt. He is the head of security for our government contracts in the States."

"Henry told me this morning you were staying an extra day. Is there a problem?"

"No problem. I'm sure he told you I went down to the storage area yesterday. I want to have the entire contents of the room shipped back home. I decided to stick around and personally take care of the project."

"You don't have to stay around, Willow. I can get someone to pack and ship the contents."

"Thank you. I would rather handle it myself."

"At least let Henry arrange the shipping company."

"Sounds great. I want the shipment sealed up here for maximum security."

* * * *

"You were right to extend our stay a couple of days," Willow said, as she sat at her desk. "The shipping company isn't able to get here until first thing tomorrow morning."

"Is there a nearby office I could use? I need to do some work," Wyatt said.

"I'm sure there is; let me contact Carol."

"I'm sorry; all the offices on this floor are currently occupied," Carol said. The three of them were gathered in Willow's office. "I have a couple on the floor below us."

"I prefer to stay on this floor."

"There are the sleeping rooms. Each room has a desk, not much of a desk though. You could use one of those if you'd like."

"Thanks. Willow, I'll pick you up here for lunch."

* * * *

"Good day, Mr. Chairman," Thomas said. "To what do I owe the honor?"

"Thomas, your assignment there is complete. I see no further advantage to having you stay on. Make preparations and leave today."

"Thank you so much, sir. I'll see to it."

"Good. Oh, and Thomas?"

"Yes, sir."

"See to it you say your good-byes to Willow."

Thomas was elated at the prospect of never having to step foot in this insidious company again. Sure the first couple of years proved fruitful and interesting. Nevertheless, he had to admit he'd become so complacent he'd nearly been discovered a few times. A situation he would take to his grave. The Chairman was *not* a man forgiving of mistakes; there were no second chances.

* * * *

A soft knock sounded on Willow's door. She called out without so much as lifting her eyes from the computer screen.

"Come in."

The person dropped a small stack of mail on her desk and turned to leave. Willow, absorbed in her work, barely registered the presence of the person.

"Have a good afternoon, Wil-loow," the stranger said and shut her door.

A frigid jolt shot straight through her. Frozen in fear, she hesitated for only a nanosecond, and when she glanced up, the man had disappeared.

"Wyatt—he was just in my office."

No response came back to her. Wyatt bolted through her door in the next instant.

"Are you okay?"

"I'm fine. He dropped the mail and took off. I didn't even look up to see who he was." She shook her head, irritated at herself for her lack of diligence.

"You stay right here. I'll be back."

"Wait." All the pieces fell together in her mind. "Please be careful. It feels as if this man has no soul. If this is the person I think it is, he's not the same man I once knew, and it threw me off."

Wyatt gave her a wink and disappeared.

"Damn it, Willow," she said, scolding herself. She stayed glued in her seat as her mind replayed the interaction. Was he really the mailman or someone else? She picked up the phone and dialed the mailroom.

"Mailroom," a woman's voice answered.

"This is Willow Winters. Who delivered the mail on my floor today?"

"Hello, Ms. Winters. I hope there wasn't a problem. It was Thomas. He wasn't feeling well today; he said he would finish his route, then he needed to head home."

"Thomas? He's worked for us for around five years, correct?"

"Yes. You've always had nothing but nice things to say about him. There wasn't a problem, I hope?"

"No. Thanks for your help."

Her office phone rang.

"Willow."

"Ah, Miss Winters. It's a treat to hear your voice," said a man's voice echoing in her memory.

A memory tugged at the corners of her mind.

"I'm afraid you have me at a bit of a disadvantage, sir. To whom am I speaking?"

"Now I am offended. Don't tell me you don't remember me. I've been in your life since the day you and your sisters were born."

Willow felt every muscle in her body tense. Her skin prickled as the wave of adrenaline seared under it, and spread throughout her body as her senses reached out.

"Dr. Ryker? Edward Ryker?"

"Yes, yes. I knew you wouldn't forget me. We have so much to catch up on."

"Where've you been? Where are you? What did you do to my mother's drug?"

"Tsk tsk. We'll have plenty of time for all your questions later. I've kept my eye on you three girls and I have to say, I'm quite impressed. I thought your mother a genius, and I'm more then pleased to learn your sister Victory is a savant. You and Payton, well, you both certainly excel in your areas of expertise. I must warn you though; tread carefully in your current quests. The contracts you have involved the company in may turn out to be the death of the Winters Corporation."

"How is it you know so much about us?"

"All in good time my dear girl. By the way, today was Thomas's last day. He's needed elsewhere."

The line clicked dead.

"I couldn't find him," Wyatt said, as he walked back into her office. "Are you sure you didn't know him?"

"I do know him. His name is Thomas and he's our regular mailman."

"Willow, are you all right?"

A fluttery feeling filled her stomach, most likely the aftereffects of the adrenaline. She stuttered as she fought to get her next words out.

"Thomas—is—not—returning. He's a spy and he works with Edward Ryker."

"What are you talking about?"

A trickle of sweat ran down her chest and she shook all over.

"Ryker phoned me. He's alive and he's kept tabs on us. His spy has also been working here for five years. This means he knows about every contract and project past, present, and future in the London office. Wyatt, Thomas must somehow be connected to Kaleidoscope Group."

Wyatt grabbed a bottle of water and rushed over to Willow's side.

"Drink this. No, don't get up. You're going into shock. Stay seated and breathe. Come on Willow, breathe."

She focused solely on Wyatt's voice and did as told. Time crawled by as the dizziness abated and the tightness in her chest began to ease.

"Better. Okay, let's move over to the sofa. I'm going to go through your mail and make sure he didn't leave you any surprises. After that, I want you to start from the beginning."

She reiterated her conversation with Ryker.

"Why do you think he phoned me now? Why expose himself? We'd no idea if he was alive or dead, and we still don't know where he is, or for that matter how he's involved."

"To show you he has no fear of you and he believes he has the upper hand."

"Doesn't he?"

"Maybe for the time being. However, now we know he's part of the game, he won't for long. I'm going to go get Angie. We need to update her and make a plan."

"She's going to be upset when she hears about Thomas. We both liked him."

"We must be positively certain everyone is safe. Even though Ryker says that Thomas is gone, we should be careful and change all the locks and combinations tonight. He won't be coming back, but let's be sure he's cut out of all forms of access to the Company. He's finished his assignment, and I'm sure his assignment consisted of more than scaring the life out of you. He had the perfect cover, an insignificant employee who had access to the entire company."

"Creepy, don't you think? I'm going to interview each employee in our mail department the first day I'm back. I wonder what his assignment could've been."

"Best guess, you called it. He kept tabs on the active projects here. I checked the storage before I returned. The security lock is in place. No one has entered since you left."

* * * *

"I don't understand," Angie said, her eyes wide. "I spoke with Thomas nearly every day. He seemed a kind and pleasant man."

"His cover. Your first concern is for the safety of your other employees, and I suggest you vet them all immediately. Make sure there are no other leaks in the company. I'm sending in a security team to beef up your system. They'll work in concert with Henry. We need to make this complex and computer system impenetrable."

"Thank you, Wyatt. I'm sorry Willow."

"For what? Don't blame yourself for hiring Thomas. I liked him, too. I picked up nothing but honesty and commitment from the man." *How could that be?* she thought. *How could this man have tricked me? I should have picked up the deceit in his aura.*

"Could that be the reason for genetically altering a person's aura, to cloak their true nature?" Wyatt pushed into her mind. The sudden invasion made her quiver. Wyatt took hold of one of her hands within both of his. *"I'm sorry, didn't mean to intrude. I thought you were speaking to me."*

"This is going to take some getting used to." This time she gave him a shy smile.

Wyatt's phone vibrated. "Jack, what'd you find?"

"Your mailman did enter the U.S. a couple days before the incident at the old complex. Paula checked with the mail department here, and they told her Thomas checked in with them and actually helped out for a day while in town. Gotta say the guy has balls."

"Why weren't we notified?"

"The department notified security per standing instructions, the same way they've always done. It's been common practice for the Washington Company and the London branch to transport highly classified mail via a personal carrier."

Wyatt looked at Willow for confirmation and she nodded her head.

"Damn it all to hell. The man was right under our noses."

"Insignificant position," Willow mumbled.

By the time Wyatt and Willow returned to the hotel, it was late in the evening. Willow succumbed to exhaustion and dropped into the first chair.

"We haven't had anything to eat since breakfast. I know it's late, but we need something. I thought I would order up a cheese-and-meat tray." He walked over to the bar and poured two glasses of merlot and placed them both on the table beside Willow and made the call. "We left this place a real mess." He picked up the scattered clothes from the night before. He spied the envelope that still lay on the floor and held it out to her. "Hope you haven't been looking for this."

Willow's eyes widened as she realized what Wyatt held.

"My mother's letter. I can't believe I forgot all about it."

Chapter Eighteen

"There's a bunch of different notes ripped from her notebooks," Willow said. "The dates vary widely." She quickly leafed through the stack of papers.

"How far back do they go?"

She pulled a page from the pile.

"I don't know for sure. There's no date on this one, but the paper is yellowed." She read from the page.

I'm positive Edward is hiding research from me. He's become a different man, secretive, mistrusting of others, almost evil in his reactions. Ever since I questioned him about the "new" drug Biotec produced, he's locked me out of his activities. He tries to justify himself by saying it was only a matter of time until they came up with their own formula. He doesn't know I've tested their "formula" and it's mine; not one ingredient is altered. Biotec signed a contract with us. It says they cannot clone or reproduce our formula. As soon as I've gathered enough information, I'll take it to Joseph. With this, he will have to move forward when he finds out.

"Sounds like your mom caught on to Ryker and Biotec fairly quickly."

"Here's another. She must have written this note sometime after the one I just read."

Edward's become more and more secretive with each passing day. Now he won't even tell me what he's really working on. I've tried to convince Joseph we should let him go, but Joseph is worried about the backlash. Besides, Edward is an extremely intelligent scientist, and I'm sure that plays into the scenario, too. Also Edward has become friendlier to Joseph and fills his head with lies. The other night at dinner I attempted to broach the subject of Edward and his research. Joseph went on and on about his daily conversations with him and the reports Edward gives him. Edward told him he feels we work better apart, and I'm having difficulty dealing with the truth. Edward has brainwashed Joseph into thinking that he only wants what's best for the company. I know it's not so. I'll gather the information and prove to Joseph this man is lying to him.

"Is she talking about another formula?" Wyatt asked.

"I think it might be; there's nineteen pages, all handwritten. Wait, here's another note tucked into the middle. There is a date on this one; it's less than a week before Ryker left for England."

I've accessed Edward's hidden files. I knew he lied to me. I found this formula he's created and worked on for a number of years with no one the wiser.

I'm not completely sure what he is trying to develop, but I am sure it's somehow related to a cloaking ability. He's attempting to hide a person's true nature by using this formula. If his formula worked, it would be a viable answer to fooling a polygraph. I discovered a few more formulas but hadn't the time to write them down. I didn't want to make copies on the computer for fear someone would discover what I'd stumbled on and inform Joseph or worse yet, Edward.

I've found some peace in my daily visits to the girls' resting place and writing in my notebooks. Writing at the grave assures I will not be discovered. I have found comfort here, but not yet closure. I'm not exactly sure how to explain my feeling, but at times I feel like my girls are not truly here and never were. Joseph tells me that's nonsense. He says it's natural to want to believe the daughters I never got to hold can't possibly be gone. I understand what he is saying. Even so, the feeling remains...they aren't really here.

I need to return to the U.S. The three daughters with me need my help, love, and guidance. I still believe it unsafe. I will tear out the pages of my thoughts from this notebook and hide them. I'll take the rest of the notebook home and work on the formulas I have jotted on its pages.

"Did she write any more?"

Willow flipped through the remainder of the sheets.

"No. Come to think of it, Victory did come across some notebooks with missing pages. We never thought anything of it. She figured Mom had torn out pages of failed formulas."

"Wouldn't she want to keep those notes too, so she could refer to them?"

"Yes. She had other formulas fail and they're written down in the notebooks. At the time we could find no other explanation."

Wyatt handed her a glass of wine, took the notes from her, and set them on the side table. He put together a small plate of cheese, crackers, and meats and handed it to her. She started to shake her head.

"You need to eat, Willow. You've gone practically all day on an empty stomach. The last thing we need is for you to become ill."

She took the plate and nibbled on a piece of cheese. He sat next to her and she curled into him and tucked her feet up on the sofa. They were simply enjoying a meal together, and yet Wyatt found himself absolutely content.

"Wyatt?"

"Hum," he answered with a mouth full of food.

"What do you think Mom meant when she said she couldn't *feel* the girls there?"

"Probably just what your dad said. Only natural for her, since she never got a chance to see her girls, to believe in her mind they were not gone."

"Maybe."

He leaned away from her and turned her toward him.

"You aren't buying it. Why? What is it you believe she meant?"

"We know Braxton was insane. I think Ryker is just as psychotic. Or maybe even more. From everything I knew about him, the man seemed eccentric and brilliant. What if the girls weren't buried there?"

"You mean he took them somewhere else to bury them? You don't mean to say he would've actually done experiments with their bodies. I can't see even him being that deranged." He shook his head and flat refused to consider it.

"He wouldn't have to keep them in order to run experiments. He could take their blood and tissue and have all he needed. No, what I mean is…what if the girls are alive?"

Wyatt stared at her in total astonishment.

"He took them away, and no one ever knew who they were or where they came from." She could see him mull the idea over and over with that faraway look he got as he worked out a problem.

"A bit farfetched. Regardless, this is the same man who's stayed hidden for over twenty years. It wouldn't be difficult to place two baby girls with parents who desperately wanted children and would ask no questions. What are you thinking?"

"First, you need to promise me this will stay between the two of us until we know for sure. Now I know how both Victory and Payton felt when they kept secrets. But there's no sense upsetting them or getting anyone's hopes up until we know for sure. This includes keeping Tristan in the dark." She eyed him warily as she waited for his response.

"You have my word."

"I realize we need to go back home tomorrow. Is there anyone you can trust to get a court order to exhume the bodies and verify whether they are or aren't my sisters? And to do it quietly?"

"As a matter of fact I do. He's not in England at the present. I'll get a hold of him first thing in the morning and see if he will do this for us."

"Thank you, Wyatt."

"No need to thank me. I would do anything in my power for you."

He pulled her to him and kissed her. His teeth nipped and tugged at her bottom lip. Their tongues danced, and she tasted the wine and the heady flavor that was only Wyatt. To her sheer surprise, she was scooped up into his arms and carried over to the bed.

He laid her down and stared at her for a heartbeat, his lapis eyes holding hers. His flaxen hair had grown out slightly and gave him an even more ruggedly handsome look. He kissed her tenderly. She could feel his hands unbutton her blouse and unsnap her bra. His lips left hers and burned a slow trail down her neck, along her shoulder, and all the way down until he reached his goal. He took her breast into his mouth, pulled and nipped. The feel of him sent her floating in absolute bliss.

Wyatt managed to slide her slacks and panties off her and continued his exploration down the length of her body. He kissed the center of her belly, and she could swear she felt butterflies. His mouth moved to her thigh, then over until he nestled between them. He spread her legs and explored her feminine core. He kissed and licked and then plunged his tongue deep inside. She heard herself whimper and say his name over and over. She felt him smile as he maintained his lavish pace. His hands and mouth on her sent her on a wave of pure ecstasy.

Before Willow got a chance to take a breath, Wyatt lifted her legs and rested them on his shoulders. He pulled her hips up and closer to him as he buried himself within her. His pace was fast and hard, and Willow met him thrust for thrust. The world around them fell away; Wyatt became her island, her haven, the place she wanted to stay forever. They reached their climax in unison, locked together mind, body, and soul as they fell back to Earth. Still inside her, he released her legs and his large frame enveloped her.

"*My A rúnsearc.*" Wyatt whispered the long forgotten words from his Irish background into her mind.

* * * *

Wyatt woke with his arm possessively around Willow's body and her arm stretched across his body. The warm, soft feel of her was truly incredible. Of course he'd had his fair share of relationships, yet in all his life he'd never woken as peacefully as these two mornings with Willow. His usual habit, if he accidently fell asleep with his lover, was to slip out of bed and leave a note. If they woke at the same time, he always felt tense and used work as an excuse to leave. He waited for the familiar feelings. When nothing came, his body fully relaxed, and he succumbed to this new experience. He wrapped his other arm around her and gently stroked her back. She lay there so quietly, he wasn't sure if she were awake or asleep until she lifted her head up to him and smiled.

"Good morning."

He placed his finger under her chin and tilted her face closer as he leaned into her and kissed her sweetly. "I could get used to waking up like this," he said. His remark made her smile all the more. "How about we grab a shower and I order us up some coffee and breakfast?"

"Sounds great. Will I have time to stop by the office and say my good-byes before we leave?"

"We have plenty of time to get done whatever you'd like to do and get to the airport on time. Now it's my turn. How do you want to handle *this* when we get back home? I don't know how excited your sisters will be to find out you're involved with another Farraday."

"Am I involved with you?"

"I'd like to think so."

"Well, I'm sure Victory would accept you; she already believes you're my soul mate. How would you like to handle this?"

"I'd prefer more time. Time to get to know one another better without others interfering. I just want to enjoy your company and learn your deepest secrets." He gave her a wink.

"I think you already know all my deepest secrets," she said. "I'm not sure I can say the same about you. I understand what you're saying and I agree. Except I don't know how long we will be able to get away with our relationship before my sisters and Tristan discover us."

"Relationship..." he muttered softly. "I like the sound of that." Wyatt pulled Willow over the top of him and relished the feel of her smooth, sensual curves. He gave her butt a light pat, and she laughed, pulled herself up, and kissed him hotly. He felt himself pulse against her taut belly. Before he knew what happened, she'd straddled him. It was the clincher in more ways than one. Yes, he did want to wake up beside this astounding woman every morning.

* * * *

"Thanks, Wyatt," Angie said. "Your security team had already arrived at my office when I got in this morning and I have to say, it makes me feel much safer."

"Good to know. Where are they now? I want to check in before we take off."

After Wyatt left the room, Angie smiled and winked at Willow. "It seems to me, you and that hunk of a man have worked things out."

"Oh my gosh! Is it that obvious?"

"An educated guess, based on the glow on your face and how he no longer appears wound up tight, like a rattler ready to strike. Don't get me wrong; he's still intense and alert, only calmer."

"Great. If you've picked up on it in less than five minutes, we have no hope when we get home."

Angie giggled at Willow's dilemma.

"I should be so lucky. Besides, why do you want to keep your feelings a secret? I think it's wonderful. You deserve to be happy, and Wyatt's a great guy."

"We want time to get to know each other better. Spend time with just the two of us, without sibling teasing and commentary."

"I understand and wish you luck."

"I didn't see Henry at his desk. Can you tell him thanks from me? He gave me enough space to pack up my mom's stuff and still be there when I needed him."

"One of his greatest qualities," Angie said.

"Ready to take off?" Wyatt asked when he returned an hour later. "They're good to go, Angie. If you have any problems, you know where to reach me."

"I'm sure I won't. It's going to be a long few days. I'm starting interviews this afternoon."

* * * *

Willow and Wyatt arrived back on campus late in the evening.

"It's good to be home," Willow said. "I suppose I should check in with my sisters."

"No need. I've already touched base with Tristan. Told him you were back safe and sound and to let your sisters know you would see them at the office in the morning."

He opened the front door for her, and she instantly panicked when Asia didn't rush out to greet her.

"Don't worry so." He rubbed his hand down her arm. "Asia is with Payton and Collin down at his bungalow. I also told Tristan to have them keep her until morning. No sense getting everyone all riled up."

"So we have the entire house to ourselves." A devilish grin spread over her luscious lips.

"It would seem so."

"There are lots of rooms in my house." Willow quirked an eyebrow at him.

"Aren't you tired? I thought you'd be ready for sleep."

"Hum…maybe in an hour or two."

"What have I gotten myself into? You're going to be the death of me." Wyatt closed and locked the door and turned on the security system. He turned and pinned Willow to the wall and kissed her. She wrapped her long elegant legs around his hips. Wyatt was astonished to discover that he'd already missed this intimate time, even though he'd woken beside her this very morning. *What the hell have I done to myself?* he thought, but only deep in his mind and only to himself.

* * * *

Willow woke to find the bed empty and was shocked by how bereaved she felt. The emotion swamped her. She sat up and found a note on the nightstand.

Morning Willow,
I need to do some things early this morning. I've arranged for us to all meet in the conference room next to your office at eight. By the way, the plant will be gone by the time you get to your office.

That was all, not a single personal mention. He'd not even written his name. He attempted to put distance between them—but why? Had she said or done something to upset him? She felt like a giddy school girl with her first crush. Did he have second thoughts? Maybe she read too much into it. She knew she tended to do that. She shook the negative feelings off and headed for the shower.

* * * *

"Morning, Willow! Glad you made it back in one piece; we've missed you," came the chorus from her sisters and the SOCOM team.

Each person came up to welcome her home while Wyatt sat at the conference table and worked on his computer, never making eye contact. When Noah gave her a bear hug, she felt Wyatt's energy shift; she glanced over to see Wyatt stiffen and immediately force himself to relax. She felt a tad guilty that Wyatt's response gave her comfort after his disappearance this morning. Now she was certain she'd second-guessed herself; he meant nothing more than what he'd written in his note.

"Okay, everyone. Grab a seat, we've got a lot to cover," Wyatt said.

"I guess someone didn't get his beauty sleep," Logan chuckled and nudged his partner, Noah.

Wyatt and Willow took turns and explained the events as they happened in London. They told the group everything, minus the one page of notes from her mom where she talked about the gravesite.

"Edward Ryker is indeed alive," Victory said, as if she were trying to convince herself.

"And Thomas, our employee, the mailman we've all known and chatted with for years is the maniac who chased you not once but twice. And he works with Ryker," Payton said, and shook her head in disbelief. "Could this situation get any weirder?"

"Probably," Morgan blurted out. Wyatt glared at him from across the table, so he added, "But let's hope not."

Willow handed Victory the pages of formula. "You think it's possible these pages go to that notebook you have with pages torn out?"

"Anything's possible. Although creating a formula able to cloak a person's true nature sounds highly improbable. It would, however, certainly be a benefit, a useful superpower to add to his soldier's arsenal."

"Yeah, especially for a criminal," Morgan said.

"I'll study this today and see if I can figure it out. From all I've read and learned, Edward Ryker is a brilliant man. A shame he chose to use his skills in this destructive manner," Victory said.

"Greed and control can be extremely powerful," Tristan said, as he rubbed his hand along Victory's back. "What's your take, Wyatt? Will he contact Willow or her sisters again?"

"I'd bet my life on it. The real questions are, when will Ryker make contact again and who does he work for. We have yet to discover the leader of the Kaleidoscope Group."

"What about Prescott? He could be the leader of this insane group," Payton said.

"I don't think so. My take is he's Braxton's replacement. Second-in-command and taking all his cues from a boss. I don't think the guy in charge has ever put himself out in the open," Wyatt said.

"How about Carl Sterling? The guy is shielded so deep, we may never get access to him," Jack said.

"I've given him some thought. He's definitely involved in KG, most likely up to his political eyeballs. Nonetheless, he doesn't seem the right fit. He's benefiting, knows every move they make, perhaps he's even the creator of a few of their devious plans. I just don't see him leading the band."

"I get the feeling you might think Ryker is the big boss," Tristan said.

"Makes sense, don't you think? Up until now, no one knew if he was even alive. He worked with Susan and Joseph Winters. He was the only other person present when Susan lost her first twins. Ryker is the one constant. I think there's a strong possibility he is the number one man."

"Think we can flush him out?" Collin asked.

"I doubt it. This man plans out every step. He's had twenty some years to plot this out. We would have to come up with something earth-shattering."

"Even then he might send one of his minions," Tristan said.

"General Roberts has requested my presence in D.C. He didn't want me to update him over the phone or computer. He's pretty convinced there is a leak within his department. As of yet he hasn't figured out who the leak is," Wyatt said. "Let's keep on target and continue our research."

"I thought we could walk back to the campus together," Victory said to Willow.

"Sounds good, give me a second to run up to my office and get my things." By the time she returned, Victory sat alone in the kitchen. "Boy, they scattered quickly."

"Wyatt wanted me to tell you he'd give you a call tonight."

"I see." She couldn't shake the feeling something had changed with him. She inhaled a breath and focused on the present. "Given this additional information you might require even more help. Would you like me to reassign Mary full-time to you for now?"

"About Mary. I wanted to speak with you about her."

"What's wrong?"

"We don't seem to be working out. I don't know what concerns me about her. She makes me uncomfortable and uneasy. At first I thought it was because she's Mom's friend and I still feel like a young girl around her."

"I know what you're saying. I felt the same way when she first showed up for the interview."

"Yeah, but that's not it, sis. There's something unsettling about her. I can't place my finger on it. Would you mind accompanying me to my lab? She should be there any minute. Maybe you can pick up on what I'm missing."

Chapter Nineteen

"Well, this is a treat," Mary said, as she walked into the lab. "Good to see you, Willow. I've enjoyed working here with Victory."

Willow picked up the same mixed signals again. Mary displayed the same conflict that Willow saw when she first interviewed her. While she appeared at ease and confident, her aura radiated a thin, muted, muddy yellow. It surrounded her, and Willow sensed no fear or regret. Now the yellow bled into muddy red, which signified anger, defiance, and vengeance accompanied with bitterness and greed. Mary's negative aura reverberated straight through Willow. Before she'd the chance to find her balance, the room tilted. She reached out and grabbed the work table, but not before both of the women noticed.

"Willow, are you alright?" Victory asked, as she reached out to steady her.

Mary grabbed Willow by her other arm. Willow felt the slither of a thick, oily push of negativity. Mary was enveloped in a shroud of synthetic energy. Willow turned toward her sister, her eyes wide with understanding. Concern played over Victory's features for a split second, before realization dawned on her.

"Willow, sweetie, I told you the jet lag would catch up with you. How about if I grab a cart and take you over to your office?" Victory asked.

"Maybe you should call Dr. Russell," Mary said.

"No, no. Victory's right. I tend to push myself; a pleasure to see you again, Mary."

"What on earth happened back there?" Victory asked, after they were a good distance from her lab. "You looked like you'd stared into the eyes of the devil."

"I did."

Victory snapped her head around in Willow's direction and practically toppled the cart over. Willow clutched the panic bar to keep from sliding out of the cart. She waited a beat for Victory to get the cart under control before she spoke.

"Your instincts were spot on. Mary doesn't know about your capability to magnify enhanced abilities."

"She has no special abilities."

"She does. And your skill of magnification has brought hers to the surface. I experienced bits of the unusual synthetic shroud the first time from the man in the basement, which turned out to be Thomas. The unnatural energy pushed at me again on the campus that night when the intruder chased me. Even more surfaced when Thomas found me in the London complex basement. I put it together when he visited my office. I knew the auras and energy felt unnatural, even synthetic. Walking into your office and experiencing you and Mary together magnified the sensation to an entirely different level. Her aura is much stronger because of you. I think Mary is a Kaleidoscope Group plant."

"You realize what you're saying? If what you say it true, Ryker's way ahead of us. He's invented a serum with the ability to cloak an individual's natural aura. Why would he create such a thing?" Victory asked.

"Because even back twenty years ago, he planned to create an invincible hit squad. He knew long ago that he and the Kaleidoscope Group would be up against other enhanced creatures like themselves. What better way to keep them hidden than by creating a veil to hide their true nature. They wouldn't be perceived as a threat—until it's too late."

They walked into Willow's office and she shut the door behind them. Victory dropped into a chair.

"Oh no! Do you think they exploit the children's abilities with their training at the schools? They could use the schools as a way to identify abilities. Then send them away to be brainwashed, honed, and if they're successful, for the final step, introduce the serum to hide them in plain sight?"

"Victory, you're brilliant. I believe you've defined the meaning behind Kaleidoscope Group's Second Wave. We need to contact Tristan and Wyatt and tell them of our discovery."

Victory sat in silence for a while. Willow glanced at over and caught her look of concentration. Of course, she always forgot about her and Tristan's telepathic connection. She remained quiet and waited.

"The guys think we are on to something. Wyatt will update General Roberts with this information. They don't want us to tip our hand to Mary. Willow, I can't work with her. How can I get her out of my lab without her becoming suspicious?"

"If we put our heads together, I'm sure we can come up with a new research project in need of her extensive knowledge." Willow winked at her sister. "I'll take her to lunch, soften her up with all the excellent help she's provided you, and offer her project coordinator of this *new* project."

"Wait. I have just the thing. I'll do some work on it tonight. Make the project appear legit and interesting to her. Mary's an astute woman; we need to make sure she falls for this."

"I'll leave it in your capable hands. Shall I schedule our lunch for tomorrow or the day after?"

"Give me a day. I'll prepare a detailed outline for you. Then you'll have something concrete to show her."

"Sounds good. The really difficult part is, how are you going to obtain a sample from her so that you can study her DNA?"

"No problem there. I know a dozen places in my lab she's left her DNA."

* * * *

Mary stood waiting for Willow in the courtyard.

"I've looked forward to our lunch since you invited me last night," Mary said. "I know we planned to stay on campus and eat at the café. But it's such a lovely day I thought we could lunch at one of the waterfront restaurants in town. I know the perfect place."

"I told Paula we'd be at the café. Let me call and update her. Shall we take the car service?" Willow asked.

"No, no. Why bother. My car is parked right over there in the front lot. Make your call, and I'll be right back."

Willow called the office phone, and the call went straight to message.

"Hey Paula, we've decided to lunch in town. See you when I get back."

She had told Victory and Paula she would be staying on campus. She couldn't very well say no to Mary; she didn't want her to have any reason to become suspicious. The front gate guard would still record their departure.

* * * *

"I haven't been here in forever," Willow said, as she looked out and admired the serene water of Liberty Bay.

"This is one of my favorite spots. I'm way too busy as of late, and I haven't had the chance to indulge myself."

"It's my pleasure to share the experience. I have a great deal to discuss with you." She pulled the file Victory had assembled and opened it on the table. "We have a brand new project, and we would appreciate it if you would consider the position of project coordinator."

"Oh, really? I'm honored you would think of me, but what about assisting Victory? She has a lot on her plate at the moment and I've enjoyed helping her."

"Believe me, she's sincerely appreciated it and that's why she suggested you lead this new project. She thinks you would do an outstanding job and it would mean a healthy raise as well. Why don't you look these over a bit? I need to head to the ladies' room."

Once inside the stall, Willow pulled out her phone and rang Paula. The phone rang and rang. Once again, Paula's voice came on telling her to leave a message. Then someone entered the ladies' room. Not knowing if it were Mary, she disconnected her call and left.

* * * *

Mary pulled out her phone as Willow turned the corner for the restroom.

"Good afternoon, Mr. Sterling, it's Mary Downing."

"I can't talk with you at the moment. I'm in the middle of something."

"But sir, I believe the sisters are on to me. What should I do?"

"Like I said. I can't talk. Call the Chairman."

She heard the click. She knew she couldn't risk returning to the campus without getting instructions. She pushed the speed dial.

"Good afternoon, Mr. Chairman, it's Mary."

"Of course, Mary. What can I help you with?"

"I followed protocol and contacted my superior. He's tied up at the moment and instructed me to contact you, Mr. Chairman."

"I see. What seems to be the issue?"

"I believe I'm compromised."

She quickly gave him the rundown and finished by telling him what she was currently doing.

"I see. Well, I've always put faith in your hunches. Do you by any chance have the drug on your person?"

"Yes, I carry it with me everywhere."

"Good. Place a few drops in her drink. Get her into your vehicle within ten minutes, or you will draw a crowd. This is a perfect opportunity. I'll text you an address by the time you reach your vehicle. Follow the instructions."

Mary replaced the bottle into her purse just as Willow came into view.

"Have you made your decision?" Willow asked, as she sat at the table.

"I have, yes. I'm honored you've asked me to lead the project." Mary picked up her iced tea and held it out. "Shall we toast to a productive project?"

Willow picked up her iced tea and clicked her glass. She took a sip of tea and started to place the glass back on the table.

"And, one more toast, to the three of you girls. Your parents would be truly proud of what you've accomplished."

Willow smiled, clicked her glass to Mary's once again, and took a few more sips of tea.

Mary waited a few moments and when she realized Willow was too confused to reply, she said, "Oh my, look at the time. I really must get back to my lab. Shall we go?"

"Yes, I'm feeling a sudden headache coming on," Willow mumbled.

Mary managed to get Willow into the passenger seat not a moment too soon. She closed the passenger door and by the time she got around to the driver's side, Willow's head lolled back; she was unconscious. Mary's phone beeped, notifying her of the directions and instructions. She started the car and headed for the highway.

* * * *

Willow felt like she had a terrible hangover. She couldn't recall the last thing that happened before she fell asleep. She tried to rub her head, but her hands felt like lead; she couldn't get them to move. Then she realized she wasn't lying down, but sitting in a chair, and it wasn't the lead feeling keeping her from moving her arms. They were tied behind her.

"Welcome back," said Mary.

Willow slowly lifted her head and opened her eyes. She looked around the large empty room with gray metal walls and a concrete floor.

"Where am I? Why have you done this, Mary?"

"You can stop the charade. I know you are on to me. Consider this my resignation."

"Great, fine. You quit. Now let me go." Willow tried to loosen the rope around her hands. "This is crazy. You do realize people will be looking for us."

"Not for a while. I texted your assistant from your phone and told her we were so excited to begin the *new project*, we were on the Seattle ferry. We needed to pick up some equipment and wouldn't be back until later tonight."

Willow heard a door open behind her and footsteps approached.

"Good to see you again, W-i-l-low."

Willow suppressed her initial fright.

"Thomas. I thought you would be long gone by now. What brings you here?" Willow asked.

Thomas sneered and paced the floor around her.

"You have no idea how pleased I am not to have to play the company idiot and cater to you, your sisters, or Angie any longer."

He stepped directly into her line of sight. His aura dripped with hate and resentment; his black eyes were feral. He stepped away and dragged a small table in front of her and placed a computer on the table. He opened the laptop and pressed a button. The computer came to life and the screen filled with a man's face. She knew his face. Somewhere in the depths of her memory she felt she knew this man. He'd been much younger when last she saw him.

"We have you, Mr. Chairman," Thomas said.

Mr. Chairman. Willow thought. Her thoughts seemed disjointed and she couldn't focus on one thing.

"Yes, I see. Willow, it's been a long time since last I saw you."

"So, you do work for Kaleidoscope Group."

He chuckled at her as if she had told him the stupidest joke.

"My dear girl. I don't *work* for the Kaleidoscope Group. I *created* it."

"What do you mean?"

"It's simple. KG is my creation. I put the pieces and people into place long before I left the Winters Corporation. I tried to convince your mother to join my quest. She wouldn't have it. For the life of me, I will never understand her loyalty to your father. She and I, we could've controlled the world."

"Obviously you didn't know my mother. Control meant nothing to Mom, and Dad and she shared the same moral center; something you never had. As for her loyalty to my dad, that's called—love."

"Love?" He spit the word out as if the sound of it left a sour taste in his mouth. "What a weak and destructive feeling. Mark my words, love caused her downfall. She never needed Joseph. He was an ordinary man and stood in her way of greatness."

"Ryker, you can justify her death however you see fit, but it's still clear to me that you had my parents killed. I choose to believe they had a wonderful life together, up to the very day you cut it short." It took every ounce of willpower to maintain her stare, but she kept eye contact with steely determination. She blinked, though, when she thought she saw a tiny spark of remorse.

"I did not kill her. I could do nothing to prevent her demise. I urged her to join me. She refused, which made her a liability."

"Stop stalling. Why am I here?"

"I thought now would be the perfect opportunity to place our cards on the table."

Yeah, not happening, she thought.

"Your little company is both a wonder to me and a pain in the neck."

"Sorry to hear."

"Yes, I'm sure you are. Tell me. Have you enjoyed my test subjects?"

"What are you talking about?"

"I've sent people into your campus a number of times. It's a perfect environment to test out some of my latest improvements. You and your sisters aren't able to read their auras or their thoughts. You had no idea they were even there or they had special abilities, did you?"

"I have no idea what you're rambling on about."

"Please, Willow. I have no patience for your false ignorance. The questions are merely rhetorical. I know you weren't able to flush them out. Only when you came face-to-face with them did you actually know they were there. Wait. There, I see it." Ryker's face enlarged as he moved closer to the camera and studied her. "You didn't know they were there, but eventually you did recognize the difference in their energy and auras. How did you discover my serum?"

She stared into the screen and said nothing.

"Your abilities have sharpened." He leaned back and thought a moment. "My decision to use your campus as a testing ground has proved advantageous. You're going to have to tighten your security. However, I don't believe you have the capability to keep my people out. A real shame to pull Mary out, she served as our greatest asset. We've had a front row seat to everything your company's worked on since the day I disappeared."

"Mary hasn't been involved with our government contracts."

"Technically correct. Nonetheless she has worked for the Winters Corporation for a long time and has many friends, and you, my dear, assigned her to work alongside Victory. Thank you for the opportunity to glean insight into her current projects."

"It was Mary who broke into my office, wasn't it?" Willow looked up at Mary. She hoped she might get a rise from her.

"You are a smart girl. The time had come to locate one of our lost employees. We can't have her running amuck and not know what she is up to."

"Aimee. You want to find Aimee. I'm sorry you didn't find who you were looking for."

"No matter. She'll come out of hiding sooner or later."

"And Thomas? What purpose did he serve in London?"

"Aw, Thomas and Mary were the first to be injected with my cloaking serum. They were long-term test subjects, along with information gatherers. Thomas did like to stir the pot and could be a bit reckless at times. Still he's the best at cleaning up others' messes." Ryker smirked at Willow. "You know dear, the three of you are my first successful test subjects. I know you discovered I adjusted your mother's fertility drug. She wanted dearly to have children and when she came to me and told me of her plans, I was elated. It was the perfect opportunity. Finally I would have the chance to create a superior being. She trusted me completely, and I had all the time I needed to *fine-tune* her drug. You're welcome."

Fury rose up in Willow at the arrogance of this man. Her body betrayed her and she began to shake. She wanted to throw in his face that she knew about the bug in her plant, the possibility the twins were not buried where he claimed, that Carl Sterling and Daniel Prescott worked for him and were part of his demented group. She yearned to see his expression. Even though she knew it would only serve to alert him and KG. No, for the sake of her family she couldn't afford to let anything more slip. Doing so would only be a setback to Wyatt, his team, her, and her sisters. They were hot on KG's trail now, and she would be damned if she'd leak any information to this psychotic creature for the mere thrill of seeing his expression.

"Now you've lost your conduit to our company. Why am I here? Are you going to try and pump me for information? Let me save you the time. I will tell you nothing. Is this a kidnapping? Are you going to hold me for ransom? Or have you decided to kill me?" She all but hissed at him.

"Hum...all legitimate thoughts, but no. I simply thought the time had come for us to meet in person. I must admit, what I've learned from you is interesting. I should inform you that your company is supporting the wrong side. I've given you and your sisters phenomenal abilities, and I can give you more. Merge with Kaleidoscope Group. I can help Victory with her research to buffer the increasing effects of the foreign DNA Braxton injected into Collin and Morgan. I know you are out of your mother's formula, and your and your sisters' abilities are evolving. Come join our quest and I'll help Victory stabilize all of you. Don't you see, Willow? Join me and the world will be at your feet."

"Don't you mean *your* feet?"

"My dear Willow, the world is already at my feet. The reach of Kaleidoscope Group encompasses every notable country in the world and includes prestigious and powerful people throughout; people who appear untouchable are my tools."

She soaked in every word he spoke. *This man is one cocky bastard,* she thought.

"Well, if you've no intention of joining my team, I believe it's time to end this meeting. Heed my warning; our next meeting will not be as friendly. This seems all so pointless. Both our groups strive for the same answers. What a pity you are too shortsighted to see the value in our merger."

"We may be searching for common answers, but there is no way in hell we intend to use our findings in the same fashion."

"Good to see you again, Willow. I have to apologize in advance for how you will be leaving—unconscious. We wouldn't want you to lead your merry band of misfits back to this facility."

Ryker nodded to Mary. The woman approached her with a large hypodermic needle, ripped at the sleeve of her sweater, and jabbed her in the shoulder. Willow passed out before she even had the chance to protest.

"Thomas?"

"Not yet, sir. Wait, I have it." A pinging sounded on his computer. Mary went over and stood behind Thomas. The layout of the building was displayed on the screen, and the pinging sound originated from the place where Willow slumped, out cold.

"Very nice, Chairman," Mary praised him.

"This will be the first true test of my microscopic tracker, untraceable by X-ray. Willow won't even know it's there."

"How long will the tracker last?" Thomas asked.

"Indefinitely, I believe. We'll have to watch and learn."

"What makes it different than the run of the mill tracker?"

"My tracker is biological. It will slowly mutate into an inert organic substance and be absorbed by the body, rendering it untraceable, even with an MRI. There's a minute chance of an interaction in some individuals, which over time would render the tracker useless. Tie my computers into the microchip. I need to follow the process firsthand."

"Certainly, sir."

"Shall we return her to the campus, Chairman?" Mary asked.

"Not yet. The amount of drug you gave her will keep her out for a good half-day. Leave her where she is for now. In four hours or so, deposit her down the road in the opposite direction of her campus. Let's watch them all scramble a while longer. Good work."

"What's my next assignment?" Mary asked.

"You need to leave town immediately, Mary. Leave Willow to Thomas. He has a new passport and identification for you. We have booked you on a flight out of the country. I will contact you when it's safe."

Mary nodded in understanding and the screen faded to black. She looked over at Thomas.

"Don't touch her," she said, in a warning tone.

"Aw, come on, you're no fun." A ghastly sneer lit his face.

"Dr. Ryker will have your head if you do anything to her he didn't instruct."

"You're right. Ryker would have my head on a platter. Nonetheless, I can give her a farewell she will not soon forget and savor her fear and uncertainty. The bitch stole five years of my life. Chasing her through the basement of both the old complex and the London site served as the only highlights of my assignment. I'm going to make her squirm."

Chapter Twenty

Victory fretted and paced the floor of her lab. She was so concerned that she hadn't heard from Willow, she couldn't concentrate on her research. She probably worried for nothing. She picked up her office phone and rang her sister.

"Willow Winters' office," Paula said.

"Oh hi, Paula. Is Willow in a meeting?"

"No. She never returned from lunch."

"Wait—what?"

"She left me a message and said they would be dining in town. A while later she sent me a text and said she and Mary went over to Seattle to pick up a few items for Mary's new project. I don't expect her back in the office until tomorrow morning."

"Oh, no."

"Is there a problem I can help you with, Victory?"

"Paula, there is no new project."

"Then where is she?" Paula's voice trembled.

"Everything will be fine. Why don't you head home for the day? I'll get this sorted out." Victory tried to reassure herself as much as Paula.

"I should stay, and…"

"No. I don't want any of our employees to get wind of this. I'm contacting the team. I know it's a lot to ask of you, but please, act like it's just the end of any other day. I'll keep you apprised, I promise."

"*Tristan, I need you.*" She sent her thought into the universe to locate her husband. She knew he was close by and would understand her call.

"*What's upset you, honey? Tell me what's wrong.*" Tristan answered her.

"*Willow took Mary out to lunch and now they're both missing.*"

"*Shit. When did they leave?*"

She said they were going to meet at the café at noon, except Mary wanted to go out in town."

"*You get Payton and we will all meet up at our house as soon as possible.*"

"Hi Victory, Collin and I were just heading down to his bungalow for dinner; what's up?" Payton asked.

"I need the two of you to come up to my house immediately. Willow's missing."

* * * *

"I checked with security at the main gate," Logan said. "Mary's vehicle left the campus at 12:10. The guard claims he saw a person in the passenger seat but didn't take the time to get a good look at them."

"Okay, start from the beginning," Wyatt said. The image of his head and shoulders filled the laptop on Victory's kitchen table. Everyone in the room could feel the layers of black rage roll off the man, even though he sat three thousand miles away in General Roberts' D.C. office.

"Yesterday, after the meeting, Willow asked if I would like Mary to spend more time with me, because of the additional work. I told her no. In fact I didn't want Mary working with me any longer. Mary gives me a strange feeling and makes me uncomfortable. I asked Willow to accompany me to my lab as Mary would soon be there, and she could give me her thoughts on Mary's aura."

"Go on," Tristan prompted as he took her hand in his.

"That's when I connected with you, and you reached out to Wyatt."

"Yes, and I seem to recall we instructed you not to alert her. Apparently our warning fell on deaf ears. What did the two of you plan?" Tristan asked.

"No, your exact words were 'don't tip your hand;' we didn't. After I updated you, I told Willow I couldn't work with the woman another day. Besides, the last thing we needed was to have her spend any more time lurking around in my lab."

"And…"

"And, we worked out a plan to get her out of my lab without tipping our hand."

"What kind of a plan?" Wyatt asked.

"Well, we came up with a new project. I fabricated a file, based on an actual project we are considering. There's no way she could have seen through my work."

"It's not your work she saw through; it was your timing."

"What do you mean?"

"Think about it. You and Willow meet her in your lab the morning of the meeting. Willow reacts strangely enough that Mary suggests you call for the doctor. One day later Willow invites her to lunch and offers her a new position. This woman is seasoned. If she is who we think she is, she's played this part for years and years, highly likely even before your parents died. She knew a setup when she saw one. Jack, have you tracked Willow's phone?"

"I've checked continuously since I first heard. Her phone is off, or dead."

A tiny dot of light lit up on Jack's computer screen.

"Wait. I've got her," Jack said.

Everyone watched as Wyatt grabbed his phone and hit the speed dial. Her phone rang and rang.

"She's not picking up. Where is she Jack?"

"Looks like she's in a state park about an hour from here."

"I can't get my chopper into a state park. Nowhere to land," Logan said.

"The chopper would draw too much attention anyway," Noah said. "I can get us there in forty minutes."

"I'm coming with you," Victory said.

"So am I," Payton said.

"Neither of you are leaving this campus," Collin said, before anyone had the chance to comment. "We could be walking directly into a trap with Willow as the lure for the both of you."

"Collin's right," Wyatt said. "Noah, Logan, and Morgan, head out, now. Jack will maintain contact."

The three men shot from the house.

"Jack, if you see or hear anything, I want to know."

"Yes, sir."

"General Roberts is insisting I stay here. If you don't locate Willow in the next hour, Roberts be damned; I'm on the next plane back," Wyatt said.

"Don't be foolish, brother. We'll find her. We're not only a team, we have all become a family. They will find Willow and bring her back. You hold tight," Tristan responded via the brothers' telepathic link.

"Find her, Tristan," Wyatt answered in kind.

"Contact me the moment the men reach her," Wyatt said to the team.

* * * *

As the foggy veil lifted from Willow's mind, the first thing she registered was the strong aroma of evergreen. She rotated her head to one side and a spasm of pain shot through her skull. She let out a soft moan, brought her hands to her head, and covered her eyes. Frozen like a statue she waited for the agony to subside. As it did, she took stock of her surroundings by sound and feel. No longer inside a building, this she knew. Now she was somewhere outside and laying on the hard, cold, dirt. The soft crunch under the movement of her body suggested the dirt also featured pine needles and dried leaves. When the pain in her head had tapered enough, she ever so slowly removed her hands and opened her eyes. She looked up into a canopy of evergreens; the light of day had turned to early dusk.

Gradually she raised herself into a sitting position. Every single muscle in her body screamed out in torment. As she surveyed her environment she got the sense of a park setting. She remained where she sat and dug into her slacks for her phone. It was there. Relief flooded her body and she hit the button. Her call for help was answered before the first ring was completed.

"Willow, are you all right?" Wyatt asked. She could hear the relief in his voice.

"I-I don't know. Every inch of me hurts. I don't know why I called you. You're clear across the country. Let me phone Victory."

"Don't you dare hang up on me. I'm contacting them now. You stay right where you are. The team should be there in the next ten minutes."

"How did they know?"

"Your phone. It powered up a little over an hour ago."

She heard rustling behind her. Then a familiar voice called out.

"Willow, if you can hear me, call out," Logan said.

"Logan, I'm here."

The three men burst through the foliage.

"Willow, are you okay?" Noah ran up to her and dropped down on his knees beside her.

"I hurt everywhere. I'm extremely grateful you found me."

"Here let us help you stand up," Morgan said. He reached out and gently took her arm, but Willow screamed out in pain and he immediately let go. "Shit, I'm sorry."

"Sit right there, let me have a look," Noah said. He ran his hands lightly over her arm and shoulder. "I don't think it's broken, but your shoulder is dislocated."

"Can you fix it?" she asked.

"I can, but it's gonna hurt like hell. Why don't you wait and let Dr. Russell have a look."

"How far are we from the campus?"

The men looked at one another.

"Yeah, I thought so. Get it over with."

"Okay. Logan, sit down behind Willow and straddle her. When I say so, you get a tight hold of her and I'll reset the shoulder."

"Are you sure about this?" Morgan asked Willow.

She nodded her head, which turned out to be a bad idea as the pain rang through her brain. Logan took up his position behind her.

"Now, Logan," Noah said, before anyone had the chance to reconsider.

Logan grabbed Willow and held tight as Noah gave her arm a teeth-rattling yank. Even through gritted teeth Willow's cry escaped.

"How does your shoulder feel?"

"Like you just yanked my arm out of the socket."

"I kinda did, but I reset it too. You're still going to need Dr. Russell to look at your shoulder."

The men helped her to her feet. She wobbled from side to side.

"Are you sure you're okay?" Noah asked, with a concerned look on his face.

"I think so. Do I look as bad as I feel?"

"Willow, your sweater is half torn off you. One leg of your slacks is ripped all the way up to your thigh and you're covered in dirt."

She looked down at her hands. They were filthy. She reached for her slacks and found the button at the waist torn off and the zipper half the way down.

* * * *

"There's no evidence of sexual abuse of any kind," Dr. Russell said, as she finished with her examination of Willow. "I'm sure if you weren't in such pain when you were found, you would have realized it yourself. How are you feeling now?"

"My shoulder is still throbbing, less than when the guys found me though. Especially here." She wrapped her hand round the base of her neck and touched the top of her shoulder. "Ahh, ouch. Is it broken?"

"X-rays show no broken bones. You could very well have a torn tendon and you can bet you are going to be badly bruised. We could do an MRI if you'd like."

"Not tonight. I'll come by in a couple of days. I appreciate everything you've done. All the same, I think I'm done being pulled, poked, and prodded for tonight."

"I completely understand." A smile quirked one corner of Dr. Russell's mouth. "Take these pain pills with you. Start them first thing tomorrow morning or later tonight if you wake in pain."

"I don't think I need those. The pain isn't too intense anymore."

"Good, the injection I gave you has started to work. Take my word, when the meds wear off, you will be grateful for these." She placed the bottle in Willow's hand and closed her fingers around it.

Willow carefully slid off the examination table, and Dr. Russell helped her into her sweats and pullover.

"I'll get a cart and take you up to the house." She opened the door to her exam room and found Victory, Payton, and the entire SOCOM team waiting. "Well, I see I needn't worry about you getting back to the house safely."

"Thanks doc, we've got her covered," Tristan said. He stepped up beside Willow, Collin on her other side, and they cautiously escorted her out to the cart. "If you're feeling up to it, we need to go over what happened."

"Not tonight, Tristan. She needs to rest," Victory said.

"I'm okay, Victory, really. All I need is a soft chair and a cup of hot tea."

"It can wait until tomorrow."

"Yes, honey it can. Except by tomorrow she might forget some of the details. We really need to go through the event while it's fresh in her mind," Tristan explained.

"Please, don't argue over me. I would rather go over this tonight and move on."

* * * *

At last the computer buzzed. Wyatt pushed the key so hard for a second he thought he might have broken it. The image on the screen sharpened with his brother's face.

"How is she, Tristan?"

"See for yourself," he said, and turned the computer in Willow's direction.

Willow reclined on the sofa and sipped on a cup. As she lowered the cup he noticed a slight shake. No wonder with what she'd experienced and with him nowhere around. General Roberts had ordered him to stand-down and remain in D.C. Wyatt had gotten so infuriated with the General he almost went AWOL.

"You're welcome," Tristan said, using their telepathic link.

"Yeah, thanks. How's she holding up?"

"She's a fighter. We all had a huge scare. When the guys found her, by all appearances they were worried she might have been assaulted."

"Yeah, I got that impression. Willow left the line open; I heard most of the rescue." Wyatt could feel his heart once again start to race and heat rush to his head. *"She wasn't, right?"* He hoped his desperation didn't echo though his mind.

Tristan shook his head.

"Thank God they found her."

"Okay you two. Either include all of us in your conversation or I'm heading up to bed. My day's been hell," Willow said.

The bruising had already started to show. One of her cheeks had a red-and-purple hue, and the color traveled down her neck. Wyatt thought he could make out fingerprints on her neck, which disappeared underneath her pullover.

"How are you feeling, Willow?" Wyatt asked.

"Like someone threw me from a moving vehicle." She attempted to smile and touched her bottom lip as a cut began to bleed. Payton appeared by her side and handed her sister a tissue.

"The quicker we get through this, the quicker you can go up to bed. Tell us what happened when you met with Mary?" Wyatt asked.

"Because it was a beautiful afternoon, she insisted we go into town and eat at a restaurant on the waterfront. I knew the guys at the gate would see us leave, and I left a message on Paula's phone. Lunch and the meeting were going well. I thought I had Mary hooked. She even wanted to toast to her new project. Right after the toasts, she wanted to get back to the campus. I can't conjure up what happened after the toast. She must've slipped something into my drink when I got up to use the restroom. I woke up inside some type of storage building or factory, a large building. I don't even know how far we were from town."

"If she kidnapped you, why did she let you go?" Wyatt asked.

"She did it for her boss—Edward Ryker."

Her news stunned the entire group.

"Edward Ryker. You finally got to see him in the flesh?"

"No. Well, sort of. Like you, Wyatt, he Skyped in. I have no idea of his whereabouts. Your hunch was correct, Wyatt. Ryker doesn't *work* for Kaleidoscope Group; Edward Ryker *created* the group. He said the reach of this group encompasses every notable country in the world and includes prestigious and powerful people throughout. He actually called these people his untouchable tools. From what he told me, the idea for the group came into fruition years before. Way back when he worked on the fertility drug for Mom, possibly earlier."

Willow explained the entire altercation blow-by-blow to the group.

"For what it's worth, you sound like you handled yourself like a pro. You obtained a great deal of information while telling him virtually nothing," Wyatt said.

"Thanks. Believe me, it took every ounce of my willpower not to rub his face in the information we do have."

"I imagine it did. I'm proud of you, Willow."

His statement caused her cheeks to pink. He noticed the color change even under the nasty bruises.

"Do you remember anything more?" Tristan asked.

"There is no more to remember. I told you everything. Next thing I know, Mary injected me with something that knocked me out cold, and I woke up in the woods." She rubbed at her upper shoulder.

"Okay then, let's call it a night. I want you guys at the office first thing in the morning," said Tristan.

"You'll have to work this thing through without me. I'll be tied up in a damn meeting. I'll touch base with you the minute I'm free," Wyatt said.

"Willow, don't disconnect yet, please," Wyatt whispered.

Her phone had remained connected when the guys located her in the park. Wyatt witnessed every grueling moment of the rescue. He experienced every pain she felt. When Noah finally called him and told him about her clothes, the terror of what might have happened squeezed every last breath from him. He hadn't started to breathe again until Tristan made contact on the computer.

Wyatt stared into Willow's eyes and willed his words into her mind.

"I'm deeply sorry this happened to you and I'm devastated you were hurt."

"I know you are, Wyatt. It wasn't your fault. But when you return, maybe you can explain to me why you left both my room and the campus without so much as a good-bye."

She gave him the smallest of smiles, which stabbed his heart clean through, as she pushed the disconnect button.

Chapter Twenty-One

Wyatt drove onto the Winters Campus. Two long weeks passed since the morning he woke beside Willow and slinked out of her house. What a chickenshit he'd been. He hadn't even phoned her, other than the video conversation after her kidnapping. Now he didn't know what to say to her. This woman confused him to no end. Even without contacting her, she remained ingrained in his mind.

"Son of a bitch," he muttered. He certainly didn't need this complication. What had he been thinking? "Man up, Farraday." He needed to find her. He couldn't avoid her any longer. Truth be known, he wanted to see her; he'd ached from missing her each and every day and night he'd been gone. "Son of a bitch," he grumbled. What the hell was he supposed to do about this? He'd no desire and no time to have a real relationship. Not being involved with anyone had served him well over the last five years. He'd noticed Willow and found her extremely attractive. They'd always been like oil and water—until they weren't. "Man up, Farraday." He parked his car in the main lot and headed for the storage building. The shipment from England had arrived early this morning, and if he knew Willow, she made sure to meet it.

She sat sideways on a sheet-covered chair, facing away from him. Her long elegant legs were crossed at the ankles and bobbed up and down to their own beat. Her glistening golden hair was pulled loosely into a single braid and hung down her back. There was only a trace of the bruise left on her cheek from her ordeal a week ago. Immersed in something she was reading, she was obviously oblivious to her surroundings. This woman would be the death of him. He tried to impress upon her over and over the importance of being aware of her environment.

"Willow," he pushed her name mentally and at the same time he lightly placed his hand on her shoulder. She wiped a hand across her face before she turned to him. Her pain consumed him, and he squatted down next to the chair. Now he could see the wet tracks running down her cheeks. "Willow, what's the matter?"

"What do you care?" She shot back at him and wiped at her cheeks once again.

He knew he deserved her wrath. But hell, he couldn't bear to see her suffer. "I know I deserve your anger. I'm sorry I didn't call you after your kidnapping."

"When you left that morning you didn't even say good-bye. You promise, no matter how you feel about me, you'll see this through to the end? You'll find out if the twins really are in those graves?"

A jab of hot white pain spread throughout his chest. He realized in one split instant how his inconsiderate action of leaving a note and not facing her to voice his fears had caused this unbelievable woman to doubt him. What had he done? The only thing he could've done to protect himself from being pulled under by…what? Commitment, happiness, love? Yep, a total ass. He thrust the train of thought aside.

"You have my word." He placed the lightest of kisses on the top of her head.

Shit. He was such a *jackass*.

"You're right; you are," she said, without missing a beat. "I may not have the ability to interpret your aura like I once did, but the unguarded thoughts in your mind become clearer with each passing day."

Holy crap. Now she could pick up his thoughts with no prompting from him. He needed to work on buffering his casual thoughts from her.

"You have every right to be pissed at me. However, can we please table it for now and discuss the issue at hand? Why are you crying?"

"I found another envelope taped to the underside of Mom's desk. Mom wrote it shortly before she and Dad died, or should I say—were murdered. She's right, Wyatt. Mom and Dad weren't innocent victims of a random auto accident. Their supposed accident was an elaborate smoke screen. Mom knew someone meant to kill her just not who. Even so the number one suspect she listed was Edward Ryker."

"Why did she suspect someone wanted her dead in the first place?"

"Mom continued to be haunted about the twins until the day she died. Haunted to the extent she eventually reached out in secret to a colleague in London who was the head pathologist. She asked him to exhume her daughters and verify their DNA. She made sure all correspondence between her and this friend were contained in a password-protected file, which she always closed after she finished with it. One morning she started her computer and the private emails between her and the pathologist appeared on the screen. She knew someone had broken into her office and accessed her files. Mom and the pathologist were working out a plan, Wyatt. She planned to fly back to London the following month and witness the exhumation."

"And that's why you believe she and your father were killed?"

"Yes, and I believe it was Mary who broke into her office and got into her file."

"Mary hammered the final nail into their coffins. Ryker knew she would never be swayed to join him, like he told you. Now with this new information he couldn't allow her to live."

"There was another note, and this came as a complete surprise. She talks about visiting Mary in her lab late one evening. Mary was upset and drunk when she phoned Mom. Mom went to Mary's lab for moral support. At first Mary rambled on about nonsense. Then she got mean and spiteful. She told Mom she and her company were the reasons she couldn't be with the man she loved. Mary said her daughter would make a difference in the world. She said Tessa was smarter than all three of us put together."

"Tessa? Are you sure she wrote, Tessa? Tessa the telepathic, brain-sucking vampire? Tessa who killed Braxton's administrative assistant and Emma's half-sister, Sarah? Tessa the bitch who nearly killed Payton?"

"Yes, that Tessa. Look right here." She pointed to the paragraph and Wyatt read it aloud.

"Could be a coincidence, there must be many women with the name. But I don't believe in coincidences. Have you met this girl?"

"No. Mary didn't keep her. I recall reading her file before Mary came in for her interview and there was a short notation of her leave of absence twenty-nine years ago."

"She left, gave birth, and put her daughter up for adoption?"

"Mom said the baby got adopted out by a private party prior to her birth."

"What the hell happened to the father in all this?"

"Mom never stated who the father might be. What she did write about was the continuous rumors the baby's father might be Edward Ryker."

"What the hell! Why would he be a possibility?"

"Mary and Ryker shared the same lab. They worked together for over ten years, a long time to work with someone. It fits. Her not being able to be with the man she loved and to have to give up her child."

"Okay, let me get this straight." Wyatt stood up and made a "hold on" gesture with his hands. "Ryker and Mary have a daughter together. She gives the girl up for adoption. What I am hearing is Ryker most likely placed her in a foster-type home. They raised her until he retrieved her to do experiments on, and now she is a tool for the Kaleidoscope Group. That's cold, even for Ryker."

"I can see all the pieces fit together. You didn't see him, Wyatt. I looked into the computer screen and into the black depths of a soulless man."

"Jesus." He rubbed his palms roughly over his eyes. "The two of them are heartless." He shook his head in disgust. "To use your own daughter in your experiments. To create a woman capable of tearing into a person's mind so viciously, she can cause a massive brain bleed...I can't even comprehend it. Even so, I think you're right; it appears the most logical fit. Did Mary recall telling your mother about her daughter?"

"Mom said she never brought Tessa up again. She figured Mary was too drunk to recollect anything from that conversation. She said even with all the other times she and Mary shared a drink, she never saw her in that frame of mind, before or after that night."

One fat tear trickled down Willow's cheek. He left her with her thoughts, walked around the storage unit, and inspected the items. After a short while he circled back to her.

"I need to touch base with the team and fill them in on all you've discovered. Would you mind if I take your notes with me? I'll get a couple copies made and return the originals to you. We need to talk, Willow. Can I see you tonight?"

She didn't so much as glance his way. Bile rose in his throat at the possibility she might refuse his request.

"Please, Willow. Give me another chance. I promise I won't let you down."

Willow looked up at him; her watery ocean-blue eyes were near to overflowing. He wanted to kick himself. He knew his callousness caused her hesitation.

"I'm going over to Cassidy's for dinner tonight. I will most likely be late. Let's make it tomorrow night." She held out the envelope to him.

"I need to assign someone to shadow you if you're leaving campus."

"I've already taken care of my security. I'd no idea you would be back today. I have one of the campus security guards escorting me tonight."

He thought about demanding he assign the security but thought better of the idea. At least she'd thought about arranging security. He knew he teetered on the edge with her at the moment and figured this would be a battle he would lose.

* * * *

Wyatt sat at his desk and waited for his team to gather. Jack wasn't even in the office when he'd arrived. He walked out and looked around the disaster in the main room. Between the men's cluttered desks and the remodeling Payton had started, the place was a wreck.

"What's up, bro?" Tristan asked, as he walked in, tossed Wyatt a bottle of water, opened his own bottle, and dropped into the nearest chair. "Hate to say it, but you look like you've lost your best friend; rough day?"

"You could say so. Can I ask you a personal question?" Wyatt asked, as he looked at his twin. If not for their different hair and eye color, no one would be able to tell them apart. Tristan's black hair and dark violet eyes were a vivid contrast to Wyatt's light-colored hair and light blue eyes.

"Since when have we not told each other everything?"

He could see Tristan study him.

"How did you know you loved Victory?"

Tristan's eyes widened for a nanosecond.

"I knew I loved her when the thought of living even one day without her by my side made me feel as if I would be swallowed up by a tornado—oh, don't tell me you think you're in love with Willow."

"What? No. Just interested in how you knew you found your true love, that's all."

"Give it up, bro. I know you better than you know yourself. You've already fallen. Hate to tell you, you're in love with her. It's written all over you."

The door to the building swung open and the rest of the team traipsed in. Wyatt exhaled. For once he thanked the powers that be for the guys' poor timing. Without wasting a beat, he gathered his team and filled them in on the day's events.

* * * *

Willow was fifteen minutes late by the time she pried herself from the office. She planned to go back to the house, change clothes, and feed Asia. Thank goodness for her sisters. Victory planned on heading to her own house shortly and agreed to pick up Asia and take care of her until Willow returned. The company car was parked right outside the door to her building. The guard leaned casually against the vehicle. He snapped to attention the instant he spotted her and opened the door.

Cassidy greeted her at the door before Willow even got the chance to knock.

"I started to worry you were going to get waylaid at the office," Cassidy said, as she hugged Willow.

"An attempt was made. I told Paula to schedule the issue for first thing in the morning. Nothing earth-shattering needs to be solved today."

"Sometimes being the boss is a good thing. Let's go into the kitchen. I've got a wonderful bottle of red wine open. Dinner should be done soon."

"Great house."

"Let me give you the grand tour."

Cassidy handed her a large glass of wine.

* * * *

"Thank you for a wonderful dinner. How in the world did you have time to cook with the long days you have?"

"Easy. I prepared the lasagna last night and whipped up the salad when I got home. I love this house. Do you know it's the first home I've ever owned? Well, I don't really own it. But I will in fifteen years."

The doorbell rang.

"That's Randy, my neighbor. He and I carpool to the ferry. I told him you were coming over tonight and invited him over to join us for a drink. You'll like him. He's a real sweet guy."

"New beau?"

"No, friends, neighbors. Nothing more. I'm not in the market for a relationship at the moment." She got up from the sofa and went to the door.

"Didn't want to come over empty-handed," Randy said, as he walked in the door with a bottle of wine.

"Thanks, Randy. You shouldn't have brought anything; I have plenty. This is my friend, Willow Winters."

"Good to meet you Willow." Randy walked over to Willow and held out his hand. "Cassidy can't say enough great things about you. She says you two have known one another for a long time." He took the glass of wine Cassidy handed him and sat down across from the two women.

"Yes, we have, a very long time."

The three carried on a casual conversation as the night wore on. Something about Randy made Willow slightly edgy, even though she picked up nothing substantial from his aura. A color would begin to halo around him and quickly disperse before she could make out any definite color.

Strange, Willow thought. She'd seen lots of strange auras over the past few months, only nothing quite like Randy's. True each aura is unique, but all the same they contained similarities. But not Randy's. She felt hemmed in; she must be more worn out than she thought. She needed a moment to clear her head. She reached out and poured the last drops of wine into Cassidy's glass.

"Looks like we need another bottle. I left the one I brought out by the door. Let me go get it." As she left the kitchen her mind cleared of the strange feelings. Still something needled her. Randy's aura contained certain similarities to Mary's and the men who invaded the campus. Not exactly the same, but not exactly different. She didn't pick up unnatural energy. She grabbed the wine bottle and stood in the doorway for a moment. Night had fallen and the starless sky enveloped the houses, the only light from a few of the neighbors' windows or porches. Willow looked out and saw the car, her driver in the front seat. He would be coming for her soon, as she had informed him she didn't want to stay past eleven. She took a few more cleansing breaths and headed back into the kitchen.

When she returned, she walked into the twilight zone. Cassidy sat tied up to a chair and gagged. Randy pointed the dangerous end of a handgun in her direction.

"Why, come join the party, little lady." Gone was Randy's smooth baritone voice, in its place she heard the distinct drawl of a Southern accent.

She didn't move a single muscle. Try as she might, Willow's brain couldn't comprehend the surreal situation.

"Who are you?" she finally asked.

"I told ya. I'm Randy. Y'all have no idea how damn hard it's been to keep up the blasted accent. Now y'all take a seat—now." He flicked the wrist holding the handgun in the direction of an empty chair.

She did as instructed and sat as close as she could to Cassidy. Cassidy's eyes were glassy; her features held a dissociative expression, as if her mind had checked out, unable to assimilate what was taking place. Willow picked up waves of fear rolling off her friend. She reached out to pat Cassidy's hand to reassure her.

"Nuh uh, there'll be no touching."

"What do you want?" Willow cried in terror and fury.

"It's not what I want, little lady. It's what my boss wants. He wants Emma and Collin McBain. We know Emma is somewhere away at school. So for now, y'all are gonna bring Collin here."

"If Ryker wanted Emma and Collin, why didn't he demand an exchange when he had me?"

"The Chairman don't dirty his hands with the day-to-day details. That's the job of the Board. Daniel Prescott is my boss, and he already had instructions in place before you met with the Chairman. He's new in his position, and it's his responsibility to secure the McBains. Now, enough with the chitchat. Pull out yer phone and call McBain."

"I need to call his Captain, Wyatt. Collin won't come unless Wyatt orders him to."

"No. Y'all call Collin. He's the one I want. He'll come—If not..." He pressed the barrel of the gun into Cassidy's forehead. Tears flooded from her eyes.

"All right. Put the gun down. I'll do as you say." She pulled out her phone. "My security guard is going to start to wonder why I haven't come out. He'll be here at any time."

"Nah, he won't be going nowhere no more." He pulled an ugly hunting knife from his back. Spots of blood dotted the blade.

Both of the women gasped.

"Call 'im. Y'all tell him he best come alone if he don't want yer purty head blown into thousands of tiny pieces."

"Hey Willow, what can I do for you?" Collin asked.

"Collin. There's a situation. I'm here at Cassidy's. Her next-door neighbor, who turns out to be an employee of Prescott's, wants you here—now."

"Do what he says Willow. I'm on my way."

"Alone, Collin."

"I figured as much."

"He's on his way," Willow informed Randy as she disconnected the call. "You can untie Cassidy now."

"Nah, I can't do it. Boss told me to take care of Cassidy. Nuttin' personal, just the job."

Cassidy's muffled scream pierced the air. She struggled to break free. Willow jumped up to block her from him.

"Sit the hell back down."

Randy backhanded her so hard she fell back into the chair and saw stars. A warm trickle of blood dripped down one corner of her mouth.

A feral look filled Randy's features. His heinous aura expanded and permeated Willow's mind. She pressed the bottoms of her palms into her temples in a futile attempt to block his aura. As if she'd lost her own free will her mind became overwhelmed with his hostile, disjointed thoughts. Randy shoved his pistol into the back of his jeans and put the knife down on the nearest counter. He grabbed a rope and tied Willow up.

"Like I said, nuttin' personal. To show y'all there ain't no hard feelings I'm gonna do her quick."

Cassidy pleaded and cried. Pitiful sounds sputtered from her gagged mouth. A horrendous sneer spread across Randy's face as he wrapped his enormous hands around her neck and squeezed. Her face instantly turned red; she fought with all her will to breathe. In a split second a purplish tint bled into the bright red color. Cassidy's eyes bulged from their sockets as the agony of her torture finally stopped and her body went slack like a rag doll.

A woman's voice cried and pleaded until it was so hoarse the room went silent. Who made those retching sounds? The room was a haze through her veil of tears, as Willow's mind finally shut out her surroundings. She withdrew inside herself, rejecting the merciless slaughter of her longtime friend.

She fought a mental battle against her need for self-preservation and telepathically reached out for Wyatt.

"Wyatt...Wyatt! Randy strangled Cassidy. She's dead."

"Stop it!" Randy ordered as he backhanded her once again, bringing her back to the nightmare.

"Stop what? What are you talking about?" The split in her lip came open and blood ran freely. She tried to rub the blood away with her shoulder.

"Don't y'all play dumb with me. Y'all just communicated with someone telepathically. You see it's a gift a mine. Can't do the talking, but I can always feel the energy. Too bad. You were almost rid of me."

Chapter Twenty-Two

Wyatt, Logan, Jack, and Noah worked out in the weight room on campus. Noah spotted Wyatt as he bench-pressed his last set. In mid-lift, Willow's voice screeched through his mind.

"Wyatt...Wyatt! Randy strangled Cassidy. She's dead."

His stomach revolted and threatened to expel his dinner. His world dimmed.

"Captain, what the hell is going on?" Noah grabbed hold of the weights Wyatt started to drop. "Logan, pull him out."

Logan raced over and yanked Wyatt off the bench by his legs.

The next thing Wyatt knew, Jack towered over him holding a wet towel on his forehead.

"What happened?" Logan asked. "Noah barely snagged the bar before you dropped it on yourself. You sick? You look sick."

"Shit. It's Willow. She's in trouble."

Across the room Wyatt's phone rang. He started to get up. Jack pushed him back down.

"Get that." Logan nodded in the direction of the ringing phone.

"Noah."

"Noah, where's the Captain?" Collin asked.

"He's right here. Hold on." Noah put the call on speaker. "You're on speaker, Collin."

"I just got a call from Willow. She's in trouble. Do you know where she is?"

In a flash, Wyatt barreled upright as he pushed Jack aside.

"Yes, she's with Cassidy. Get hold of Morgan. Meet us all at the main gate, now," Wyatt said.

"She said I need to come alone."

"Bullshit. Willow's there and Cassidy is dead. You know damn well this is a trap. I'm not losing either of you." He reached out for his phone and ended the call.

"What about Tristan?" Logan asked.

"He's staying here, along with Jack."

"He's not gonna be happy," Jack said.

"*Tristan, Willow's in trouble. She said Cassidy is dead.*" Wyatt reached out telepathically for his twin.

"*Damn it all to hell. What the hell happened?*"

Wyatt relayed all the information.

"*Where are we meeting?*" Tristan asked.

"*We're not. I'm taking the team, minus Jack. You two are staying here. Hold down the fort.*"

"*The hell I am. That's my team. You're the captain. Which means you should stay and I should be on the front lines.*"

"*You're right. I am your captain. My orders stand. There's no way in God's green Earth I'm sitting this one out. I need you here.*"

Silence floated through Wyatt's mind for a few heartbeats.

"*Yes, sir. You sure as hell damn well better call if you need me—you hear?*"

A black SUV sat idling outside the side door of the training facility. Morgan jumped out of the driver's seat; Collin got out of the passenger's side.

"We brought everything you requested, Captain," Morgan said.

"Good. Let's load up."

"It's gonna be a tight fit, especially on the way back with Willow," Logan said.

"We can manage. One vehicle will be much less conspicuous than two. Besides, you forgot about the security guard and the vehicle already on site. That guy better have a damn good reason for not knowing what's going on in the house. Logan, you take the wheel," Wyatt said.

Logan, Collin, Morgan, Noah, and Wyatt, all crammed into the SUV.

"Feels strange not having Tristan with us. How'd he take it?" Noah asked.

"He's fine. He got his assignment and he's seeing the job through." Out of the corner of his eye he saw Morgan look over at Noah. "Problem, gentlemen?"

"No, sir," the two men said.

"Permission to speak freely, sir?" Noah asked.

Wyatt could swear he heard a collective moan from the other three men.

"What's on your mind?"

"Well sir, it's just that you've been out of the field for a while now. In fact, I can't recall the five of us ever working a mission together."

This time he was positive he heard the men groan. Wyatt turned to face the back seat and stared at Noah.

"Point taken and exactly why the five of us are going out on this mission now. Consider it a real-time operation readiness inspection. You guys are the elite of the elite. I want to make sure you perform. As far as not being in the field, I've been in the field—often. Just not with you." He turned back around.

The three men gawked at him.

"Any other questions?"

"No, sir," the men said.

"Good. Logan, find a place to hide this vehicle a few blocks from the house. Collin will approach from the front. Morgan, you cover his six. Check on the security guard on your way; we don't want to spook him and cause him to alert Randy. The three of us will fan out and come in from the back and sides. Remember, we're going into a residential area, so double check your silencers now. We need to get in, secure the situation, and get out of there with none of the neighbors having a clue we ever set foot here."

"Do you want the hostile taken alive?" Collin asked.

"In a perfect world. Yes, alive if possible, but Willow is our priority. Capturing a KG henchman would be a big plus and a great opportunity to question him."

"*Willow, we're on our way. Willow, please answer me.*" Wyatt sent his thoughts into the atmosphere. He waited, but got no response.

Logan pulled the SUV into a parking area a block behind the target house. The men armed themselves and scattered into the night. Collin kept watch as Morgan approached the guard's vehicle. Morgan's voice came over the comm in a whisper. "Something is off here. The guard's head is tilted at a strange angle. Hold on." He got closer to the vehicle, and looked inside. "Shit, the bastard slit his throat from ear to ear." He shook his head at Collin and the two of them approached the front of the house. Morgan hung back out of sight, to give the illusion that Collin came alone as instructed by Randy.

Collin walked up the steps of the porch and banged on the front door. He was armed with only his enhanced skills and a knife tucked in his boot. He stopped and listened. He didn't hear anything that sounded human, and with his keen sense of hearing he wouldn't miss a thing. He closed his eyes and focused on the sounds within. He heard the electronic humming of the refrigerator, television, computer, and various other appliances, but no breath sounds, no whispers, no shuffle sounds. He turned the doorknob and found it unlocked.

"I'm going in," he whispered into his wireless comm. "I don't hear anyone inside."

Morgan joined him on the porch, and the two entered, back-to-back to each other.

"Clear," Morgan said.

"Clear," Collin said.

The living room was lit by a single table lamp. Willow's coat and purse hung on the coatrack by the door. Collin nodded at Morgan to clear the bedrooms and he started toward the kitchen. He saw Cassidy the second he entered the room. Cassidy's torso slumped forward, held in the chair only by the rope tying her wrists together.

"House is clear," Morgan said, as he walked into the kitchen. "Ah damn."

Collin shook his head. "No pulse," he said, as he removed his hand from her neck.

"Asswipe. He had no reason to kill her," Morgan said.

The corner of a paper caught Collin's eye, wedged between Cassidy's chin and chest. He carefully pushed Cassidy back into the chair, slid the folded piece of paper out, and began to read.

What part of alone didn't you understand, McBain?
You forced me to take Willow. Not the plan. But I'm not the jackass who can't follow a simple instruction.

Wyatt, Noah, and Logan walked into the kitchen. "What the hell happened? Where's Willow?" Wyatt asked.

Collin handed Wyatt the note.

"How the hell did he know you weren't alone?" Wyatt asked.

"I have no idea. I told Willow I'd come alone. He had no reason to think otherwise."

"Think taking Willow was his plan all along?" Morgan asked.

* * * *

"Why bring us here? No. Kaleidoscope Group wants Collin and Emma. They already had Willow. If she was the person they were after, they would have kept her when Mary kidnapped her. Something spooked him and he wasn't going back to his boss empty-handed," Wyatt said. He pushed his doubts and fears aside and focused on the situation at hand. He'd find Willow. He'd bring her home. He'd kill Randy. "We have little to go on. The only thing we know is his name is Randy, and he works directly for Prescott."

"He's Cassidy's next door neighbor," Collin said. "Willow told me when she phoned."

"Let's go take a look at the neighbor's house, then," Wyatt said. The team headed out into the front yard. The house on one side had the front porch light on. The rest of the house was dark and looked locked up tight. The house on the other side was also dark, except the garage door stood wide open and empty.

"Let's check it out, carefully now; it might be booby trapped," Wyatt said.

The team moved stealthily into the dark garage. The search for clues found nothing. Wyatt signaled to Logan to take the lead into the house. Logan crept up the stairs and inspected the door for alarms, found none, and tried to turn the knob.

"Hold tight, door's locked," he whispered to the team. He pulled a lockpick kit from one of his pockets and expertly worked the lock. The team heard the click as Logan hit his mark, and one by one they filed up the stairs and into the blackness. They entered in formation and cleared each nook and cranny.

"No indication anyone is here, but spread out. Search every inch of this place. This house is our only lead. Maybe taking Willow was a last-minute change in plans, so he had no time to gather all his stuff," Wyatt said.

Noah and Logan were at the end of the hall clearing the master bedroom.

"Clear," Logan said as the two stepped out of the room.

"Captain, you need to see this," Collin said.

"What'd you have?" Wyatt asked.

"This isn't right," Collin said. "Look at the length of this hall." He started tapping on the wall as he moved down the length. "Listen." He knocked in one place and again a couple inches away. "Hear that? It's hollow."

"A hidden room," Wyatt said.

"That's my guess," Collin said.

"What about an exterior window?" Noah asked.

"Just looked, no window. Might've been one initially, but nothing now, only exterior wall," Morgan said, as he returned to the team.

"Can't very well cut into the side of the house. Sound alone would draw the neighbors' attention," Logan said.

"Check the garage. He needed a way to get in and out of the room. My guess is a floor access," Wyatt said.

Morgan and Noah took off for the garage, while Collin and Wyatt continued to search the rest of the house.

"So, Randy works for Prescott not Ryker," Collin said.

"Potato, potahto. Still all boils down to KG," Wyatt said.

"I won't argue with that. It does, however, show Prescott has been here and active for some time now, well before the sale of the old complex. I'm confused though. Why did Prescott order Randy to murder

Cassidy? Seems to me they could gather more information had they left her alive," Collin said.

"I guess acquiring you and Emma was the higher priority, and they didn't want any loose ends," Wyatt replied.

"We located the entrance," Morgan said.

They all followed Morgan back down to the garage. The two men had pulled the garage door down; in the darkness a shaft of light came from an opening in the ceiling. One by one, they followed Morgan up an A-frame ladder and into the hidden room.

"Holy crap. There's a lot of shit in here," Logan said.

The room was full of computer equipment. There were newspaper articles, pictures, notes, and messages covering the entire length of one wall. They took photographs of every part of the room and then gathered every file, slip of paper, and USB they found. They collected every last slip of paper taped to the wall. Even the trash was emptied into its own bag. Lastly they unplugged all the electronics and readied them for transport.

"Noah, go get our ride," Wyatt said.

Noah went back for the SUV and with the motor and lights off rolled the vehicle into the garage. The team loaded in everything. Two of the men pushed the SUV back out of the garage. They shut the door and rolled the vehicle an entire block before starting the engine. As they started down the two-lane road, they were passed by the clean-up crew. The crew's job would be to erase all evidence of Willow, the team, and Randy from Cassidy's house. They would stage her house to make it look like a break-in and remove the security guard and his vehicle from the scene.

"*What's your status, Wyatt,*" Tristan's thoughts penetrated Wyatt's crowded mind.

"*We're on our way back to the campus. Randy left with Willow in a hurry.*"

"*They weren't there when you arrived? How did they know Collin wasn't alone?*"

"*I have no idea, but I intend to find out. Tell Jack we're bringing him back a computer. I need him to start on it right away. Have you told Victory what's happened?*"

"*No, she was sleeping when you first contacted me. I let her be. She'll probably be madder than a hornet tomorrow, but there's nothing she can do now except worry.*"

"*I agree. Let's gather everyone in the conference room next to Payton's office first thing in the morning.*"

"*You don't need me now?*"

"*No. I want you to stay with Victory. First thing in the morning, Tristan.*"

Wyatt attempted once again to reach out telepathically for Willow. A process he'd performed over and over since she'd contacted him earlier.

"*Willow. Willow. Where are you? Willow, can you hear me?*"

He closed his eyes, hoped and prayed. He mentally reached out over and over. Each time, he met with dead air.

Chapter Twenty-Three

The entire team met in the conference room with Payton and Victory. Both of the women's eyes were red and puffy. Collin and Tristan were tasked with informing them of their sister's disappearance first thing in the morning.

"I'm sorry for the loss of Cassidy," Wyatt said, as he greeted each of the sisters. "Don't worry, I promise we'll get Willow back safely."

They all gathered around the conference table. Victory began the conversation.

"I don't understand why he kidnapped Willow. As far as anyone outside of your team knew, Collin followed instructions."

"He did, yes. However, he didn't go in alone. Most of the team served as his backup."

"But how could Randy have known? You said he was gone before you even arrived," Payton said.

"I'm hoping Jack can answer at least some of these questions."

Jack sat at the far end of the table focused solely on his computer.

"Jack, what do you have for us?" Wyatt asked.

"On the bright side nothing encrypted. A little complacent if you ask me. Thinking he'd never get caught. He deleted his inbox each day but didn't know enough to wipe his hard drive. Geeze." He shook his head, "When will these guys ever learn?"

"Never, if we're lucky," Noah said.

"True…looks like he moved into the house a week after Cassidy bought hers and he sent daily reports of Cassidy's every move."

"Reports to whom?" Wyatt asked.

"Best guess, Daniel Prescott. I'm not sure. The IP address is dynamic, meaning temporary and changing. It didn't originate from one certain place; the signal hops all over the globe. However, Randy refers to the person he sends his email to in the identical way each time: DP. Original right? The sender never reveals himself, but he's definitely the person in charge."

"Did he know Cassidy met up with Willow at the conference and visited the campus?" Payton asked.

"Oh yeah. Cassidy mentioned her plans to go to the conference on one of their daily ferry rides. She said a good friend of hers could possibly be attending. She was on the fence with whether or not she would approach Willow. Randy gave her the shove she needed. No details on what they discussed, which means no bug on Cassidy. He'd been pushing her to invite Willow to the house to renew their friendship," Jack said.

"Are there any instructions for him to kidnap Willow?" Wyatt asked.

"Nope. DP wanted Collin. He wants Emma too, but he doesn't seem as hot to get her as Braxton. Sounds like Collin is the cash cow. DP believes he was the successful outcome of the DNA experiment. They want Collin's blood, bad. I also found mention of Second Wave. All facilities were abandoned, orders direct from the Chairman. They weren't certain which facilities we knew about, so they closed them all. They have set up two new schools in the U.S. and one somewhere abroad."

"Those poor children; every day they spend being *educated* in those facilities is one more day they are brainwashed into believing they have no free will. Until their turning point, when they lose all humanity and become *tools* of destruction for the Kaleidoscope Group." Payton scrubbed her hands over her face in a futile attempt to push away her frustration and the threat of tears.

"Jackpot," Jack said. "Randy sent an email to Prescott at 6:22 last night. Cassidy phoned him and told him she invited Willow for dinner. Sly bastard even got himself invited over for a drink. He was confirming a go on the plan, since he'd little time to prepare. He received the green light thirty minutes later. Since he'd have no time to clear out the room, his plan was to apprehend Collin, move Willow to the hidden room, and transport Collin. After which he would return to the house, clean out the room, incapacitate Willow, haul her off, and text the sisters to tell them where to find her."

"Evil bastard," Payton said.

"He got an update five minutes later. Prescott wanted Cassidy taken care of. Randy didn't want to do her at that time. He impressed upon Prescott that he couldn't make it back to the house and finish the job in what was left of the night. Prescott didn't care; he wanted it done," Jack said.

"They start referring to C and M," Jack said.

"Original, don't ya think? Numbnuts," Logan said.

"I don't understand why they are so hell bent on getting Collin, but not me," Morgan said.

Wyatt watched the sisters. Naturally they were beside themselves and agitated.

"Victory, if you and Payton would prefer to sit this one out while we dig through all Randy's information we can contact you when we know more," Wyatt said.

"No, we're staying," Victory shook her head. "It's difficult to be patient, when our sister is in the hands of some enemy. But we want to hear every detail."

"This might answer your question, Morgan," Jack said. "Prescott says they want to acquire C because he had no special abilities prior to the injection. They need to study him to figure out why his system merged with the DNA when all their *experiments* didn't. They don't have the amount of children they want and are getting more and more limited on these *test subjects*. Prescott says the Chairman believes if they can figure out why C's system accepted the merge, then they can build their army."

"Victory, you're right. They have no idea Collin had abilities from birth," Tristan said. "What I don't understand is, if these abilities were created from the vitamins before birth, shouldn't there be lots of people with enhanced skills?"

"I'm sure there are more people. Still, genetics will play a part," Victory said. "We may discover many of the people didn't develop abilities, or possibly, as with Willow, they believed their abilities to be the norm."

"And, they're focusing on children in order to control them more effectively," Wyatt said.

"Here's something else interesting," Jack said. "And I quote: 'While M showed increased speed with regards to running and jumping, no other useful traits surfaced.'"

"Morgan, didn't you display your full skills?" Wyatt asked.

"No, I didn't. I only used what I needed to keep Collin safe. I figured, 'Why the hell give Braxton what he wanted.' The less I showed him, the less interested he appeared to be in me. Of course, I knew I also ran the risk of becoming obsolete in his eyes, but I was willing to run the risk." Morgan shrugged his shoulders.

"So basically you screwed with Braxton and presented bogus results," Tristan said.

"Yeeeeap."

"That's my partner, understated." Collin slapped Morgan on the back.

"Based on Braxton's conclusions, Ryker and Prescott are heading down the wrong path," Payton said. "Nice job, Morgan."

He flashed a huge grin.

"Nice indeed. This will certainly slow Ryker down. However, let's not forget the man is exceptionally astute. It's only a matter of time before he figures out something is not right and starts the entire process over. Nonetheless, it does give us some breathing room," Victory said.

"Sounds like the rest of the data you need to cipher through has nothing to do with locating Willow," Wyatt said.

"I would agree, Captain."

"Okay, this is my take on the situation. Willow was to be used only as bait. Somehow Randy surmised he was being set up. He killed Cassidy per specific instructions and fled with Willow as his bargaining chip. Is there anything I missed, or any other conclusions?" Wyatt asked.

"Nope, that's my take," Tristan said. The team agreed.

"Alright then. Now we narrow down where Randy might have fled to. Payton, when does Daniel Prescott take control of the old complex?" Wyatt asked.

"He already owns the complex. It was a cash deal and a quick close. That's the main reason he got the place. There's a rumor they've started work on the place. In fact, I know someone whose husband is a contractor involved in the remodel."

"Any chance you could get some information from her?" Tristan asked.

"It shouldn't be a problem. I'll talk with her right after we're done here. You don't really think they'd take Willow there, do you? Not with contractors going in and out."

"Probably not," Tristan said. "All the same, I think Noah and Logan should check it out." He eyed Collin.

"Good idea. Go in undercover. Put your ears to the ground and see what you can find out. If the opportunity presents itself, plant a bug or two," Collin said.

"Jack, Tristan, and I will develop a list of possible places they might be holding Willow. Collin and Morgan, I want you staying on campus."

Both men started to argue.

Wyatt shot the men a look and stopped them cold.

"You two are on KG's radar, and we're not giving them any opportunity to nab you. I want you to go to Willow's office and search for any information we could use. Speak with Paula. Fill her in with what's happened and pick her brain. After you're finished, head to Mary's lab and search the place, top to bottom. Let's keep this quiet. The fewer people who know the better. Keep in touch with Tristan. I want you guys touching base with any new information."

* * * *

Collin, Tristan, Wyatt, and Jack went back to the campus SOCOM offices.

"It sure is going to be a bummer when we have to give up this place," Jack said. "It's super-convenient to be right here on campus, since ninety percent of our time deals with the Winters Corporation contracts. Guess they've tried to give us the hint with this remodeling Payton has been doing, smells like fresh paint."

"Shit, I forgot all about that," Collin said.

"About what?" Jack asked.

"Payton told me a few days ago they'd decided to give us this building permanently, or for as long as we need. They think it's perfect for the team. The building is remote from most of the campus. She's reworking the layout to suit us better."

"Plus it keeps you and Collin close at hand," Jack winked.

"What about their original plans for the place?" Wyatt asked.

"Now that the last office complex is completed, they don't think they will need our building. At least not for the foreseeable future, Payton calls it kismet."

"Great news. I'll run it by General Roberts, but I don't think we'll have a problem."

"Have you tried to contact Willow telepathically?" Tristan asked.

Jack's interest was piqued. "Wait. You can talk telepathically to Willow? Since when? You know what Victory believes. Every sister develops a telepathic connection to their soul mate."

"Yeah, I heard. And I have tried to reach her. I've tried over and over again, and I get nothing, like she's vanished into thin air."

"Maybe they drugged her." Tristan said.

"Here's another question. Why haven't they contacted Collin again?" Jack asked. "Did Randy take her phone? I could ping it if he did."

"We found Willow's phone on the floor in Cassidy's house. Even under pressure, he made sure not to leave behind anything we could use to track Willow," Wyatt said. "Her phone is right over there with her coat and purse," he nodded to the corner. "Thought I'd go through it and see if anything jumps out at me."

* * * *

Willow floated between dreams and nightmares. Part of her mind fought to wake and another part wanted to drift. Her consciousness hovered just below waking, as if she was aware of her dire situation. Inch by grueling inch she became cognizant that her surroundings were unfamiliar. A razor sharp pain took up residence in her brain and a dull ache radiated from her shoulder down through her back. With her eyes still closed she lifted her arms and rubbed her eyes.

"Sit up and I'll give ya something for the after-effects."

Randy's voice startled her. She hadn't realized anyone was with her. She cautiously turned her head and looked directly into his eyes.

"Where am I and what in the world did you inject into me?"

"Something that dropped y'all like a rock. You tried to set me up. Collin wasn't coming alone."

She focused on Wyatt and reached out. He would come for her the second she knew where she was being held.

"Y'all might as well save your energy. The facility you're in has the same hi-tech security grid they used on the island. There's no way you can telepathically reach anyone. Now take these damn things or I'm gonna let ya suffer. Y'all ready caused me too many problems."

She reached out, took the pills and water, and swallowed them down. Never did her searing glare leave Randy's stone cold eyes.

"You still didn't tell me where I am."

"Give the woman a prize." He stood and walked out the door.

Chapter Twenty-Four

Four long stressful days passed, and still they'd yet to hear from anyone about Willow's abduction. Wyatt knew the tactic: wait your opponent out until they were willing to do or say anything to get the person returned. He'd even put the tactic into practice a time or two. Still the knowledge didn't make a damn bit of difference. He stalked the campus offices like a rattlesnake trapped in a corner. Only five in the morning as he gulped down his fourth cup of coffee, his stomach protested as acid rose in his throat. The door swung open, and Tristan strode into the building.

"What in the name of hell are you doing here at this hour?" Wyatt scolded his twin.

"I came to check on you and to bring you food." He handed Wyatt a covered plate. "It's eggs, bacon, and pancakes; Victory made it."

"Why on earth is she up? Tell her thanks, but I'm not hungry." He swatted in the direction of the plate and nearly knocked it out of Tristan's hand.

"Damn, you're one ornery jackass. You're gonna sit your ass down and eat this breakfast my wife made for you. And the answer to your previous question is you aren't the only one who can't sleep. Victory's paced ruts on the living room floor. When's the last time you've had anything but coffee? Hate to tell you bro, but you look like shit. At this rate you aren't going to be a damn bit of good to anyone, especially Willow."

Wyatt could feel the anger and concern roll off his brother. Tristan was right. He needed to pull himself together. General Roberts would arrive today, and he wouldn't give a second thought to pulling him off of Willow's rescue. Of course it wouldn't stop Wyatt. He'd handle her rescue alone if need be. In the process he most likely would lose his job, but at this point he didn't give a damn.

"Thanks." He took the plate and sat at his desk.

"Sorry. I know you're right. Just burns the hell out of me. We've searched all the facilities we can think of, even the two Biotec sites. Where the hell did they stash her?"

"I know how you feel, Wyatt. Believe me. But you know we'll find her. Someone will contact us soon. We still have something they want."

"Unless they already killed her." He couldn't believe the words actually slipped out of his mouth. A world without Willow wouldn't be a world he could live in.

"Knock that shit off right now." Tristan challenged him with his fiery stare. "She's alive. They'll keep her that way. I for one have no intention of telling her sisters she's dead. Don't you dare say or even think anything different ever again. Besides, you would know if she were gone."

"What in the bloody hell are you rambling on about? I can't reach her. Don't you think I've tried until my head feels like it'll split from my neck? There's nothing, no response."

"My point exactly," Tristan said.

This time it was Wyatt's turn to stare his brother down. "Look, Tristan, I know you're trying to help. But all you've accomplished is to piss me off."

"She's become your life. The only person you think of when you go to sleep and the first one you think of when you wake. Willow's a part of you. The two of you have developed the special telepathic connection exclusive to soul mates."

"Oh, for the love of—not you too?"

"Hear me out. How many times since Victory came into our lives has she been wrong about this scientific stuff? She might have been off target a tad, but never totally wrong."

Wyatt slumped into his chair as his indignation deflated.

"Fine, Victory's right. I *love* her; are you happy? I love Payton and Victory too. They're family now. It doesn't make a damn bit of difference. I still can't locate her. I'm drowning here, Tristan."

"It's not the same thing and you know it. You're not drowning Wyatt; I won't let you. You've always been there for me. It's my turn now. The team has your back. We'll find her. Right now you need to get a couple hours sleep. I'll hold down the fort. You can't look like this when Roberts arrives."

"I can't sleep. I tried last night. Sleep just won't come. Besides, I'm not going back to my apartment and when the guys start rolling in, there's no way I will be able to sleep here."

"Tell me, before all this when was the last time you were at your apartment?"

Wyatt crossed his arms over his chest and thought. He rubbed his chin between his finger and thumb.

"I thought as much. You might as well move out of the place. You can store your stuff cheaper in a storage locker."

"Funny."

"Payton, Victory, Collin, and I talked about your living arrangements last night. The sisters want you to move into one of the bungalows. They figure you're always here, you might as well have a place to call your own."

"I can't..."

"Yes, you can," Tristan said, as he held up a hand to silence his brother. "Jack got your palm print entered into the bungalow's reader; here's the unit number." He pulled a slip of paper from his pocket and handed it to him. "Oh, and a little something to help you sleep, courtesy of Dr. Russell. She claims the pills are pretty potent and said you should take it within ten minutes of lying down. When Willow is back and this thing is over, we'll all help you move into your new place. For now I'll send one of the guys over to get some of your stuff."

"But the team—"

"Are all big boys and know how to do their jobs. I'm the team leader, and believe me, I can handle them in the office as well as on a mission. Now get your ass out of here and get some sleep; there's a bed already in the bungalow. General Roberts won't be in until around four this afternoon. I'll come down and wake you in time for you to get yourself together."

Wyatt looked down at the slip of paper and the pills. Emotion threatened to overwhelm him at the thought his brother and the sisters had offered him a home. He looked back up at Tristan. "Thanks bro. I really mean it." He left the building and headed for his new place.

* * * *

"Wyatt, come on, time to get up," Tristan said, as he shook his shoulder.

"I just got to sleep, what's up?" Wyatt woke and groaned at his brother. He looked at the clock next to his bed; it read 8:00 a.m. "It's only eight. I just got into bed an hour or so ago—do you have something on Willow?" He popped up the instant his mind came to life.

"No. We still haven't heard anything, and it's eight in the morning the following day. You slept over twenty-four hours. Dr. Russell was spot on about her pills. I don't think you've ever slept longer than six hours."

"Shit! Why didn't you wake me? General Roberts should have…"

"He postponed his arrival. He should be here in two hours. I sent Logan to pick him up at the airport. Jump in the shower, and eat the breakfast Victory made you; I left the plate in the oven to keep warm. See you in an hour."

The office buzzed with the SOCOM team, minus Logan. Much to Wyatt's surprise, they'd cleaned up the entire place. Wait—it wasn't only cleaned up, the main room was twice the size now. He looked around the room, made a point of stepping back out of the door, and came back in.

"What in the world? Is there an inspection I'm not aware of? Did an army of elves rearrange this place in the day I was gone?"

"Kinda, Payton pushed the builders. They finished up a couple hours ago. By tearing down those walls, they made the main room twice as big. They even helped rearrange the place for us," Jack said.

"Where's your office, Jack?" Wyatt asked.

"Gone, I spend so much time here alone. I really wanted to be in the main room, works better. The only office left is yours. Payton had the supply department order me a new desk. Check this out; it wraps around on all three sides. Made especially for computer geeks like me. It's sizzling. I promise to keep it orderly," Jack said, as he made a sweeping motion with his arms.

"Like a kid in a candy store," Noah said shaking his head. "Took us all a couple hours to get that monstrosity assembled. Except when we got finished, the thing looked so good the process bled over to the whole darn building. We all got new desks."

"Payton observed how each of us use our spaces and has designed them accordingly," Collin said.

"Kudos to you guys and to Payton. This place looks great. With all this investment, I expect you all to keep it exactly this way."

A groan ripped through the men as Morgan mumbled, "I told you this would happen."

Morgan's comment made Wyatt grin. He loved taunting the guys. It felt good to be in charge, and it dawned on him this was the first time he had smiled since Willow went missing. The shadow of hopelessness must have been mirrored on his face.

"Yes, sir. The sisters were kind enough to give us this building, the least we can do is show our respect for the place," Tristan said.

"Check this out." Collin led Wyatt to their Situation Room and pointed up. The title was etched into the header above the door and above the title was a domed light. "There's a switch right inside the door." He walked in and switched the light on. It lit up bright red with the words 'Confidential—Keep Out.' "Look what else we have now."

The plain table was now replaced with a state-of-the-art conference table, with computer pop-ups all around. Jack had a main station where he could switch between the individual units or the oversized screen on the front wall. Ergonomically-designed chairs finished off the layout. In the corner was a brand new coffee bar with a sleek refrigerator and supply cabinet housed under the bar.

"The Winters Corporation paid for all these upgrades? Why?" Wyatt asked.

"They did all of this for us and for the company. Payton said it's an investment in the future. They want us to have every possible cutting-edge piece of equipment. She says the upgrades keep us on an even playing field with Kaleidoscope Group."

The main door opened as Payton walked in followed by a string of people carrying enormous covered platters and a variety of drinks. She led the group into the Situation Room, and they arranged the feast on the long counter on the back wall, which ran the length of the room.

"Hi everyone. Wyatt you're looking better," she said, as she gave him a sad smile. "I just received a text from Logan. They'll be here shortly. I didn't want to disturb you once General Roberts arrived. All the hot dishes are on warmers and should stay warm all day. The cold dishes are on coolers. If you need anything, please send me a text."

"Thank you for all you've done for us, Payton. Please pass my thanks to your sister and the company."

"You can thank us by bringing Willow back." She gave him a slight smile as a sheen of tears coated her eyes. "It's helped to focus on finishing this project. It's kept my mind busy."

"Captain, is it okay if I take her back?" Collin asked.

"Make it quick."

* * * *

"Well, I know I've seen no requisition for this new equipment," General Roberts said, as he entered the Situation Room, followed closely by Logan. "Is this the sisters' doing?"

"Welcome, General. Yes sir, it is," Wyatt said.

"You all must being doing a good job, current situation excluded."

Everyone filled their plates and took their seats around the massive table.

"Tell me where you stand," General Roberts said.

"We've covered all the known facilities of KG within the country. Morgan took a quick trip to London. I even sent Noah and Logan out to take a quick peek at the old complex Daniel Prescott recently purchased from the sisters."

"And?"

"There's a lot of activity, but no sign of Willow."

"I see."

"Sir, I'd like to put someone on Carl Sterling. See what he's up to. At this point he is our most reliable lead."

"Absolutely not. Wyatt, you know as well as I do the delicacy of the situation. Sterling is the blasted CIA Director. Before we attempt to shut him down we have to have an air-tight case. Translation, no wiggle room—none."

"He thinks he's untouchable. He's not God. He needs to answer for his actions."

"And he will. Believe me, I'm working on it. It'll take time, but we're gonna take Sterling down. If we go in half-cocked it will give him all the ammunition he needs to shut *us* down. Right now we're a burr on his ass and he can't touch us. If you go in and get caught or worse yet, piss him off, he will take us down. All of us. With us out of the way there would be no stopping the bastard. We'll get him, but not today. You need to find Willow without him," Roberts said.

"I understand. The next best person is Daniel Prescott. Like I said, the guys took a look at the old complex. We checked out the Biotec facilities on San Juan Island and the Hawaiian facility. We haven't checked his other personally held facilities yet. Do we have a green light on that?"

"You do, yes. All I ask is to use your best judgment. If at all possible, get in and out without being noticed."

"Question, sir?" Jack asked. "Would it be possible for us to send in our new Whisper Drone first?"

"Our what?" Tristan asked.

"When I went to D.C. last month I got a chance to play with the new drone. I believe I can put it to good use as early as tomorrow, if you'll let me have immediate deployment authorization. We could put it in play by surveilling Prescott's personal facilities. "

Perplexed, the men looked from Jack to General Roberts.

"Our Whisper Drone is virtually soundless and nearly indestructible. The drone's covered in a high-tech coating which reflects its environment, allowing it to blend in with any backdrop. At this point in time there are only seven drones ready for service. Are you sure you can pilot this thing?"

"Positive, sir."

"Okay then. I need to make a few calls and pull in a marker or two. Shouldn't be too difficult; I do manage the elite teams."

Wyatt showed the General into his office and returned to the Situation Room.

"Sure glad you're on our team," Wyatt said, as he slapped Jack on the back.

A while later the General returned.

"It's a go. You impressed the D.C. team so much they are deploying a drone for this team immediately. Don't make me sorry." Roberts eyed the men. "The drone will be here tomorrow afternoon along with a tech person to help you get the thing set up."

Chapter Twenty-Five

Randy threw the door open. Willow popped up in her bed and pulled the sheet securely up to her neck. She could swear she felt the slimy heat of his stare as it traveled up and down her body.

"If only I had the time, sweetheart," he said. "Pull yourself together; I'll be back in a half hour."

He slammed the door shut and re-engaged the lock before she even had the chance to ask him where he planned to take her. *Didn't really matter*, she thought. At least it would be away from this depressing room. There were no windows and no clocks. Based on the number of meals brought in, she guessed five days had passed locked in this dreary place. She walked over to the dresser and pulled out one of the light-beige pairs of scrubs, which served as the extent of wardrobe offered. She headed for the bathroom to shower off the nightmares from the night before.

Willow patiently waited in the only chair when the door disengaged.

"Let's go," Randy said. "No tricks. There's no place for ya to go."

She followed him down a short hall toward the door. As he swung the door open sunlight spilled through the threshold. He motioned to go out. She stepped out into the blazing sun and was taken aback by the arid, sweltering air. She shaded her eyes with her hands and glanced around. Willow saw she was hostage in some type of a compound, enclosed by a single-story high-security fence. Beyond the fence, the view for as far as the eye could see consisted of flat, parched landscape; the only movement was tumbleweeds blowing by. She shut out the world around her and focused all her energy on reaching out for Wyatt.

"*Wyatt, are you there?*"

"Don't bother," Randy said. "When I said an impenetrable grid covers the place, I didn't mean just the building yer in, I meant the whole damn compound. Yer words—so ta speak, are falling on deaf ears." He chuckled at his own joke.

Willow sneered at him and remained quiet. Fine, if she couldn't reach Wyatt, this would be a good time to further explore Randy's aura. She'd now encountered a number of Ryker's people with buffered auras and needed to discover a way to identify these people. She cleared her mind and focused on Randy. Hoping he wouldn't notice, she relied on her assumption that reading auras would work despite the buffer. This time she opened her mind to what already existed in the atmosphere. Discovering a pattern would allow her to spot these individuals. The colors of his aura flared and dissipated, not a one remained for more than a few seconds. The colors flashing by were dark and muddy, representing a deceitful, lying, untrusting individual.

She'd unearthed a thread. The dissipating, flashing, muddy colors *were* the identifying factor. Or perhaps their auras had been masked by Ryker using the muddy overlay to disguise the intentions of his altered employees. But as far as she knew, Ryker would have no way of knowing this, since he couldn't see auras.

"Right here," Randy said.

He turned her in the direction of an impressive two-story stone house. The house was situated clear across the compound from where they'd come. The front of the house faced away from her and in the direction of the compound's fence. She glimpsed an ornate bronze gate which towered over the front of the house. They approached the back side of the house. A sprawling, covered stone-paver patio adorned the full length of the building. A number of decorative ceiling fans spun cooling the entire patio. Beautiful climbing plants served as two side walls. Elegant tables, chairs, and loveseats were scattered about. Glass panels made up the back wall of the house; he pulled one open and gestured for her to enter.

They walked through a tastefully decorated formal living area, down a huge hallway and into an oversized dining room with an enormous table. Everything in this house appeared larger than life. Two servants scurried about while a lone man sat eating at the far end of the table. Willow recognized him from the news articles; Daniel Prescott, his jet-black hair now speckled with gray. His features and black eyes looked harder in real life. He put down his utensils and sized her up.

"Wait outside, Randy," Prescott said. "Sit down, Willow. Bring her a plate," he said to the closest servant. "You and your two sisters certainly have caused us havoc."

The servant set the plate down; it smelled heavenly. She'd hardly eaten over the past five days. Willow picked up her fork and dug into the Steak Diane, roasted beets, and roasted baby red potatoes. She figured it wasn't drugged or poisoned. If he wanted her dead, she wouldn't be here.

One of the servants refilled Prescott's wine glass and then traveled the length of the table to fill Willow's glass. She took a quick glance at the bottle, a Château Margaux of good vintage. She'd only tasted a Margaux once in her life, the day she and sisters opened the doors to their campus. She estimated the bottle cost somewhere around one-thousand dollars. Prescott lifted his glass and made a "toasting" gesture.

"I'm aware red is your favorite. You simply must try this, quite delightful, to good health and good fortune." He sipped at his wine.

Unable to deny herself this once-in-a-lifetime wine, she lifted the glass. She inhaled aromas of ripe cassis fruit, spicy vanillin oakiness, and violets. The rich liquid ambrosia delighted her senses as it slid down her throat. *If only this was another place, another time, with Wyatt sitting here,* she thought.

"Ahh, I see I'm right. My selection tonight is not wasted. A good bottle of wine is quite civilized don't you think?"

She didn't answer, feeling a trap being set.

They ate in silence for some time. At last, Prescott nodded his head and the two servants instantly cleared the plates and left the room with alacrity.

"I wanted to thank you personally for selling me the old Winters' complex. When the renovations are complete, you will have a rival on your hands."

"What do you mean 'will'? You're part of the Kaleidoscope Group, are you not? You've been our rival since the day you tampered with our mother's drugs. Believe me. Had we known who you *really* were, we would've burned the place to the ground before we sold it to you."

"Well, then. Apparently your lack of knowledge served as my good luck." He gave her a sinister grin.

"Shall we stop playing games? What exactly do you want and why did you kidnap me?" Willow asked.

"I am not like Braxton. I don't play games. I'm not a scientist. I hire them and only the best. I'm what you would refer to as a multi-millionaire businessman. I'm exceptional at what I do and I never let sentiment cloud my judgment."

"Bully for you." The words slipped out before her brain engaged. What astounded her more than her uncensored comment was Prescott's reaction. He laughed at her.

"You're a feisty one. What a pity we find ourselves on opposite sides of this playing field."

"Like Cassidy? Why did you have to kill her? She knew nothing. You could've just let her be."

"Unlike yourself, Cassidy was not held in high esteem. She was here merely to be studied. Once my scientists learned she held no enhanced abilities, she was set free. The product of a simple culling, she no longer served as a productive tool and Randy's skills were needed elsewhere. So to protect his identity, she needed to go. If it makes you feel any better we have test tubes upon test tubes of her blood, along with a multitude of DNA samples."

Her stomach roiled and threatened to expel the Steak Diane and Margaux. A *tool.* Not a person to him, but a tool and a useless one at that. Prescott's cool demeanor made the tiny hairs on the back of her neck stand straight up.

"You never said why you kidnapped me?"

"You my dear, happened to be the one easiest to take. I believe your sisters, who have both been taken a time or two are now suitably paranoid. Any one of you would've worked; you are merely the bargaining chip. I can't very well trade, if I have nothing to trade with. I might have gone straight to the source and kidnapped Collin. However we all know he would be too difficult to kidnap."

"How long do you intend to keep me here?"

"Only as long as necessary. The Chairman believes you and your sisters can be of good use to us. Frankly I feel he's being a bit sentimental. No matter. As long as we reach our goal I will heed his wishes. Be warned, Willow. The Chairman may want you alive, but accidents do happen. Behave yourself. Don't become a statistic. I hope you enjoyed your meal; now if you will excuse me, I have more pressing matters to attend to."

He looked over at the servant. "Get Randy to take Ms. Winters back."

Prescott rose as Randy entered the dining room and motioned for her to leave.

"Let's go, all this food is making me hungry," Randy said.

* * * *

Wyatt watched as Jack and the tech from D.C. maneuvered the Whisper Drone through the campus. Not one employee walking around the campus showed any reaction. The next trial would be Collin and Victory. Wyatt texted Collin and asked him to escort Victory down to their SOCOM office. Jack flew the drone over the couple's vicinity once they were clear of the buildings, but neither reacted at first. When Jack turned the drone around and headed it back in their direction, the two glanced skyward.

"Collin said you needed us. Is there information on Willow?" Victory asked.

Wyatt felt a pang of guilt at getting her hopes up. He hoped this drone would be his redemption.

"I guess I can say—in a way."

Both looked puzzled.

"Did you notice anything unusual on your walk down here?"

They shook their heads.

"Nothing?" Wyatt pressed.

Victory closed her eyes. He could read his sister-in-law well now. She was replaying the walk in her mind.

"Hold on," She said, still keeping her eyes closed. "Now that you mention it, I did hear a soft, muffled buzzing."

"Yeah, me too," Collin said, "Sounded like something way off in the distance."

"It didn't alert you enough to be of concern?"

They shook their heads again.

"Great. Jack, it looks like your Whisper Drone is a go."

"The drone's already here? You tested it on us?" Collin asked, eagerly looking around the sky.

"Yes and yes. The drone passed with flying colors on all the employees we've tested it on today. You two were the cherry on top. If the drone didn't alert the two of you enough to investigate, I'd say we're good."

"Wait—what?"

"Show her, Jack."

Jack pressed a button on his handheld control and the drone appeared directly in front of him.

"Meet my newest toy. The Whisper Drone."

"Oh my gosh. I didn't even hear it. It's nearly invisible, too!" Victory said.

"Yes, almost. The drone's covered in a high-tech coating which reflects its environment; this allows it to blend in."

"Amazing. No one has seen it either?"

"I notice a slight shift when I look at it while it's moving. It reminds me of a heat wave you would see on a hot day," Wyatt said. His phone vibrated in his pocket. He pushed the button and read the text from Dr. Russell.

Can you come to my office as soon as possible, please? I have information regarding Willow.

He jammed the phone back into the pocket.

"Collin, why don't you walk Victory back. I gotta go meet with Dr. Russell."

The door to Dr. Russell's office stood ajar when he arrived. He knocked lightly and called out her name. No answer. Did one of Ryker's goons manage to break through the security system again?

"Wyatt," Dr. Russell called from across the hall. "I'm in the lab."

He let out his breath and walked across the hall. He needed focus. Given his enhanced skills, he should have detected her movement on the other side of the half-open door. He scolded himself and entered the lab.

"I'm glad you could respond quickly. Let me preface this by saying, normally I would *never* give out patient information. However nothing's normal lately and I sincerely believe my findings will help locate Willow."

"What do you have, doc?"

"I did an MRI of Willow's shoulder the day before she disappeared. I feel terrible. I never looked at the results until today. I figured there was no reason to review the report until she returned home safe. I got an itch this morning. You know the one you get when you feel like you've overlooked something?"

Wyatt nodded his head in agreement and waited for her to continue.

"Come over here. Take a look in this microscope."

"I'm no doctor, doc," he said, as he walked up to the impressive piece of equipment.

"You don't need the license for what you're about to see. I have a very microscopic section of her shoulder showing. Tell me what you see."

Against his better judgment he played along and looked into the microscope.

"Wow, this is pretty awesome. But I still have no idea what I'm looking for—wait. What's the little blotch?" he asked without breaking contact with the machine.

"Exactly."

Her remark caused him to lift his head and stare at her.

"You mean you don't know what it is?"

"No, not specifically. So I pulled up her last blood panel. Take a look as this." She handed him the report. He looked the report over feeling like an idiot because she made it sound so simple. "Wait a minute; they told me my white blood cell count was high at 14,000; this is higher than that. That's bad, right?"

"An infection. And what can cause an infection? The body's reaction to fighting off a foreign body. Mary injected Willow with a serum to knock her out. I believe something more filled her syringe."

"Can you enlarge the section anymore?"

"I've tried multiple times. It always blurs. This is the closest I can get. I could run the MRI results into the electron microscope; we might see something more."

"Let's do it." Wyatt watched the doctor as she moved around her lab working her equipment as a pianist would play her piano.

"I have something," she said. "The blurred image looks like a microscopic computer chip. I've seen tracking devices look like this." She stepped back to allow Wyatt a chance to look.

"Ryker has created a microscopic tracker? Can you make me copies of all this?"

She pressed the button on a machine and the image of what they saw printed out. She picked up a large envelope and tucked the picture inside.

"Thanks doc. This is our first real lead. Let me know if you find anything else."

Wyatt kissed Dr. Russell on the forehead. Her surprise made him chuckle. This was the first time since Willow's kidnapping he felt hope.

Chapter Twenty-Six

"This is Wyatt Farraday. I need to speak to General Roberts immediately. It's high priority."

"General Roberts is in a closed door meeting and can't be disturbed," Roberts's assistant said.

"Make sure he calls me ASAP."

Wyatt disconnected the call and hit a speed-dial number.

"Yes, sir," Jack answered.

"Jack, finish up what you're doing and get back to the office, now."

Wyatt explained to Jack what Dr. Russell told him and showed Jack Willow's reports concerning the injection. Jack nodded as he listened.

"What's your take?"

"It's certainly plausible," Jack's eyebrows raised. "I can reach out to my contacts and see if they know anything. The microchip is most likely located through GPS, Global Positioning System. GPS is detected with radio signals. Cell phones, the most common identifiers with GPS, have recorded phone numbers which are used as identification. We don't have any sort of a marker. In order to locate Willow we would need to triangulate her position with three or more satellites, to do that we need an identifying number or at the very least, a general location. What did General Roberts think?"

"He's in a damn meeting. I'm waiting to hear back from him."

"I'll see what I can find, but it's like the old needle in the ocean."

"You mean a needle in a haystack," Wyatt said.

"Nope. In this instance it's an ocean."

"Tell me this. If we used the Whisper Drone and identified a general position, could you locate her then?"

"Yes, if we have a marker to trace."

Jack got up from the chair next to Wyatt's desk and went over to his station.

Wyatt paced his office like a caged animal. Each minute that ticked by heightened his anxiety. *Son of a bitch, how the hell long can one meeting be?* Wyatt thought.

"What meeting?" His brother asked.

Shit. With his anxiety sky-high, Wyatt inadvertently sent his thoughts directly to his brother.

"Sorry bro, I didn't need to involve you."

"What's up, Wyatt? You don't make that kind of a slip unless you're super-pissed."

He wasn't getting out of this. He'd hoped to have some concrete information before involving the rest of the team. Thanks to his lack of focus, he would have to fill Tristan in now.

As Wyatt finished updating Tristan, his phone rang. The caller ID read "General Roberts."

"My assistant told me you have something urgent. What do you have?" Roberts asked.

For the third time in the past few hours, Wyatt relayed his story.

"Are we working on anything along those lines?" Wyatt asked as he finished.

"You know technology. We're always working on the next best toy. I personally haven't been updated about anything like this, but I can do some research and get back to you. It's after eleven out here. We're going to have to wait until tomorrow to get any real answers without raising red flags. My first thought is to go with Jack on this, so we don't stir the pot. I have my sources, except I'm still not one-hundred percent sure who I can trust."

"Maybe you're right, sir. Why don't you sit on this for the next twenty-four hours? Let's give Jack a shot."

"How's the Whisper Drone working out?"

"C'mon, it's Jack. It took him all of an hour to have the thing humming his tune."

"Sure glad that kid's on our side," General Roberts chuckled.

"You and me both."

Wyatt leaned against his office door and watched Jack work. The guy really was a genius when it came to electronics and analyzing.

"Hey Jack, when will the Whisper Drone be ready to go?"

Jack answered without looking at Wyatt.

"Drone's ready now, sir."

"Good, send it out. The sooner we get the drone over Prescott's Texas compound, the sooner we'll find out if Willow is being held there."

* * * *

Wyatt yawned and stretched his arms over his head. He sure was grateful to Payton for setting up this new quiet room. She furnished the room with six twin-size beds and a sleep chair. A full bathroom was installed and included two showers. She told Wyatt they needed a place to sleep when the team pulled all-nighters. She'd walked in on them sleeping at their desks for the last time. She'd also said this room in no way should serve as Wyatt's nightly sleeping place. Last night it'd come in handy. He and Jack took turns all night monitoring the drone's progress to Texas.

Wyatt picked up his phone off the night stand and checked the time. He nearly bolted out of bed when he saw it was nine-thirty in the morning. He headed to the shower, dressed, and walked out the door in under ten minutes. The building was abuzz with the entire team.

"See, I told you he would wake up the minute we got breakfast," Tristan said.

"Funny guy. What's the status, Jack?" Wyatt took the plate of food Morgan offered and his first sip of coffee.

"The drone is approximately sixty miles away from target. I just switched on the video feed. We'll see everything the drone sees and it's being recorded." Three out of four of Jack's large computer screens lit up and filled the screen with flat, dry landscape whizzing by.

"The place really is out in the middle of nowhere," Noah said.

"Make sure to keep the drone a good distance up. The thing may be camouflaged, but that might not stop it from triggering whatever type of security the compound has," Wyatt said.

"It's set to go in at two-hundred feet. Drone's on the approach now. Doesn't look like there are any buildings over three or four stories," Jack said.

Wyatt's phone rang. He pulled it from his pocket. The caller ID displayed "private number."

"Wyatt Farraday."

"This is Daniel Prescott, Mr. Farraday."

Wyatt drew his hand across his throat, and the entire room went as quiet as a tomb.

"It's Captain. How did you get my number?"

"Willow Winters was kind enough to give me your number. I thought it high time we discussed a trade. I'm thinking Collin for Willow."

"How do I know you actually have Willow, or if she's even still alive?"

"I just told you. She gave me your number."

"Doesn't demonstrate she's still breathing." It took every ounce of restraint for Wyatt not to crawl through his phone and murder the man on the other end.

"I'll call you back in ten minutes, as soon as one of my people can take the phone to her."

"It doesn't work that way, Prescott. You could have a recording with her voice. Forgive me if I don't believe you. But the only way I'm going to consider the discussion of a trade, is for *me* to speak with her and then with you."

"Fine, fine. Let's stop wasting time, shall we. Give me fifteen minutes." The line went dead.

"Everyone keep your eyes on the computer screen. If Prescott is in his compound, chances are he's not keeping Willow in the same building, since he needed fifteen minutes to get the phone to her."

"There." Logan pointed at the screen closest to him. "Right there, a person just came out of the building next to the fence."

"I'm zooming in on the figure. I'm going to bring the drone down to seventy-five feet."

"Be careful Jack, don't push it," Wyatt said.

The team could now tell the person was a male. The figure got into the backseat of a waiting cart and headed to the heart of the compound. The cart stopped outside a large plain gray building, and the man went inside.

"Everyone stay quiet. If it's Prescott, he should be calling back any second. I'm going to answer on speaker phone. I want all ears focused on this call. Collin, come closer. I want you to specifically listen for any background noise."

Wyatt's phone rang. He let it ring a couple of times before he answered.

"Farraday."

"Wyatt, it's Willow."

For a split second Wyatt stopped breathing and thinking. The only thing that registered was the thumping of his heart.

"Willow, are you okay?"

"Yes, I'm fine, I—"

"Satisfied, Farraday?" Prescott asked. "She's here with me and she's fine, now about our trade."

"Collin is out of town on a mission," Wyatt jumped in before Prescott could finish his demands. "I can have him back here in twenty-four hours."

"In twenty-four hours and one minute I want him on his way to meet me."

"Where?"

"I'll tell you when the twenty-four hours are up. This time—he comes alone."

"I take it he can get to the meeting place by car."

The line went quiet.

"Have a pilot standing by. You might need one. But only the pilot. We'll speak again in twenty-four hours."

The team's eyes were all fixed on the screen as they watched the door the man entered. A few minutes after the call ended the same man left the building and once again got into the backseat of the cart. It headed back in the direction it'd come from.

During the exchange between Prescott and Wyatt, Jack triangulated his GPS and targeted the building Prescott entered.

"I think we have him," Tristan said.

"I think we have Willow, too," Jack said. "See the ping on the screen? I weeded out all the cell phones and that single ping remained on screen. I would bet my next paycheck the ping is Willow." Jack pointed at the flashing dot.

"Great job, Jack." Wyatt slapped him on the back. "What did you hear, Collin?"

"I'm not positive, but I think this compound has the same security grid as the island."

"Which means no one would be able to telepathically connect with the outside world," Wyatt said.

"Exactly."

"Jack, map out the compound with the drone and as soon as you're finished bring it home," Wyatt said.

"The team's ready to go. I'm assuming you want us entering the compound under darkness," Tristan said.

"Yes. The C-27J Spartan is being fueled and ready to go. We'll touch down at Cannon Air Force Base in New Mexico. There'll be a chopper waiting for us there. Logan will take us the rest of the way in. Logan, work with Jack and figure out where the best place will be to put the bird down. I want us skids off the ground the second we have the compound layout," Wyatt said.

"Wait a minute, you said 'we.' I understood you heading out for Willow the couple times she went missing locally. Are you telling me you're leaving HQ and going with us to Texas?" Tristan asked.

"I am, yes. Jack is more than capable of holding down HQ. I'm going out on this one, and I don't want to hear another word."

"Oh man. You got it bad, bro. You do know my team is more than capable of bringing her back," Tristan said in Wyatt's mind.

"Don't start, Tristan. I'm going with you. End of conversation."

"Okay men, let's work out our plan. Is there any possibility of shutting down the security grid?" Wyatt asked.

"It's pretty sophisticated. I say we do it the same way I did on the island," Tristan said.

"Which is how?"

"I blew the control panel up." Tristan grinned.

"Subtle."

"I'm telling you, the blasted thing is complicated. Jack could probably figure it out. But the quickest way is to disable the main panel."

"Not exactly quiet."

"You got a better idea?"

"Jack, any ideas?" Wyatt asked.

"You might be able to fry the circuits without the explosion. Call me when you're ready to disable the system. You can put the panel on your phone screen, and I can take a look at it. I think I can talk you through the process if I can get a good look at the panel."

"Won't be as much fun," Tristan said.

* * * *

A couple hours later, Wyatt, Tristan, Collin, Morgan, Logan, and Noah loaded up their gear and got into the C-27J Spartan. When the plane touched down at Cannon Air Force Base in New Mexico it was well into the evening. The team grabbed all their gear from the plane and loaded a waiting helicopter. Logan sat in the pilot's seat and went through his takeoff checklist.

"Read me, Jack?" Logan asked through his headset.

"Loud and clear," Jack said. "Let the team know Prescott just left the compound by helicopter."

"Roger. Jack informed me Prescott has left the compound by chopper."

"Means one of two things," Tristan said.

"Either he doesn't plan on handing over Willow, or he doesn't plan on being at the exchange," Morgan said.

"Chickenshit. I'm betting it's the first. He thinks he's keeping Willow," Noah said.

"Let's get this bird in the air." Tristan rapped the back of the pilot's seat.

Chapter Twenty-Seven

Logan killed the exterior lights to the chopper the last hundred miles. He switched the interior red lighting on for the final approach. If anyone looked into the night sky, the chopper would be unseen. Due to the flat terrain which enveloped the location of the Texas compound, Logan landed the helicopter a good eight miles away. The team disembarked the chopper, unloaded their gear, unfolded the camouflage netting, and pulled it over the aircraft. If anyone happened to fly over, their aircraft would blend into its surroundings, both night and day.

"Morgan, I want you manning the radio," Tristan said. "We might need Noah's tracking abilities, and he doesn't need the distraction."

"Okay, let's load up. Logan, I want you staying put," Tristan said.

"Oh good! I missed my sauna this morning, and the chopper's gonna be a great sweatbox," Logan said.

"Good, it's about time you got clean. But if we need you to fly into the site to pick up Willow, you need to shorten your beauty regime and fly right into the compound. Morgan will give you a heads up when we make our final approach. That should give you plenty of time to get the netting off, stowed, and get your bird airborne," Tristan said.

They each loaded up their gear and tested their wireless earpiece comms. All but Collin and Wyatt donned night-vision goggles; their vision remained as clear in the middle of the night as the middle of the day. Tristan gave the team thumbs up, and each returned the gesture. Noah in the lead, they vanished into the darkness.

* * * *

Willow paced her room. Sleep eluded her as her mind played out different scenarios of what could happen at tomorrow's exchange. She knew the exchange would never happen and was trying to anticipate what plan the team orchestrated. If only she could reach Wyatt, she wouldn't be as antsy.

She put her ear up to the door, straining to hear any movement in the hall. It sounded to her like the place was empty. She walked over to the bed and sat, closed her eyes, and concentrated on her breathing for a good while. Centering all her will, she sent her plea into the night.

"Wyatt. Wyatt, can you hear me?" she called to him via her telepathic link. No answer came back to her. Not willing to give up so soon, she called and called until her body became physically drained. Eventually she lay back down and drifted off to sleep.

The next thing she knew, Randy was kicking her bed again and again.

"Hey, if ya want breakfast ya better get your ass outta bed. This ain't no fancy bed and breakfast."

Boy that's an understatement, she thought.

He rattled her bed again.

"I'm up. You can stop with the shaking now."

"Food's on the table. I'd advise y'all to eat now. I'll be back in a few hours, be ready to go."

"How will I know when it's been a few hours? There's no clock in this room."

"Knock it off with yer smartass answers, just be ready." Randy slammed and locked the door behind him.

* * * *

The SOCOM team had hunkered down a few yards from the compound, partially buried in the dust behind sparse, tiny shrubs. They'd covered themselves with their personal camouflage netting. Tristan ordered the team to remain outside the fence until Wyatt received his instructions from Prescott. He didn't want to risk the chance of Wyatt being overheard inside the compound, and he thought it better for the team to stay together, get the phone call from Prescott, and then enter the compound at the same time. They had no idea what type of security they might run into aside from the security grid.

Wyatt's phone vibrated in his hand; he answered on the second ring.

"Farraday."

"Is Collin ready to go?" Daniel Prescott asked.

"He's ready. What are your instructions?"

"I'm sure he's familiar with the San Juan Island facility. He has two hours to get there."

"And Willow will be waiting there for the pilot to take her home?"

"Per our agreement. She's been here all along. Two hours. No Collin, no Willow."

"That lying sack of shit," Wyatt muttered. "Prescott wants Collin at the San Juan Island facility. He claims Willow's been there all along," he whispered to the team through his comm. "He wants Collin there in two hours."

"Okay," Tristan said. "We need to disable the security, locate and retrieve Willow, and get out of this hellhole in ninety minutes. I'm going straight for the security building. Noah's in charge of the perimeter once we get inside. Morgan will be with him and on the radio. Wyatt and Collin, you start for the building Prescott entered when he let you speak to Willow. The second I get the grid down, I'll let you know."

Noah left first; like a snake he slithered up to the fence and checked to see if it was hot. When he found nothing, he reached into his side pocket and pulled out his wire cutters.

"I'm in."

One by one they crept out of their hidey holes with Wyatt and Collin bringing up the rear. The men wasted no time in taking up their positions.

"Hold up," Noah said. "There's a guard headed directly for you, Tristan."

"Roger," Tristan said.

The guard came into view as Tristan blended into the few shadows on the corner of one building. The guard passed and continued to stroll away from Tristan and in Wyatt and Collin's direction.

"Wyatt. He's heading your way."

"Roger."

"I'm at the security building," Tristan said. "There's a guard smoking a cigarette a couple feet from the door. Everyone hold up. Let's see what he's going to do."

A few minutes passed in radio silence. Wyatt could swear hours passed and he bit his tongue to keep from demanding Tristan's status.

"Shit. He's taken up his post right at the door."

"The only way in or out," Morgan said.

"Dammit. Okay, I'm heading in." Tristan left his wireless comm open so the team would get a play-by-play of the event. "Hey, bud. You got a smoke I could bum?"

The guard studied him. Unfortunately for the guard, he hesitated a beat too long.

"Wait a minute. Who the hell—"

Tristan reached out and roughly grabbed the guard around the neck, choking him until he was unconscious. He dragged the guard to the far side of the building, taped his mouth shut with his trusty roll of gray duct tape, zip-tied his hands and feet, then taped him to a concrete post next to the building.

"I'm on my way in."

Plastered to one side of the doorway, he glanced inside to see if anyone else had hung around. Seeing no one, he quietly entered. He'd stepped only a few feet inside the room when the door in front of him swung open. Tristan glued himself to the wall. A guard walked out still tucking his shirt back inside his pants.

"Quick smoke," he said to Tristan, without turning as he continued walking away.

"There must be some sort of alert in the room when someone enters the front door," Noah whispered in Tristan's ear.

"I thought you said you'd be gone ten minutes." The guard said as he turned in Tristan's direction. His eyes widened and he reached for his weapon. Tristan leapt and reached the other man before he could discharge his gun. The two struggled for the weapon, the guard dragging Tristan closer. Tristan felt when the guard's finger found the trigger and in one abrupt maneuver he twisted the barrel of the gun toward the guard. Registering the movement too late, the guard pulled the trigger and shot himself squarely in his chest. Confusion played across the guard's features as he went lax and dropped to the floor. Tristan reached down and checked for a pulse.

"Clear," he said, into his comm and went to the security panel. "This is interesting. There're only two cameras here. One fixed on the main gate and one on the back of the house Prescott exited."

"There must be more cameras somewhere," Noah said.

"Not necessarily. The remote location may have made Prescott overconfident."

"Yes, but if they hold prisoners regularly like Cassidy and Willow, then that building may have more cameras.

"Probably a good bet," Wyatt said. "We'll keep our eyes open."

"I'm contacting Jack now. I'll get back to everyone as soon as I have something to report."

Wyatt and Collin reached the far side of the compound.

"I'm going in," Wyatt said.

"Captain, don't you think it would be best if we give Tristan a few minutes?" Collin asked.

He knew Collin was right, and it didn't make the situation any better. As the two men approached the building, the door clicked. They vanished as the door opened. Three men walked out of the building. They leaned against the building under the eaves, which provided a tiny bit of shade. The first man pulled out a pack of cigarettes and offered it to the others. The second man took the offer; the other shook his head.

"I told you, I'm giving those cancer sticks up. Those things will kill you, besides they're too expensive," the third man said.

"Yeah, yeah, yeah," the first man commented. "You're worried about these killing you. I'd worry more about this hell hole of a post. Shit, everything here bites and can kill you. My buddy found a nasty scorpion in his boot the other day. I'm counting the days until my post is up."

"Did I hear right?" the second man asked. "Prescott left the compound and isn't coming back any time soon?"

"That's right. I heard him say something about some island. I want to go there, got my name on the list to get out of this miserable desert."

"Stop your bitching, will ya?" the third man said. "I swear you spend all your days bitching. You'll be lucky if you keep this job at all." He turned to the other man. "Yeah, he's gone for a while. I think Randy and some guys are going, too, along with the latest arm candy they got in lockdown."

"Hey, maybe they'd take me? I wouldn't mind a ride with—or on—that blonde and a chance to see an island."

"I doubt it. Besides, the pilot said they wouldn't be there long and then they were off to somewhere else. Okay, enough shooting the shit, you two get back on duty. I'll be at the security building if you need anything."

The trio dispersed.

Wyatt started to telepathically connect with his brother, until he remembered the grid. "Tristan, move your ass. You got company coming," he said, through his comm.

"I need five more minutes. Jack's figured the system out; he's walking me through it now."

"Then you're gonna need to do something with your new company. He's gonna be on top of you in three."

"I've got it covered...Okay, grids down. You're good to go."

Wyatt looked at Collin.

"Think you can keep those two dickheads outta my hair while I hunt for Willow?"

"Please, a Cub Scout could keep them busy," Collin said, with a snicker.

"All right then Scout leader, let's get this done." Wyatt snuck up to the door to survey what type of locking mechanism he was dealing with, when he noticed it was left ajar. He looked back at Collin and rolled his eyes. Collin shook his head and joined Wyatt. They took a quick glance inside, saw no one in the area, and slipped inside the building. Collin quietly closed the door behind them. Wyatt directed Collin with hand signals. He nodded his understanding and started down the hall. Wyatt stepped back into the shadow of a doorway and reached out telepathically for Willow.

"Willow, can you hear me? I'm here."

Chapter Twenty-Eight

Willow felt like climbing the walls. She'd paced her small room nonstop. Randy had made it sound like she would be leaving any minute when he dropped off breakfast this morning. By the way her stomach was grumbling, it had to be hours later.

"Willow, can you hear me? I'm here."

She froze and actually looked around her. *"Wyatt?"* His name played in her mind.

"I'm here. We're going to get you out. Hold on a little longer and be ready for anything."

"But how are you able to reach out to me telepathically?"

"Tristan disabled the grid. Do you know what room you're in?"

"Last door on the left. There's a couple halls that shoot off in both directions. I'm on the main hall."

"Okay. Hang tight."

A few seconds later, the door to her room flew open and she smiled. Her smile instantaneously fell when instead of Wyatt, Randy bolted in. His aura flamed around him, the muddy colors flashing and fading.

"Who the hell are you communicating with?" He snarled at her.

"I have no idea what you're talking about. You said this compound has an impenetrable grid."

"Obviously it's compromised. So I ask again— who are you talking to?"

"I only tried to reach someone and failed! Nobody heard me."

"Bullshit, I know two-way telepathy when I feel it. Who is it?"

Resolute in her mind she would not give him what he wanted, Willow stood her ground and didn't utter a word.

"Fine. No more mister nice guy."

He walked over and slapped her, sending her onto the floor with the force of it. He towered over her and glared down into her face. Deep inside she felt her body start to shake, but she refused to show him how afraid she was.

"Well?"

His irises were deep, empty black holes that promised no mercy.

"I have *no* idea what you are talking about."

"We're leaving." He seized her by the upper arm and drew her against his chest. "If you make any attempt to contact anyone, I'll make you pay."

From out of nowhere a seven-inch buck knife pressed against her throat. With only a touch the scalpel-sharp blade laid open a small cut and blood dripped down the length of her neck.

"Understand me?"

Panic-stricken from the evil vibrating from this man she whispered assent.

"Good. Let's go."

He all but carried Willow as they walked out of her room and headed in the opposite direction of the door.

"Hey, asswipe," they heard behind them. "If you want to get out of this alive, you better release her this minute," Wyatt said.

Randy turned and grinned at Wyatt as he pulled Willow in front of him as a human shield and put the knife back to her throat. She watched as Wyatt's face drained of color and his eyes went flat.

"We're leaving together or she's gonna develop a serious leak." Randy emphasized his words by pressing the side of the blade into her skin. Another tiny trickle of crimson ran down her neck.

"Tell you what, you let her go and I let you live. How does that sound?"

"Like you think I'm some kind of an idiot."

Collin appeared in the hallway behind Wyatt.

"Get out of my way," Randy said. "Call off your goons. We're leaving together. This is your last warning."

"Stand down," Wyatt said to Collin and to the team listening.

Wyatt lowered his gun and stepped to the side.

"Not happening. I want you and your pal there to leave in front of me. When you get outside the door drop your guns and hit the ground."

"Do what he says," Wyatt said, as he and Collin walked back down the hall. As Wyatt got to the door he placed his open palm on it, turned and focused on Willow's eyes, and sent one quick message: "*Drop as you exit, one chance.*"

Willow stiffened in fear, thinking Randy had caught the brief interchange, but Randy was totally engulfed in watching the men and keeping Willow close, so Wyatt's words slipped by unnoticed. The door closed before Randy and Willow reached it.

"Open it. Take one step out and tell me where they are and what they're doing. If ya try anything I'm gonna drill this blade into your back."

Willow did exactly as instructed and stepped out the door. But instead of telling him where the men were, she tried to slam the door behind her. Randy realized at the last second what she intended to do and thrust his knife at her as she dropped to the ground. Randy pushed open the door and attempted to retrieve his human shield, but instead he got inundated with a hail of bullets. The knife slipped from his fingers, and he dropped next to Willow. Wyatt ran to her.

"It's over Willow, get up; we have to get out of here."

Willow moaned as he rolled her over and she held her side. Blood trickled between her fingers.

"I knew you would find me," she said, slipping away from the immense pain into unconsciousness.

* * * *

When Wyatt realized all the blood didn't belong to Randy, his mind went into hyper drive.

"What the hell is going on? Sounds like the shootout at the OK Corral," Noah said.

"Morgan, get the chopper here now," Wyatt said.

"Already done. Logan should be landing right outside the gate in two minutes."

"Logan, do you have enough room to land inside the compound?"

"Possibly, maybe—why?" Logan asked.

"Willow's been stabbed, and she's losing blood fast."

"Son of a bitch," Tristan said.

"Copy. I'm coming in. The center of the compound has just enough room to set this bird down. I'll be there in two."

"Okay, I don't know how many unfriendlies we got, but our goal is to cover Wyatt and Willow and make sure no one blows a hole in our ride. Let's go," Tristan said.

"*Wyatt,*" Tristan reached out to his brother. "*You can do this. Go north of your position 300 feet to chopper landing.*"

The sound of his brother's words via their telepathic, helped Wyatt suppress his rising fear for Willow's life.

"*Roger. Thanks, Tristan.*"

Wyatt scooped Willow into his arms trying to apply pressure to her wound at the same time. Shots rang out behind him, and Collin dropped the shooter with one shot as Wyatt ran, his bloody hands full. The chopper dropped from the sky a building length ahead of him. Morgan, Noah, and Tristan surrounded the chopper, shooting at any resistance.

"You ready?" Collin asked.

"Ready," Wyatt said.

"Then go, I've got your back, Captain. I promise."

He nodded to Collin and shot out toward the bird at his top speed. He bounded into the aircraft, followed by the other men.

"Let's get the hell out of here," Tristan yelled over the sound of the rotating blades and gunfire.

As soon as they were clear of the compound, Noah spread out blankets between the seats.

"Lay her down here, Captain. Let's get a look at the wound."

Gently Wyatt placed her on the blankets, still applying pressure to her wound.

"Damnit, she's lost a lot of blood," Noah said, as he reached for the bandages in the first aid kit.

"Can you do anything for her?" Wyatt asked Noah.

Noah looked up at him. The two spoke often about his growing ability to aid in healing. Wyatt knew Noah couldn't repair a heart or fix major damage; all the same he was capable of slowing bleeding and decreasing pain.

"She needs a hospital, now," Noah said. "The knife entered between the ninth and tenth ribs on the left side. Most likely hit the spleen, hence all the blood."

"Noah, help her."

Noah looked from Wyatt to Willow. He rubbed his hands together, closed his eyes, and centered his energy. Noah slowly lowered his hands and placed them over the gash. Blood ran from under his palms, but gradually the bleeding subsided to a trickle.

"I'll bandage this," Noah said, "I've done all I could. Her bleeding's controlled for now, but she still needs a hospital."

"Jack contacted General Roberts. The General found us a hospital," Logan said. "I'm heading directly back to Cannon Air Force Base. Jack is taking care of the details. We should touch down in less than twenty minutes."

"She needs the best doctor." Wyatt questioned the decision.

"She'll get him, Wyatt. General Roberts contacted the hospital at Cannon. There was a large medical conference earlier today. One of the best internists is there right now. The General caught up with the internist in the process of leaving and requested he stay on to work on Willow. She'll be in great hands."

"She better be." Wyatt's hand never left Willow's the entire trip. His full attention remained on her as he sent her thoughts of holding on.

The trip seemed to last an eternity. At long last the base came into view. Logan requested landing clearance. A medical team of four people stood at the edge of the helipad, a stretcher between them. Wyatt scooped Willow into his arms and exited the chopper at the same time the skids kissed the concrete. He ran over to the stretcher and laid her down.

"Who's the doctor?"

"Dr. Latham is preparing in the surgical suite," a female nurse said.

"Tell him the minute he gets her stable he needs to remove the tracker here in her right shoulder," Wyatt pointed to the spot.

"Sir, the tracker isn't a priority at the moment," the same nurse said.

"You're wrong. It isn't one of ours. As long as she has the thing inside her there are people aware of her every move who may kidnap her again. Do I make myself clear?"

All four nodded.

"Good, anyone got a marker?"

One of the men handed him a sharpie. Wyatt ripped Willow's sleeve away and marked the spot.

"Tell him he's going to have to use a microscope to locate it."

The group looked at him in bewilderment.

"And I want her tracker."

They rolled Willow away, and Wyatt felt as if they ripped out his heart and soul.

"She's in good hands bro," Tristan said, as he patted Wyatt on the back. "Come on. We'll find a waiting room and a source of nonstop coffee."

The team gathered around the brothers as they entered the hospital.

Wyatt paced the waiting room for a couple hours and then moved out to pace the hall. He pestered a nurse until she told him where the surgical suite was located. He hovered at the door, shoulders stiff and jaw clenched. His team waited in the hallway as he paced back and forth across the width of the surgery doors, continually rubbing the back of his neck. He kept replaying one scene over and over in his head: one moment Willow turned to slam the door and the next she laid on the ground.

Six hours later a man dressed in blood-spattered light blue scrubs partially covered by a crisp white doctor's jacket walked through the doors. He pulled off his scrub hat, stuffed it in his jacket pocket, and ran a hand through his dark red hair. *This couldn't be the internist,* Wyatt thought. *He doesn't look much older than a kid.*

"You're showing your age, bro," Tristan laughed in his mind.

337

"Are you Ms. Winters' family?" The man asked.

"Yes. Yes, we are," Wyatt said.

"Doctor Latham," the man said, as he extended his hand to shake Wyatt's.

"How is she?" Wyatt asked, almost afraid to hear the answer.

"She made it through surgery. It was touch and go for a while. The knife made an utter mess. It chipped her eleventh rib. Both the bone fragment and knife punctured her spleen. I tried to save her spleen, but it had too much damage and I had to remove it. The bone fragment lodged itself in her intestine. I removed the fragment and patched her up. I had to do major cleanup inside. Frankly I don't know how she survived the trip; she lost a lot of blood."

Wyatt could hardly hear the doctor's words with the thrashing sound of his heartbeat blasting through his ears. For just an instant his legs felt weak and black spots flashed in his eyes. He couldn't lose Willow now. He'd only just really found her. He sent out prayers and made bargains for a chance to tell her how he felt. He needed to tell her she was his whole life. Without her, he felt nothing.

"Take a breath, Wyatt. Willow made it. She needs you now. She needs you to be strong for her," Tristan murmured in his mind.

"So, she's going to be fine, right doc?" Tristan asked.

"The next twenty-four hours are crucial. We'll be keeping a close eye on her. If she makes it that long, I'll feel better telling you she's going to make a full recovery," Dr. Latham said.

Wyatt forced his fears farther back in his head. Tristan was right. She needed him now, and hell would freeze over before he failed her again.

"When can we see her?" Wyatt asked.

"She's in recovery right now. She will be moved to ICU in the next few hours. You will be able to see her then. I'd advise you all to take a break. Go get dinner in the mess hall. A room's set up for you all to nap. Get some rest. Something tells me you won't be leaving her side once we move her. I need to warn you, she probably won't wake up until at least the morning. Her body is dealing with an immense trauma."

Doctor Latham nodded at the group and turned to leave. As he did he stuck his hands in his jacket pockets.

"I nearly forgot." He pulled a flat glass jar from his pocket. "You wanted this."

He handed Wyatt the jar. There were two microscope slides stuck together inside the jar.

"It's in there. I've never in my life seen a tracker that miniscule. I'd ask you where it came from if I didn't believe my question would fall on deaf ears. Thanks for informing my nurse about the size. I nearly missed the thing, even using my microscopic equipment."

"We need to call her sisters," Wyatt said, after the doctor left. "Shit. How could I forget to call them? They're going to hate me."

"Don't worry, Wyatt. Collin and I phoned them. General Roberts arranged a private jet. They should be here in the next few hours," Tristan said.

"Are they aware how severe her injuries were?"

"We told them she needed surgery. We thought it best to leave out the details until they arrived."

"Probably a wise idea. I think I'll head up to the ICU and wait for her."

"No you won't. We are all going to take the doctor's advice and head to the mess hall. And then we're all catching a quick nap, so we can be awake to greet her."

Wyatt looked around at his team. These men were loyal; no they were more than loyal. They really were family.

"You guys don't need to stay. I'm sure there's something you can do back at the campus."

"There's no way we're leaving," Morgan said.

"Unless of course by order of our captain," Noah said, jumping in.

"She's family, sir," Logan said.

"Okay then, let's go grab some grub. Here's the tracker, Tristan. See that it gets back to General Roberts for further study," Wyatt said.

Chapter Twenty-Nine

Victory and Payton ran through the hospital with Tristan hot on their heels. The women stopped cold in their tracks as they took in the scene of Willow hooked up to monitors and IV drips. Wyatt held Willow's hand and murmured to her. Tristan and Collin hugged their wives.

"She's going to be all right. Tell me she's going to make it through this," Payton said, weeping in Collin's protective embrace.

"She'll come out of this better than ever, I promise. We won't accept anything else," Collin said, as his and Tristan's eyes met.

"What exactly did the doctor say?" Victory sniffled into Tristan's shoulder.

"Honey, we've told you both everything he said. We need to wait until he makes his rounds if you have more questions."

Payton and Victory both cried a while longer. Then they pulled away and faced their sister's room. Wyatt turned and looked at them. He attempted to smile, but it wouldn't come.

"Are you ready?" Tristan asked the sisters.

"Victory, we need to support Wyatt," Payton said.

The quartet slipped into the room. The sisters walked up to Wyatt and each laid a hand on his shoulder.

"I can't begin to tell you how sorry I am," Wyatt said.

"About what?" Payton asked.

"I told you I'd bring her home. I promised you."

"You did bring her home," Victory said.

"Not like this! Willow getting stabbed was not part of the plan. I would take her place if I could, for the love of all that's good. I'd die if it would bring her back to us."

"Stop it, Wyatt Farraday. Willow would be furious if she heard you say that. Tristan told us what happened. You had no other options. This is that psychopath's fault; who knows what he would've done to her had he escaped."

"She shouldn't have been in the crossfire. I knew better."

"She made her move as you instructed her. We don't want to hear another word of this nonsense. The only person at blame is Randy. I for one am glad he no longer walks this world." Tears trickled down Payton's cheeks.

"We'll leave you alone with her," Wyatt said, as he got to his feet. "I'll be right outside."

* * * *

"How's she doing, Doctor Latham?" Wyatt asked, as he watched the man examine Willow.

"She's holding her own. Please call me Ben. She's stable, a very good sign."

"Thirty-six hours have passed. Shouldn't she be awake by now?"

"She'll wake up when she's ready. All you can do now is what you've been doing. Be here, hold her hand, and talk to her."

Two days passed and still Willow hadn't wakened. Victory and Payton spent all day with Willow; but each night the men insisted they go back to the hotel and rest. The team hadn't left the hospital. They'd taken turns standing watch outside Willow's door. Wyatt left when forced out by the medical staff, and then he went only as far as the other side of the window to her room.

As the third day dawned Wyatt's nerves were starting to fray. Willow's color had not returned; she remained as white as the hospital sheets. Her body was still cool to the touch. Dr. Latham greeted him as he walked into the room.

"How's our girl?" He tested the reaction of her pupils with a light.

"She's in a coma, isn't she?"

"No, Wyatt. She's not. She just needs to want to wake up. It's the body's defense mechanism shielding her from the trauma. When the worst is over she will wake up." He patted Wyatt on the shoulder. "When's the last time you got any real sleep? Have you left her at all?"

"No, and I don't intend to," Wyatt said.

"Don't get yourself rundown. She's going to need you when she wakes. I'll be back to check on her later this afternoon."

Wyatt dropped his head on the bed, still clutching Willow's hand. For a brief moment tears ran down his cheeks. Angry with himself, he rubbed them away with the backs of his hands without releasing Willow's.

"*Please, A rúnsearc, come back to me. No one will ever hurt you again. You have to come back, Willow. I can't spend another day without you. You are my everything,*" he pleaded into her mind.

"What does that mean?" A groggy, slurred response came from Willow.

Wyatt snapped his head up and stared at her, certain the words he'd heard were made up in his mind. She lay in the bed eyes closed, not moving.

"Willow?" He stroked a hand through her silky golden hair.

"You've said the phrase before. What does it mean?"

"In my native Irish language it means my *soul mate* and *beloved*. I heard this often growing up. Dad would say it to Mom nearly every day. Only now do I really understand its true meaning. You, Willow, are my soul mate, my beloved." He smiled down at her and kissed her forehead.

Her lids fluttered open for the briefest time and she looked into his eyes.

"How beautiful." She closed her eyes. "*I heard you, Wyatt. You've been here, with me, all along.*" Her words lightly fluttered across his mind, before she drifted off to sleep.

* * * *

Two weeks later…

"I have information on the DNA verification of the twins," said Wyatt.

Willow looked up at him but said nothing.

"Once again your gut feeling proved correct. The two girls buried in those graves are no relation to you."

Willow gasped, and her hand flew to her chest.

"Bastard! Ryker is pure evil in every sense of the word. What did he do with my sisters? Did he experiment with their bodies? Or do you think they could still be alive?" she asked and looked squarely into Wyatt's eyes. Pain, confusion, and sheer rage pulsated in her dark stare. She collapsed into a chair, as if the additional pain were too heavy for her to bear. "Wyatt, what if they lived? Mom and Dad left this world never knowing their girls. They believed them dead and buried. How terrible. How could any human being do such a thing to another?"

The intensity of Willow's sorrow bombarded him. He made a silent vow to locate Ryker and kill him. He pulled Willow from the chair and wrapped her in his warm embrace. She felt cold and lifeless. Terror filled him as his mind flashed back to the hospital. The weight of the past two weeks was too much for her injured body. As she cried disconsolately in his arms, he swore this man would not destroy her. He lifted her up into his arms and left the house, followed closely by Asia who'd been by Willow's side since she returned home. He carried Willow out into the sunshine, walked out into the lush green grass, and sat down as he cradled her in his lap, in tune with her emotions and thoughts. Willow felt confused and devastated, as if she were giving up. No, he would not allow her to be destroyed by this dickless son of a bitch. Not after she'd fought her way back to life and to him.

"*Willow—honey, come back. You will get through this terrible pain. You have no choice. You must explain everything to your sisters, and the three of you will need one another's support to carry on. Your parents' belief that your sisters were dead is nothing short of a tragedy. If they are still alive, you know with all your heart your parents would want you to locate them. Please, don't let this bastard destroy you. You've come too far. You fought your way back from the jaws of death. If the twins live, we need to find them and bring them home. I will be by your side every step of the way, I promise.*"

Wyatt continued to hold her and rub her back, to try to console her and bring her back from her grief. Time slowed to a snail's pace as he waited for a sign from her. Then the most unexpected thing happened. He felt her center herself, the shift of energy around him undeniable.

"What do we do next?" She sniffed into his shoulder.

"Well, I'll go back to the office and get Jack on this immediately. I'll have him check every birth and death of newborns in the London area around the time your mother gave birth. If we're lucky it will give us a baseline."

"Victory and Payton are coming up to the house in fifteen minutes." Willow said, as she pulled her phone from her pocket and checked the time. "I'll tell them what we've discovered. Let's contact the guys, we need them here, too."

* * * *

"I'll start by checking all births and deaths for the weeks prior, during, and after Sharon's delivery," Jack said, after Wyatt and Willow told the group of their findings.

"Good idea. With any luck we'll catch a break," Wyatt said.

"Could your source tell from the DNA if the newborns found were twins?"

"He said the DNA of the two were not related. However, he believes they were born and died within hours of one another."

Payton and Victory remained quiet through the interchange.

"I know this is a lot to digest," Wyatt said to the two women.

"I'm sorry I didn't tell you before now. I just didn't want to get your hopes up until I knew the results of the test," Willow said.

"You're saying the twins, our older sisters, are alive," Payton said.

"No, they didn't say that, Payton. They said the two bodies buried in our sisters' graves are not them. Our sisters could very well be dead," Victory said.

"Or they could be alive," Willow said. "I say we make it our priority to discover what actually happened to them."

"Payton, could you and Collin stay for a while?" Willow asked as the group dispersed.

The four of them moved into the living room, Willow safely tucked into the warmth of Wyatt's arm.

"I realize you have already put work into the redesign of the house. I've given this much thought. You and Collin need your own space. He needs a place where he is shielded from everyone's energy."

"But Willow. We don't want you to leave," Payton said.

"I don't intend on going far. With your blessing I would like to build a house near the backside of our ten acres. There will still be plenty of space for the dogs to run. I've already spoken with Victory. She and Tristan were planning on adding some footage to their home this summer. She thought the new house and their addition could be done all at the same time."

Payton looked at Collin. He squeezed her hand, smiled, and nodded at her.

"I think that's a wonderful idea." Payton walked over, dropped down to her knees, and hugged Willow.

After they left Willow and Wyatt sat quietly. Willow snuggled into the warmth of his body, and Asia wormed her way up and nestled into Willow's other side.

"I know you've only recently moved into the bungalow. Even so, I hoped you would help me design *our* new home and live there with me after it's complete."

"Your plan sounds much better than mine. I hoped you'd build a large deck with comfortable lounges, since I planned to spend every night on one."

"Have you forgotten your promise to me already, Mr. Farraday?" Mischief sparkled in her aquamarine gaze. "You promised to be by my side every step of the way."

"And so I shall, *A rúnsearc*." Wyatt gathered her up in his arms and kissed her soft lips. The journey which lay before them would not be all calm winds and smooth sailing. Not with the Kaleidoscope Group lurking out in the world. Still, he would make it his life's quest to live and love this amazing woman with every ounce of his heart and soul.

* * * *

Two months later...

A charcoal-colored Rolls Royce Phantom pulled up to the imposing gate. The driver rolled down his window as the guard approached.

"Good afternoon, sir," the guard said, immediately recognizing the passenger.

The guard stepped away and pushed the button to open the gate. The Phantom glided through and followed the winding two-mile drive, flanked with pristinely manicured gardens up to the villa's porte cochère, where a four-man security team stood guard.

As the driver got out and opened the door for his passenger, one of the security team stepped up to the vehicle. A distinguished middle-aged man emerged from the Rolls.

"Good afternoon, sir," the man said. "May I take your things?"

The man nodded and handed the security guard his items.

"Both men are here. They are gathered in the conservatory."

As the man approached the door to the villa another of the security team nodded and opened the door.

* * * *

"Nice to see you again, Mr. Chairman," Daniel Prescott said, as Edward Ryker strode into the conservatory.

Carl Sterling sat holding a cigar in one hand and a glass of brandy in the other.

"Good to see you, Mr. Ryker," Carl said. "I hope your drive here was pleasant."

"I didn't notice," Ryker said and sat down.

A servant set a sterling silver tray, which held a single Waterford crystal snifter containing two-fingers of Tequila Ley .925, on the side table next to him.

Ryker picked the snifter up and inhaled the exquisite fragrance.

"How are you settling in, Daniel?" Ryker asked, as he slowly rotated the snifter in his hand.

"It's an adjustment," Prescott said.

"I heard you had some issues in Texas," Ryker said, as he looked at the man in a leisurely fashion. By Prescott's expression, Ryker knew he'd hoped his debacle had gone unnoticed.

"There were some issues, I admit," Prescott said.

"Issues?" Sterling said, while puffing on his cigar. "Your whole damn plan fell apart; you lost both Willow and Collin."

"Now Carl, we all have our off days," Ryker said.

"Off days? We can't afford anymore off days. We've lost a number of good men recently."

"If they were good, we would not have lost them," Ryker snapped, and felt his face begin to flush. He held the snifter up and savored the ambrosia.

"With what has recently happened, I wonder if it's still in KG's best interest to move forward with the old Winters' complex?" Prescott asked.

"Feeling a bit under the microscope are you, Daniel?" Ryker asked.

"It's a small town. We have a variety of other facilities to choose from," Prescott said.

"For now you move forward. You don't have to personally be on-site if you can find a reliable replacement. I want to keep the pressure on the sisters. Having KG set up shop close by serves that purpose," Ryker said.

"Might I ask why the interest in Willow?" Prescott asked.

"There are a good number of reasons. Recently I learned that Willow's ability to read auras and energy has evolved into being able to ferret out my cloaking serum. I need to determine how she manages to do so," Ryker said.

"Sounds to me like one more reason to be rid of all three of the sisters," Prescott said.

"Daniel, you have much to learn and little time to learn it. The Winters sisters are a treasure trove of enhanced abilities. They are the result of my first and most successful tests and are not to be destroyed. There is much we can gain from them," Ryker said.

"I'm concerned, Mr. Ryker," Sterling said. "Between that bastard Roberts's SOCOM team and the triplets, we could one day find ourselves in a heap of trouble."

"Nonsense," Ryker said, waving a hand at him. "The Kaleidoscope Group is much too massive and powerful to worry about such trivial matters. Speaking of Roberts, have you gleaned any new information?"

"Not recently. My plant has gone to ground. Roberts is aware of a leak in his department and is on an active hunt," Sterling said.

"I see."

"Might I ask how the rebuilding of Second Wave is coming along?" Sterling asked.

"We are proceeding with caution. The three new schools are up and running. We've cut the number of children down by over half. We are finding that many children do not demonstrate a true special ability and have been weeded out of the program. We need to gain control of Collin. His DNA is the answer. If I can study his DNA, then I can reproduce it, introduce a serum into the children we do have, and build an invincible soldier," Ryker said.

"I have a list of potential buyers, Mr. Ryker. The faster we get that done, the faster we all get rich," Sterling said.

"My dear Carl, there is so much more to this plan than money."

Books by Joanne Jaytanie

The Winters Sisters series~

Chasing Victory
Payton's Pursuit

Other Titles

Love's Always Paws-Able
P.I. ~ I Love You
Christmas Reflections
Building Up To Love
Uncharted Love

About the Author

Joanne was born and raised in Sherburne, New York, a quaint village surrounded by dairy farms and rolling hills. From the moment she could read she wanted to explore the world. During her college years she slowly crept across the country, stopping along the way in Oklahoma, California, and finally Washington State, which she now proudly calls home. She lives with her husband and Dobermans, in their home located on the Olympic Peninsula with a panoramic view of the Olympic Mountains.

Joanne writes romantic suspense, paranormal, and contemporary romance. She loves to submerge herself in the world of her characters, to live and breathe their lives and marvel at their decisions and predicaments.

She enjoys a wide variety of books including paranormal, suspense, thriller, and of course romance. Joanne is a member of Romance Writers of America, and past President of Peninsula Romance Writers, which was Debbie Macomber's home chapter.

MEDIA LINKS~

Website: http://www.joannejaytanie.com/
Blog: http://www.authorjoannejaytanie.blogspot.com/
Facebook: https://www.facebook.com/pages/Joanne-Jaytanie-Author/146892025475388

24694467R10203

Made in the USA
San Bernardino, CA
04 October 2015